PRAISE FOR *Lucky Girls*

"Every story in this remarkable collection reveals the emergence of a truly prodigious talent." —RICHARD FORD

"Thoughtful and entertaining . . . Freudenberger is . . . inventive and piquant when she probes characters' relationships to their adopted homelands—which, she shows, are often more passionate and grounded then their ties to the people in their lives." —*Publishers Weekly*

"Little gems." —*San Diego Union-Tribune*

"At 22, Nell Freudenberger—arguably the summer's hottest young writer—turned down a job at Random House. Smart move. She went to Bangkok instead, teaching English to fifteen-year-olds, and then spent the following summers exploring India. Her exotic travels, and the inevitable loneliness a foreigner feels in a borrowed country, shape the five stories in her eagerly awaited debut collection." —*Entertainment Weekly*

"Nell Freudenberger's highly anticipated debut, *Lucky Girls* . . . exceeds expectations. Freudenberger deftly conveys the intellectual and artistic advantages of dysfunction and its staying power—regardless of how far away one strays from home." —*Nerve*

"Freudenberger possesses a keen intelligence, a confident, unadorned style, a brilliant ability to vividly sketch a character through telling details . . . and a deeply appealing narrative voice." —*Village Voice*

"Throughout the book . . . are moments of sharp humor and wise insight." —*Los Angeles Times*

"'Lucky Girls' is a beautiful story that has a graceful simplicity." —*People*

"Well-written, well-plotted, intelligent and surprising." —*Salon.com*

"Freudenberger succeeds nicely in creating sharply focused pieces in which each detail directs the reader along a clear path. And in crafting these tightly knit pieces, she sidesteps the mushiness that is the downfall of many contemporary short pieces . . . If the girls in these stories have missed out on some of the good luck, maybe it's because it is all going to the reader fortunate enough to peruse this collection." —*Denver Post*

"An excellent addition to all short story collections." —*Booklist*

"Freudenberger writes with a self-assurance that is engaging, carrying the reader . . . into solidly constructed fictional worlds." —*The Oregonian*

"Freudenberger has a sophistication and worldliness that eludes well-traveled authors twice her age. More important, whether her stories are set in Thailand, India, or the U.S., she makes even the dreariest of situations seem auspicious." —*Seattle Weekly*

"Skillful and assured . . . Freudenberger's prose is smooth." —*News & Observer*

"One rich motherlode of writing talent . . . *Lucky Girls* is an irresistible marvel. Freudenberger is a writer with a strong sense of history, a merciless and often hilarious eye for family dynamics, and an equally sharp eye for cultures in collision. Her love of language and literature registers on every page she writes." —*Seattle Times*

Nell Freudenberger

ecco

An Imprint of HarperCollins Publishers

LUCKY GIRLS

stories

HarperCollins books may be purchased for educational, business, or sales promotional use. For information please write: Special Markets Department, HarperCollins Publishers Inc., 10 East 53rd Street, New York, NY 10022.

First Ecco paperback edition published September 2004.

Designed by Cassandra J. Pappas

The Library of Congress has cataloged the hardcover edition as follows:

Freudenberger, Nell.
   Lucky girls : stories / Nell Freudenberger.
      p.   cm.
   ISBN 0-06-008879-6 (alk. paper)
      1. Asia—Social life and customs—Fiction. 2. Americans—Asia—Fiction. 3. Women—Asia—Fiction. I. Title.
PS3606.R479L83 2003
813'.6—dc21

                                                            2003044875

ISBN 0-06-008879-6
ISBN 0-06-008880-x (pbk)

04 05 06 07 08 ❖/RRD 10 9 8 7 6 5 4 3 2 1

For Alex

Contents

Lucky Girls

Lucky Girls

I had often imagined meeting Mrs. Chawla, Arun's mother. It would be in a restaurant, and I would be wearing a sophisticated blue suit that my mother had sent me soon after I moved to India, and Mrs. Chawla would not be able to keep herself from admiring it. Of course, in those fantasies Arun was always with me.

As it happened, Mrs. Chawla appeared early one morning, in a car with a driver, unannounced. I was sitting at the kitchen table in my painting shorts, having a cup of tea. There was no time to straighten up the living room or take a shower. I went into the bedroom, where Arun and I had often slept, and put on a dress—wrinkled, but at least it was clean. I put my cup in the sink and set a pot of water on the stove. Then I watched through the window. Mrs. Chawla had got out of the car and was standing with her arms crossed, instructing her driver how to park. The car moved forward, backed up, and then inched forward again.

Mrs. Chawla shaded her eyes to look at the backyard: the laundry line with my clothes hanging on it, the grackles perched on the telephone pole, the pile of soft, rotting bricks. I had a feeling that had come to seem familiar in the eight months since Arun had died, a kind of panic that made me want to stand very still.

The bell rang.

"Hello, Mrs. Chawla," I said. "I'm glad you came." From her handwriting, I had expected someone more imposing. She was several inches shorter than I was, and heavy. Her hair was long and dyed black, with a dramatic white streak in the front; and she was wearing a navy blue salwar-kameez, the trousers of which were tapered at the ankles, in a style that was just becoming fashionable.

"Yes," she said. "I've been meaning to. I can't stay long." She gave me a funny smile, as if I weren't what she had expected, either.

"Will you have some tea?" I offered.

"Do you have tea?" she asked, sounding surprised. She looked at the drawn blinds in the living room. There was a crumpled napkin next to the salt and pepper shakers on the table, where I had eaten dinner the night before, and which I had asked Puja, the servant, to clean. Now that it was summer, cockroaches had started coming out of the walls.

"Please don't go to any trouble," she said. "Puja can do it—is she in the kitchen?" Arun had hired Puja to do my cooking and cleaning; when he told me she had worked for his mother, I'd hoped that Mrs. Chawla was making a friendly gesture. In fact, Puja was a terrible housekeeper and a severely limited cook. She lived in a room at the back of the house, with her husband and four little girls; at night I often saw her crouched in the backyard, making chapatis on a pump stove with a low blue flame.

Mrs. Chawla walked confidently toward the kitchen, calling Puja in a proprietary voice, and I realized that Arun's mother had been in my house before. She could have come any number of times, in the afternoons, when I taught art at the primary school or went out shopping in Khan Market. Puja would have let her in without hesitation.

When Mrs. Chawla reappeared, she scrutinized the chairs, before choosing to sit on the sofa. She smiled, revealing a narrow space between her teeth. "Where exactly are you from?" she asked.

"My father lives in Boston, but my mother is in California now," I told her.

"Ah," said Mrs. Chawla softly, as if that explained everything. "An American family. That must make it difficult to decide where to return to."

I had no plans to return, as I should have explained. "It rules out Boston and California," I said instead.

Mrs. Chawla didn't smile.

My brother, I added, was getting married in Boston in July.

"And you like the bride?" she asked.

"Oh," I said. "I only met her once." I could feel the next question coming, and then a thing happened that often happens to me with people who make me nervous.

"What's her name?" Mrs. Chawla asked.

Her name, which I knew perfectly well, slipped into some temporarily unrecoverable place. "Actually, I don't remember," I said.

Mrs. Chawla looked at me, puzzled. "How strange," she said.

Puja brought the tea. She knelt on the floor and began placing things, item by item, on the coffee table: spoons, cups, saucers, milk, sugar, and a small plate of Indian sweets that Mrs. Chawla must have brought with her. The tea, it seemed, was no longer my hospitable gesture.

"How is she doing?" Mrs. Chawla asked, nodding at Puja.

"She's wonderful," I lied. Now that Arun wasn't here to tell her what to do, the house was getting dirtier and dirtier.

Puja's little girls were watching us from the kitchen doorway. When Mrs. Chawla saw them, she said suddenly, "Girls," and repeated it sharply in Hindi. "I have told her that if she has another baby"—Mrs. Chawla paused and looked at Puja—"*Bas!* Enough, I'm sending her back to Orissa." She turned back to me. "That's east India," she informed me, as if I had never seen a map of the subcontinent. "The people there are tribals. Did you know that? Puja is a tribal. These people have nothing, you know, except floods and cyclones. Now they're having terrible floods— have you seen them on television? Thousands of people are sick, and there isn't enough drinking water. I tell her that, and what do you think she says?"

Puja knew only a few words of English. She seemed to be smiling at her feet, which were bare, extremely small, and decorated with silver toe rings.

"She says she needs another child because she wants to have a boy," Mrs. Chawla said. "Stupid girl." Puja giggled. "Stupid," evidently, was one of the English words she did know. Then Mrs. Chawla said something else, in Hindi, and Puja stopped giggling and left the room.

"Did you understand?" Mrs. Chawla asked me.

"A little," I said. "You said she was a woman with girls?"

"Very good," said Mrs. Chawla. "I said she was the kind of unfortunate woman who has only girls."

"Oh," I said.

Mrs. Chawla eyed me craftily. "You think I'm cruel to them."

"No," I said. I was used to this kind of frankness from Indian women of Mrs. Chawla's age and station, and I liked it.

Mrs. Chawla looked as though she were going to say something else, but just then the electricity went out.

"I'm sorry," I said. "It usually comes on again in a second."

"This is a good area, a government area," she said approvingly. "Did you know that?"

I had been living on Pandara Road for almost five years, a fact that Mrs. Chawla knew, so I didn't say anything. The lights came on about halfway, low and flickering, and the fans spun just enough to move the air. Often this happened at night, when I was sitting in the living room, pretending to read.

Mrs. Chawla put her hand on my arm. "The point is—what's wrong with girls?"

"Nothing," I said.

"Then . . . good," Mrs. Chawla said. "You can help me teach her." She leaned back, and the cheap wicker sofa creaked. I had bought it because

Arun thought wicker was cool. I didn't know why a sofa needed to be cool, and now cockroaches were living in the little wicker spaces. I said a short, fervent prayer that Mrs. Chawla wouldn't see a cockroach. Puja started to pour the milk in my tea, but Mrs. Chawla stopped her. "Let the lady do it herself," she said, in English, and then turned to me. "She's never seen a woman like you, living so well on her own."

• • •

When I met Arun, I was wearing borrowed clothes. It was my first time in India and I was visiting Gita Banerjee, the most glamorous friend I had made in college. My parents had bought the ticket for me—"To see the world," my father had written on a card, "before you come home and settle down." I was twenty-two.

A few nights after I arrived in Delhi, the Banerjees had a party. Gita's father had once been some kind of ambassador, and the entire extended family seemed constantly to be entertaining important visitors in their extravagant houses. Gita's younger sisters thought it would be fun for me to wear Indian clothes, and they spent a long time dressing me up in a dark pink sari with a matching blouse underneath. I was wearing glass bracelets, and my hair was braided like theirs—they even painted my hands with mendhi, which left intricate brown patterns across my palms. We spent so much time making me look like them that no one had a chance to teach me to walk in the sari, which turned out to be more difficult than I had imagined, like finding yourself in the street wearing only a bath towel.

After a while, I left the party. I had meant to go back upstairs to my room, but I opened the wrong door by mistake and there was a man sitting on a bed, in the light of a small reading lamp. He had taken off his jacket, and the sleeves of his white shirt were rolled up.

"I'm sorry," I said, and started to back out of the room.

"Hello," he said. "Are you hiding, too?"

I laughed.

"You're Gita's friend, the college graduate," Arun said.

"I was Gita's roommate," I said. "Do you know Gita?"

"Since she was born." He stood up and shook my hand. "Uncle Arun," he said. There was a bottle of imported whiskey on the table, and he asked me if I wanted a drink.

I did, but I wondered if that would be inappropriate. I had noticed that although there was wine downstairs at the party (which Gita and I had liberally sampled), most of the women weren't drinking. "Is that OK?" I asked. "I mean, in India?"

This was the first time Arun really looked at me. His eyes were green, like a Kashmiri's. "I think it's up to you," he said. "Even in India."

Arun was twenty-three years older than Gita and me. He was tall, with broader shoulders than most Indian men I had met, and he had a trimmed black beard with some gray in it. I couldn't help staring at his hands as he poured my drink—the long, thin muscles of his fingers, and a raised white scar, straight as an incision, across the top of his left wrist.

He asked if I was enjoying my visit. I admitted that I hadn't been out much, but that I liked the parts of Delhi I had seen.

Arun smiled. "You want to go to Agra, of course."

"Not just Agra." I wanted to sound as if I knew more about India than that.

"Do you know what the Taj Mahal looks like?" Arun asked.

"Of course."

He leaned forward. "Did you know that the emperor meant to build another one across the river?"

I nodded, although I hadn't even known that there was a river. I had always pictured it in the desert, surrounded by raked yellow sand. "He built it for his wife, right?"

"Mumtaz," said Arun. "But what you see is only half his plan. There was going to be another one for him, exactly the same but in black marble."

I thought he was teasing me. "I don't believe you," I said.

"But when he died they simply buried him next to her—his grave is the only thing that isn't perfectly symmetrical." Arun smiled slightly. "He had a vision. They ruined it."

We were quiet for a minute.

"Can I ask you something?" he said.

I wondered stupidly if he was going to kiss me. I had never kissed a man with a beard.

"Why did you come to India?"

"I wanted to see where Gita was from."

Arun sipped his whiskey, as if he were waiting for more. "So if she'd been from Paris you might have gone there instead?"

"But I've been to Paris."

Arun laughed. "You're just like these diplomats' children," he said. "World-weary at twenty."

"Oh, yes," I said, indicating my clothes. "Very cosmopolitan."

"I wasn't going to ask."

"You don't like them." I pouted. I was already a little drunk.

"They're nice clothes," he said. "I just don't like Western girls in Indian clothes, but I'm perhaps behind the times."

"Why?"

Arun paused. "Because clothes mean something here. Historically. And when you wear them it's for romance, glamour—you don't mean anything."

I stared at the patterns on my hands. Suddenly, it seemed as if Gita's sisters had played a practical joke on me, like dressing up a cat or a dog.

"I've offended you," Arun said sadly.

"No, you haven't."

"I'm always offending women. I don't know how to behave around them."

"Making fun of their clothes isn't the best strategy," I told him.

Arun smiled. "Have another drink. Prove we're still friends."

"I think I'm extremely drunk already," I said.

Arun seemed to consider this. "You're extremely pretty," he said. "Even in Indian clothes. And since we don't want anything to happen to you, maybe I should take you back down to the party."

To this day, I remember that as the most thrilling thing anyone has ever said to me.

•   •   •

I am not extremely pretty, a fact that Mrs. Chawla noticed right away. The second time she visited, I was sitting in my studio, in front of a canvas, staring out the window at Puja's children, who were playing hide-and-seek, running in and out between the rows of hanging laundry. The studio was a prefabricated one-room structure, which I used because the rooms in the house were too dark. There was a single bed where I used to sleep if I was working late. Now I slept here all the time.

Mrs. Chawla must have rung the doorbell and, not finding anyone, walked around to the back. Or maybe she was accustomed to coming in through the garden. I looked up and there she was, directly in front of me, peering in the window. It took me a few seconds to realize that she couldn't see through the screen at this time of day. I was wearing my painting shorts again.

"Just a minute," I called, and then changed my mind. I had no reason to pretend.

Mrs. Chawla was dressed in moss green, and her hair was braided down her back like a girl's. She looked at the paints spread out on the table, at the straw mats on the floor, and the bed with a mosquito net, a foreigner's thing. Then she looked up at the fan, which was dusty, with a black layer of grease on one side of the blades. She sighed and sat down at my table. "You're not sleeping here, are you?"

"Sometimes. I like it out here."

Mrs. Chawla looked shocked. "But he never slept here?"

"Mrs. Chawla . . ." I began. I could hear the milkman calling from his bicycle.

"I mean, I could see why you would want to sleep here now, if the two of you used to—if that was the bed where you slept, as it were."

"It's not really any of your business," I said.

Mrs. Chawla ignored me. "What I do not understand"—she paused, as if we were thinking aloud together, collaborating on a difficult puzzle—"is how he could stand to stay somewhere so dirty. He was always so particular, and his house—the house where he lived, I mean—was immaculate."

"Leave if it bothers you," I said.

"Ah!" said Mrs. Chawla. "I see what he meant. You're not beautiful, but you're strong-willed. That's appealing for a man like Arun, who always got exactly what he wanted." She lowered her voice, as if she were telling me a secret. "I used to think we might have spoiled him."

"Yes. If he hadn't had all of these people coddling him, he might have learned how to make a decision," I said, surprising myself.

Mrs. Chawla put her palms in the air and shrugged theatrically. "But would any of us have been happy with his decisions? Do you think you would have been?" She smiled. "It's a Catch-22 situation." She stood up. "This afternoon I have to go see Laxmi and the boys. She's upset, you know, that I am visiting you."

I pretended to start painting.

"She doesn't understand why you're still here," Mrs. Chawla told me. "I'm sure she'll ask me."

I wondered if finding the answer to this question—why I was still here—was the purpose of Mrs. Chawla's visit.

"Maybe she should come ask me herself." I hadn't meant to say it, only think it, but it didn't matter. I didn't expect to see Mrs. Chawla again.

She gave a short, barking laugh. "You seem quiet," she said. "But you're sharp."

After Mrs. Chawla was gone, I realized that I had wanted her to look at the painting, which was the view out my window, with the laundry and the drying okra plants against the main house. It wasn't especially good—I was going to scrape it away and use the canvas again—but I didn't think Mrs. Chawla would have known that. She would have seen the perspective and the colors, and the way I had reproduced the backyard of her son's second home, and she would have known that I wasn't a phony. At the same time, it annoyed me that I should care what she thought.

•   •   •

That first trip to India had been at the invitation of Gita's family, the Banerjees, and they went out of their way to insure that I saw nothing I would not see in New York. We went to a restaurant in Defence Colony, the elite shopping enclave, and to the Lodi Gardens, where women in salwar-kameez and running shoes promenaded briskly down designated exercise paths. Gita had compared it to Central Park, but Central Park didn't have ancient stone architecture. Great ruined domes, purple in the last bit of light, appeared to float above the wet grass. When I asked what period the ruins dated from, Mrs. Banerjee laughed and said that she had no idea.

The only real tourist attraction I saw, on an overplanned excursion in the care of the Banerjees' driver, was an old Mughal fort, the Purana Qila, one chipped blue tile of which Gita forced me to take when we found it lying on the grass. No one else wants it, she said, picking it up and secreting it in her jacket. I protested but was privately pleased—it might be my only souvenir. Then, one morning, Arun showed up for breakfast and announced that he was taking Gita and me on an overnight trip to Agra, to see the Taj Mahal.

As soon as we were on the train, Gita took over her mother's role, commandeering an extra seat from an old man in a Nehru jacket and then, hours before we were hungry, spreading out an elaborate lunch that the Banerjees' cook had prepared. The first-class cars were air-conditioned to a luxurious, wintry temperature, and my arms, in the thin blouse I had chosen, were covered with goose bumps. But when Arun said that we should sit between the cars, where the men went to smoke and where you could see the green country streaming past, Gita looked at him as if he had suggested that we paint our faces and sing in the aisle for change.

"Arun is constitutionally a bachelor," she told me after he left the compartment.

"I thought he was married." I still don't remember how I knew this; I may have just assumed it.

"Oh, he's married now, but he waited forever." Gita looked at me. "Living that long by yourself, you develop habits." I knew she wasn't talking about smoking on trains, but I didn't particularly feel like being warned.

Gita and Arun agreed that I had to see the monument for the first time at sunrise, from the gate, and so we spent our first day in Agra trying *not* to see the Taj Mahal. It wasn't easy. The parapets of the Agra Fort opened, in an orderly progression of cusped arches, onto view after view of the tomb. There was little else besides the monument: men beating clothes on the riverbank, water buffalo in the mud, the river itself, skittering into the flat, tan distance and sending silver flashes into the smog like a child playing with a mirror.

"Don't look," Arun said, coming up behind me. "Careful," he gasped, as we passed the arrow slots along the steep red stairs.

That night, we ate in a restaurant Arun knew, avoiding the rooftop tourist cafés, strung with colored lights, that all boasted a "Taj view." It was the middle of the summer, and the number of tourists was relatively low. Arun had suggested that we stay in one of the cheap hotels near the monument instead of the colonial palace near the airport where Gita's mother had reserved rooms: "This way, we can stumble out of bed and be standing in front of the Taj."

Because of our sunrise engagement, Gita and I went to bed at ten. I had expected that we would stay up talking, but after a few minutes I could hear her quiet breathing. The room had an air cooler, which made a fierce grating sound and did nothing else. I tried to lie absolutely still, but I was already sweating when the power went out. The fan clicked to a slow halt, and the rectangles of light from outside, my only orientation, disappeared in a dark so heavy that it was like a soft cloth in my mouth.

After a few minutes, my eyes had still not adjusted to the dark, and I was now sweating uncontrollably. I got up and walked toward the door, my hands in front of me, hesitating for a moment before going out. There was a breeze. Some buildings nearby must have had generators, and the faint, reassuring sound of a television came from the street. A few auto-rickshaws sat outside the hotel gate; you could see the tiny lights hanging from the dashboards, like clusters of lantern fish.

Beyond the patio was a kind of thick Indian garden familiar to me now: overgrown and ripe-smelling, where you might be afraid of stepping on something rotting in the grass. I had been standing at the edge of the garden for several minutes before I saw the smoke. On a hammock suspended between two low, knotted trees, Gita's uncle was smoking a cigarette.

"Hello," he said.

"The fan went off," I said. I put one foot on top of the other, as if that would conceal the fact that I was standing outside in a camisole and shorts. I tried to think of a polite way of excusing myself, to go back inside. "Can I have a cigarette?" I asked instead.

Arun got up and lit one for me.

"This is another of those things I shouldn't be doing in India," I said.

"What do you mean?" Arun asked.

"Well, I mean, Indian women don't really smoke," I said.

"Are you trying to blend in?"

"No," I said. "I mean, not especially."

I smoked the cigarette down to the filter. The roots of my hair were wet, but Arun didn't seem to be suffering from the heat at all. He had taken off his blue oxford shirt, which was draped over the railing, and he was wearing a dark blue T-shirt. Something hung from an almost invisible silver chain around his neck. I am surprised today by what I did. I was, in general, very shy.

"What is this?" I stepped close to Arun and took the tiny amulet in my hand.

"It was a gift from my wife."

I let go of the amulet. "I think I might take a shower," I told him. Arun didn't say anything, but as I turned away he grabbed my wrist.

"I'm sorry," he said.

"Sorry for what?"

"I'm afraid I can't stand that, listening to the shower."

"The walls are very thick. I don't think you'll hear it."

Arun was stern. "I refuse to let you wake my niece, with your profligate American water use. I insist that if you are going to shower in the middle of the night you use the one in my room."

Although he was teasing me, he let me know that it would be silly for me to pretend that this wasn't exactly what I wanted.

In his room, Arun lit a fat white utility candle. The things he'd brought with him—a notebook, an extra shirt, a toothbrush, a flask—were laid out on the bed, as if he were preparing for some kind of emergency. He looked at me directly, with a sudden focused intensity. It was a quality of attention I hadn't experienced before, an ability he had to suggest that everything that had gone before had led to this precise moment. There was something almost desperate about the sex—it was like skydiving in a dream. I had no illusions about being in control.

"You seemed to be enjoying yourself," he said afterward.

"I was." I said it so quickly that I was embarrassed.

"You might make more noise next time," Arun said, as if he were suggesting a book for me to read or someone I really should try to meet.

*   *   *

The alarm went off at five. In the room next door, Gita's would be ringing as well.

"What do I do?"

He was lying on his back, with one hand on my hip. "She's probably not even awake," he said. "Go back now."

"What do I tell her?" I was panicking.

"Tell her the fan went off," he said. "Nobody's up yet."

In fact, many people are awake in India at five. The waiter from the hotel restaurant, the rickshaw drivers, and a hopeful-looking beggar at the gate all saw me leave Arun's room and dash barefoot back to mine. I opened the door slowly, being careful with the noisy key. It was an unnecessary precaution. Gita was sitting fully clothed on the bed, the guidebook in her lap.

"The fan . . ." I began. I didn't think that she was going to believe me.

"We missed it! We have to go back to Delhi, and you missed it."

"What?"

Gita looked at me as if I were a total idiot. "The Taj."

"It's only five." I wondered if this was some kind of punishment. "We can still go," I said, but Gita was shaking her head. Neither she nor Arun had bothered to read the guidebook, and, like theaters and hairdressers in America, the Taj Mahal was closed on Mondays.

We spent the morning before our train left looking at the Taj as best we could. We even went to one of the rooftop restaurants and ordered Cokes.

"It's nicer, in a way," Arun said. "You have to pay more attention."

Arun liked to say that our lives are composed of accidents. I remember the profound appeal of this idea then, when I fell in love with him, and three years later, when I went to India for no reason other than that Arun, with whom I had been corresponding all that time, had asked me to.

•   •   •

After I moved to India, Gita and I continued to see each other, but we never talked about Arun. The rest of her family were not so welcoming. I thought that the reason they never invited me to their home was out of a kind of prejudice. They did not like the combination of Arun and me. Their taste was conservative; and I thought they believed that people, like the drapes and the sofa, should match.

It is embarrassing to admit that I simply didn't consider Arun's wife. I had only the vaguest impression of Laxmi: a mental image of a woman's back as she put the children to bed in the vivid hours of the early evening, while Arun was with me. They lived in Defence Colony, in a house I knew only as the background of a photograph that he carried in his wallet. It showed two boys holding each other in an affectionate headlock in front of a new white Ambassador, barely reaching the top of the sunlit silver grille. Although the photograph was clearly worn, I somehow failed to understand that it had been taken years ago. It never occurred to me that those two boys were now young men, almost in university.

Not long after Arun helped me find the house on Pandara Road, his mother wrote me. "You must be curious about my son's wife, Laxmi," she began. "You are very young, but Laxmi is still ten years younger than Arun. He was lucky, to wait so long and still find a girl like that. (Laxmi is the goddess of wealth and good fortune, you may not know.) She is as beautiful as a goddess as well. In America, I know women want to be skinny, so that you can see the bones. Laxmi is the kind of woman Indian men like: plump and round. She does not need to wear kohl, because of the thickness of her lashes. Her lips are like the inside of a plum." She closed with what I understood to be a warning. "We do not know each other, but, if you will allow me to be frank, I would say that to a man it is the issue of will that is most important. Laxmi is devoted to my son and, if he asked, she would do anything."

All day, I thought about not showing the letter to Arun. But as soon as I heard the front door open I was up and in the hall with the evidence in my hand.

He walked past me to the table where I kept the Scotch and poured himself a drink. He took off his jacket, transferring the letter from hand to hand, and sat down with it. He read it through, and then patted the space next to him on the couch, as if this were a funny thing we could share.

"Lips like the inside of a plum," he said. "My mother is a terrible writer."

But I didn't think Mrs. Chawla was a terrible writer. The words she chose had made another person appear in the room, where before there had been only Arun and me. Mrs. Chawla had started a competition, and she seemed to relish the prospect of being a spectator.

"It's sick," I told Arun.

He thought I was talking about Laxmi. "She would not do anything for me," he said. "She's not particularly happy with me at the moment." He took a sip of his Scotch. "At any moment," he corrected himself.

He didn't understand, but it didn't matter. Mrs. Chawla hadn't addressed the letter to him. That evening, I unbuttoned my blouse in the living room and held his hand and slipped it underneath my bra, like a high school girl, and climbed on top of him with my skirt around my waist. We had sex on the sofa, with only the screen door between us and the people outside. "Look at me," I said, and he looked, but already I was talking to two women: Laxmi, in a tight blouse that stopped just beneath her breasts, her stomach behind gauze, her bitten lips; and Mrs. Chawla, who had brought her into my house.

Until that point, I had been pretending at adulthood; I felt now that I had crossed a divide. I was dating a married man, I had told a friend in a long letter, because I wasn't sure I wanted to get married. I was twenty-five, and it seemed to me that there were two kinds of marriage. One hits a crisis and decisively fails. The other weathers the crisis, with both parties insistently declaring they have been made stronger: I couldn't imagine living with that kind of compromise. Secretly, I was hoping that in a few years Arun would remove the obstacles and arrive with his things on the doorstep of the house that would be, from then on, not just for me.

• • •

When Arun died, my family said, "Come home." My mother said it first—half invitation and half formality, because of course everyone assumed I would be coming home. But I procrastinated. I didn't like to think that I had spent five years in India entirely because of a man. Then, after several months, my father called. I don't think he had ever said Arun's name, and it was difficult for him. He said it was hard to deal with a friend's death alone, and he talked about when his father had died. I thanked him and said that I wasn't alone, that I had friends in Delhi.

In fact, I didn't have so many friends, although there always seemed to be people around. I often had lunch with Gita and her colleagues, and in the afternoons I shared a rickshaw with the other teachers who lived in my neighborhood. At home in the compound there was sometimes an audience when I painted: the boys who came from across the road with their cricket bats to stand at my door, and the girls who followed them. I always left the door open.

One day, I noticed Puja's daughters standing just outside, with a girl named Pinky, who was in my class at the school.

"Why don't you bring the girls inside?" I asked Pinky. Her English was good, but she looked confused.

"Ma'am," she struggled. "Because, ma'am——"

"Please bring them inside," I said.

Pinky smiled broadly and brought the children into the studio, carrying Ruma, the youngest, and leading one of her sisters by the hand. Ruma whined to be put down and immediately emptied a bowl of dirt onto the floor. Pinky looked at me with the sympathy of a much older friend.

But after a while it got quiet. I was making so much progress that I didn't hear the girls arguing on the floor or, a few minutes later, the sound of the gate in the yard. It was Mrs. Chawla's third visit.

"That's a good likeness," she said. She was standing alone in the doorway. I noticed Puja hovering nervously a few feet behind her. You could see that she wanted to collect her children but was afraid to make a move with Mrs. Chawla there.

"It's just a sketch," I said. "I'm going to make a painting."

Mrs. Chawla came in and leaned over the canvas, studying it. "And then what will you do with it when it's finished?"

"I don't know," I said. I could feel the pulse in my right hand, which was holding the pencil.

Mrs. Chawla straightened up and looked at me. "Do you think you could paint the Sultan of Oman?"

I thought I might have misheard.

"You can make a good living, just from that—if you know the right import-export man."

"How many paintings of the Sultan of Oman do they need?" I asked carefully.

"One for every family," Mrs. Chawla said. "And you can charge whatever you want. They have so much money that they would burn it for fuel, if they didn't have so much fuel."

I laughed, and Mrs. Chawla smiled. It occurred to me that we were having a moment of understanding, and the need for Arun opened, all of a sudden, like a cut.

Puja chose that moment to duck in and scoop up her children, and abruptly Mrs. Chawla whirled around and slapped her, hard, across the face. Mrs. Chawla started speaking Hindi, very fast, so that it was impossible for me to follow. Puja's face was blank, and Ruma began to wail. When Mrs. Chawla was finished, she turned back to me, continuing our conversation as if I were not only uncomprehending but blind as well.

"Of course," she said, "it gets easier."

"What?"

"Painting the sultan. You could start with a photograph, and then you might not even need a photograph after a while."

"Mrs. Chawla," I said, "what did you say to her?"

"To whom?"

"To Puja," I said. "Just now."

Mrs. Chawla looked out the window, where we could see Puja hurrying across the yard, an awkward S shape with one child on her hip. I thought she wasn't going to answer me. I was suddenly dizzy and a bit nauseated.

"Mrs. Chawla? I know I need to learn more Hindi."

She put her hand on my shoulder, almost tenderly. "Why would you do that? It isn't necessary." She sighed. "I only asked her please not to bring the children into the house."

"But I asked them to come," I said. "I *told* them to."

Mrs. Chawla looked from the unmade bed to the empty water bottles on the table, through the open door to the bathroom, where my towel was lying on the gray cement floor.

"That is why your house is so dirty," she observed.

* * *

A few days later, a young woman appeared with a note from Mrs. Chawla. Her name was Lata. According to the note, she did not have to be paid. She had been working for a friend of Mrs. Chawla's who no longer needed her, and she wanted a place to sleep until a more permanent situation could be found. The exchange seemed more than fair, and I said yes, although I hardly needed another servant.

Lata had fair skin and arched eyebrows; she was lively and tall, and wore a salwar-kameez rather than a sari. I disliked her right away. I felt she was laughing at me, the way girls will laugh at an older woman behind their hands. She was, however, an excellent cook, and the house started to look better immediately. She didn't speak much English, but her Hindi was simple and clear, so even I could understand her.

Lata had noticed the cockroach problem, too. One morning, there was a white line, drawn in chalk across the back doorway. When I went into the kitchen, I saw another line ringing the drain in the floor. A small red-and-yellow box had been left on the counter, with instructions in Hindi and English: "For the prevention of vermin within the home. These insects will not dare to cross the powerful line. Highest quality poison but not harmful to humans." Inside was a white stick, like the kind of thick chalk children use to draw on the sidewalk.

I made coffee, and then went into my bedroom, where I found Lata crouched on the floor in front of the armoire, the door wide open to reveal my things inside.

She jumped up, and then smoothed her hair. "Madam," she said breathlessly. "You have such beautiful clothes."

I was aware that I should have reprimanded her, but somehow I let too much time elapse, and in my hesitation she rushed out of the room. The clothes swung gently from their hangers. They had been mostly purchased in Delhi, and were neither beautiful in the Indian sense nor exotic in the American one. Nothing seemed to be missing, and glancing through them I couldn't see what Lata had been looking for.

That night, she stood just outside my yard, laughing with a boy, and for the first time since Arun died I thought about going into the house to sleep. But when I stood up to leave I was uncomfortable at the prospect of walking past Lata and her suitor, and I stayed where I was, fighting off the familiar panic. If only I could stay still long enough, I felt I might turn myself into an object, something solid and inanimate, like the chair or the unreliable air-conditioner.

* * *

Arun's death was unnecessary and stupid. It was an insect-borne hemorrhagic fever called DHF, or dengue. Arun died of a mosquito bite, at an emergency clinic in the Golf Links, in a part of town I had never seen. Like almost all the bad news that I received in India, word of the illness arrived in a blue envelope from Mrs. Chawla. "I will leave pleasantries for happier times," she began. "My son is sick. You may think that you know what that feels like. I do not know you so I will not judge. But I do know that I, who have no daughters, would not presume to know about them. I ask you not to see him, as it would upset the family, who are with him all the time."

I read Mrs. Chawla's letter again and again, like a page in a high school science textbook. I put the letter in a drawer and made a deal with myself: I wouldn't see him, and, in exchange, he would be all right. Then I revised the terms: I didn't need to see him, because of course he was going to be all right. And if he wasn't, I thought that Mrs. Chawla would tell me. My day was now structured around the delivery of the mail and the sounds of people approaching the house. Mrs. Chawla didn't call; and I didn't know; and for me the hours before Arun's death were no different from the ones immediately after them.

. . .

I hadn't planned to return to America for my brother's wedding, and then at the last minute I decided I would go. I told Lata that I wanted her to help me prepare a lunch for Gita and her friends before I left, and she insisted that we go all the way to Defence Colony for the groceries. On the morning of our outing she dressed carefully, in ironed clothes and a pair of gold earrings that I had never seen before.

I didn't realize why I had agreed to drive so far out of my way until I was in the auto with Lata. By the time we got to the market, I was disgusted with myself, and still I couldn't turn around. I wouldn't let Lata buy meat, because the legs of lamb, marbled with white fat and twisting in the open air, made me queasy. She sulked for a while before becoming enchanted by a small, dark vegetable market that sold a species of fancy Chinese lettuce and miniature round green eggplants. While she shopped, I stood in the shade of the awning and watched the street. It wasn't that I believed I would be able to recognize Arun's wife from Mrs. Chawla's description, but I thought we might know each other by some other identifying mark or smell, the way a bitch can recognize her puppies, even after they have been taken away.

The market was U-shaped, and though Lata was carrying most of the groceries, she insisted on walking all the way around to the other end, and then out to the road. She wanted, she said, to find the same driver who had brought us.

"If he'd wanted to take us back, he would have stayed with us," I said. I raised my arm, and there were instantly three rickshaw drivers in front of us, fighting among themselves.

"We can take a taxi," Lata said urgently. The thought of a taxi, particularly an air-conditioned one, was appealing and I gave in. "This way," Lata told me, pointing in the direction of the taxi rank, and I followed her. It was the route she had originally wanted to take, down a shady street and out of the market. Here the houses had prominent alarm systems and the walls were very high, so only the second stories were visible.

"It's pretty," I told Lata.

"It's rich," she said, which was perhaps more accurate. We turned a corner, to get out to the main road, and almost collided with two teenage boys fixing a motorbike. Or pretending to fix a motorbike; they had the tools out on the sidewalk, but they didn't appear to know what to do with them. Lata stepped into the street to avoid the tools, and the boys stared at me.

When I went out in public, I wore a skirt that touched my ankles and a shirt with sleeves, no matter what the weather was. Inevitably, I was dressed more conservatively than the young women who wore Western clothes in this kind of area. These boys, who made no effort to conceal their interest, made me feel dowdy and conspicuously white.

Lata looked at me sideways, with quick, excited glances. When we were about halfway down the block, one of the boys gave a long, low whistle. With their tools and their expensive motorbike, they obviously belonged to the neighborhood. About a minute later, there was the sound of the motor, and then they were behind us, following very slowly.

"Lata," I said sharply. "Do you know those boys?"

Lata giggled. "Madam, they want to look at you."

"It's very impolite," I told her.

The boys came closer, and Lata glanced at them over her shoulder, teasingly. I turned around and stared, the way I would stare at a child who was talking in class until he became self-conscious and stopped. But it didn't work. The boys had longish hair that fell in their eyes and thick, curved lips; they were wearing T-shirts and cargo pants that looked as if they had been bought abroad. The one driving was maybe sixteen or seventeen, and the other was a couple of years younger.

"What are you doing?" I said, as icily as possible.

"What are *you* doing?" the driver asked. His accent was British in its forbidding crispness.

"What are you doing?" the other repeated, falsetto.

The older one smirked. Then he leaned forward, pursed his lips as if he were going to kiss me, and spat, very neatly, hitting the top of my foot, in its open sandal. He revved the engine. The younger boy, who had been looking on with a kind of enchanted shock, whooped loudly and over the sound of the motor he shouted, "Whore!" Then they arced out into the busy street, banking so sharply that their cuffs dragged on the ground, and disappeared into the traffic.

It astonished me that I had not recognized them before.

Lata bent down and was wiping my foot with a handkerchief, sobbing. "Madam," she said. "Madam, I do not know. I am sorry." Her cheeks, when she looked up at me, were wet.

"Which house is it?" I asked her.

Lata got up and led me back the way we had come, to the driveway where the boys had been repairing the bike. I rang the bell. I also ran my fingers very lightly over the numbers, where you would enter the code every day, if you lived there. Then I stepped off the curb and walked back out into the middle of the road, until I had the best view of the upstairs windows. I turned around slowly, and pretty soon Laxmi came down.

Was she a goddess, as everyone said? She was certainly very beautiful. Her *chuni* had bits of silver thread woven into the cloth, and she was wearing pearls in her ears. Her hair was hanging down her back, and her eyes, with their celebrated lashes, were deep-set and dark.

Lata set the groceries down and hurried through the gate without looking at me, like a citizen seeking asylum in an embassy. Laxmi waited until we had heard the door to the house open and shut.

"I don't want to talk to you," she said.

"I wanted to thank you for the loan of your servant."

She said nothing.

"She was helpful," I added. "I hope it wasn't difficult for you without her."

Laxmi seemed to consider this. "It was," she said finally. "But I thought you might need her more than I did."

I was ashamed. Laxmi looked confused, and it seemed suddenly touching that she had engineered this moment, wanting to see me for herself. She began to close the gate.

"Thank you," I said, and she stopped.

She pushed her hair behind her ear, almost flirtatiously. "I have my sons," she said casually. "And you have no one."

I did not cry until I returned to the compound and got to my room. Then, standing in front of the mirror, covering my breasts, I cried. I cried in the shower, and after I got out and dried my face the tears kept coming. For hours, they wouldn't stop; the second I wiped them away there were more. And then I was calm. It was five-thirty, exactly the time when I might have heard Arun's car coming around the circle. The compound was so quiet that I thought I could hear the cockroaches rustling in the walls.

·   ·   ·

I wanted to see Mrs. Chawla before I left India; I thought about calling first but didn't, and I was shown into the living room by a servant. I waited a long time, looking in a floor-to-ceiling glass cabinet crowded with mementos: a medal on a green and orange ribbon; a collection of ceramic animals—a deer, a Chinese carp, a giraffe; and an image of the monkey god Hanuman, opening his chest to reveal the faces of Ram and Sita in the place where his heart should be.

"You've come to tell me you're leaving," Mrs. Chawla said. She stood in the doorway, with her hair hanging down on either side of her face. She didn't want to have a conversation, or even, it seemed, come into the room.

I had planned to tell her that I'd confirmed my ticket. "I don't know," I said instead. "I'm afraid I may not be able to leave."

"Why?"

"I don't know. I like it here."

She was incredulous. "What? The heat, the brownouts? These people, coming from the country all the time with their filthy children?"

"Maybe."

She shook her head. "It always looks better from the other side."

"I'm not on the other side. I'm here."

"You're not charming, but you're stubborn," Mrs. Chawla said. "You're like me—like a daughter of mine would be."

"Luckily you have no daughter," I said.

Mrs. Chawla looked surprised. She ran one finger across the top of a small, spotless table. "When is your brother getting married?"

"Friday."

"The bride—what's her name—will be very disappointed."

"Very," I said.

"It will be a crime to miss that wedding."

"Mrs. Chawla?"

"You're going to regret it your whole life."

"I should have been there when Arun died," I said.

There was a brightness in her voice when she answered, a gold wire of fury.

"You didn't belong there," she said. "Nobody would've known what you were."

• • •

On the evening my brother got married, I watched a BBC news report of a dead buffalo that had been polluting the wells of three villages in Gujarat. There were shots of the dry, cracked ground, and the children with flies at the corners of their eyes, and the old people who wouldn't look at the camera. Then you saw the buffalo, a dramatic black shape in the dun-colored water. The reporters must not have wanted to get close, but there was a teenage boy who walked down to the brown river with a stick. He grinned at the camera and waved, and then poked the buffalo three times in the stomach. I had assumed that it was recently dead, because of the shininess of its black coat, and was surprised to see that once the explosion of black flies had risen off the corpse, there were large white spots, especially on the head, where the bones had already been picked clean.

After the news, I went into the bedroom and lay down. I thought about the people in a tent in my parents' backyard, proposing toasts. When I imagined myself there, I was afraid of something new—not just of being lonely but of what I would be lonely for.

Once, when Laxmi took the children to visit her parents in Calcutta, Arun spent four nights with me. On one of those nights, as we were lying in bed, I heard a bird outside, making a sound I recognized: a long swoop and then a two-note trill. I had thought that a nightingale lived in our compound and had asked Arun about it. He'd said it might be a mockingbird or a myna, but he would have to hear it to know.

"Arun," I whispered. I put my hand on his shoulder. "Arun, listen." I was afraid it wouldn't come again, but it did; far away. Then it was closer, and then it was right outside our window, in the dusty leaves of the mango tree.

Arun rolled over, and I could see his eyes in the dark. He was laughing.

"What?" I asked. He kissed my forehead and pulled me on top of him. "Why are you laughing?"

"It's the night-watchman bird," Arun said solemnly. "Sh-h-h, or he'll report us to headquarters."

Since then, I'd often heard the night watchman whistling, and once or twice I'd seen him on his bicycle, a skinny young man in an olive green civil servant's uniform, with a wooden stick against his hip.

I tried to picture Arun's face, but I couldn't—the image wouldn't stay clear. I could picture the compound, though: the women walking in pairs to the green-tiled vegetable shop across the road, the mango tree, a red cricket ball that had rolled underneath my hedge months ago and now looked like some kind of exotic bloom. Was it Arun, or India? Or was it that, for me, Arun was India?

It was six o'clock, and I recognized the whiskey-colored light on the white sheets: Arun pinning my wrists down with his hands, holding me tight beneath him so I couldn't move. It was not like with other people; he took it seriously, as if these were necessary things we were doing. Those evenings—Arun's car in front of the house, everyone knowing we were there—the whole world was in our room: tiny inscrutable figures moving in a pattern across our sheets.

And then the light was gone, and the windows were long and green, the walls steep. I sat up, and, in that moment, when my feet touched the cool cement, I had such an immediate sense of what had been blotted out: a white slice of dome, like an eye behind a half-closed lid—the unexpected view of something everyone in the world has seen a thousand times.

The Orphan

. . . .

When Alice picks up the phone there's no one there. "Hello," she says, "hello," and she almost hangs up before the recording of the operator comes on to ask whether she'll accept a collect call from—there is a caught breath, a sob, and she knows before they give her the tinned rendition of her daughter's name. There's a pause in which she's saying, "Mandy, Mandy?" and it seems like they've been cut off.

"Mom?"

"Mandy I'm here. What is it?" There's a delay on the line.

"Mom, I got hurt."

She becomes the mother of small children again: the competent, monomaniacal, emergency version of herself: "Mandy, how are you hurt? Tell me how."

"He hit me."

Her daughter is in Thailand, a place she knows is somewhere below and to the left of China, and someone—a him—has hit her. "Who hit you?" But Mandy's crying. The crying comes, after the pause, like a package delivered by the phone company, a sample of distress.

"Mom, he raped me."

"Who did?"

"Jew."

"A Jew raped you?"

Incredibly, Mandy laughs. "He's not Jewish—his name is Jew. It's J-O-O, except the *J* is kind of like a *Ch* in Thai, so you could also spell it C-H-O-O. They have forty-four letters so there are all these letters that we don't even have."

"It's someone you know?"

"Yeah—Mom—I met him through the program. We, you know, go out?"

"Mandy, where are you?"

"The bakery."

Mandy has called from a bakery before. It's one of those confusing new things that now have to be accepted as givens: she is forty-seven; her husband is living in a furnished studio downtown; in Thailand people make phone calls from bakeries. A bakery is a place where her daughter can be found.

"Mandy," she says. "It might take forty-eight hours before I'm there. Is there a place where you can go until then?"

"Is Dad there?"

"He's walking the dog," she says stupidly. There are plenty of true things she could have said. "He isn't here, but he can call you back. Give me the number where he can call you back."

"Don't tell Dad," Mandy says. "Don't come here."

"Of course I'm coming. I'm saying it might take forty-eight hours." As much as she doesn't want to admit this, it might take longer. They've had their Christmas tickets for months already, and it's only October. "It might take three days," she says. "You have to go to the hospital. Is there a hospital there?"

"Is there a hospital? Mom, I'm in Bangkok—maybe you've heard of it? Is there a *hospital*?"

Her daughter is upset and so she is—what is it—disassociating. "Then you can go there. Get in a cab and go there." She refrains from asking whether they have cabs.

"I don't usually take cabs here, Mom."

The conversation is somehow getting away from them. She thinks this is almost certainly the fault of the phone company. "Is someone with you? Can someone wait with you?"

There's a long pause, longer than the delay.

"I knew I shouldn't have called."

She thinks, bizarrely, of fishing. Her daughter is like a shiny trout, and it's up to her to reel her in. Any sudden movement, and it's over. "Mandy?" she says. She's relieved, this time, to hear the sobbing. "It's OK," she says. "We're coming. Or I'm coming. Dad doesn't have to come."

"I want you all to come at Christmas," Mandy says. "I want everything to be the way it was."

"You can come home now. Let me call and get you a ticket." She knows she's not doing this right, but she doesn't understand what she's doing wrong. She doesn't understand where Mandy *is*.

"Mom," she says. "Let me call you in the morning."

She's forgotten that it's night in Bangkok. The bakery takes on a sinister aspect. A glass front with a neon sign, a girl on the phone in between reflected headlights, everything dark except for one fluorescent light in the back.

"Who's with you?"

"A friend, Mom, it's OK."

She can't help it. "Not him?"

"A girlfriend," says her daughter.

Hank comes in from the dining room as if this answer doesn't satisfy him either. He stops a little way from her feet, cocks his head, and barks.

"Is that Hank?" Mandy asks.

"Yes."

"Put him on the phone."

"What?"

"Come on," she says. "I want to talk to Hank."

The dog allows himself to be picked up, allows the receiver to be held to his floppy ear. She hears Mandy's tiny voice: "Hank, Hank, hi, Hank. It's Mandy. Do you miss me? I miss you, Hank." Hank yelps, not because he is on a long distance call to Bangkok but because he has hip dysplasia. Someday in the not distant future they are going to have to put him to sleep. She knows this for sure. She is going to have to take him to the vet on Second Avenue and sign the papers to put him down. Who else is going to do it?

"Mom!"

She drops the dog, possibly robbing him of months of his life. "I'm here."

"So Dad's back?"

"What?"

"Dad came back with Hank?"

"He must have."

"Promise you won't tell Dad."

She hears herself agreeing to this.

"Thanks," Mandy says. "I'll call you in the morning."

"Wait," she says, but she doesn't know what to say. "Where are you going?"

There's the familiar impatience in her daughter's voice. She can picture the way her lower lip is jutting out, the sigh at the density of her mother and the world. "Home," she says, as if it were perfectly obvious that she would be going home at night, alone, in Bangkok. Or not alone.

"When?" she manages. "Can you just tell me when you'll call?"

"Nine. Or ten."

Nine or ten. She forgets to ask whether this is her time or Mandy's time, night or morning, today or tomorrow.

"Good night, sleep tight," Mandy says, which she could not intend in a horror movie kind of way, to terrorize her mother, but it feels that way, especially after Alice has hung up, and is standing in the kitchen, listening to the singing Subzero, punctuated by the loud second hand of the antique grandfather clock in the hall, and less regularly by the zipper sounds of cars, which she might count, or at least involve in some calculation, since she realizes she is holding a pen, which goes with the pad pinned to a cork message board on the wall below the phone, on which is written the number of a dermatologist, and that her left hand is touching the counter, not balancing but just making sure of the cold gray and white veined marble supporting three glass jars, flour and sugar and granola, with screw tops the same blond wood as the kitchen table underneath the window, where the sun is doing a kind of Mondrian thing of its own. It is eleven o'clock in the morning. That means at least ten hours to wait until "nine or ten," except that Mandy said she would call in the morning, which would mean her morning. Nine o'clock in Bangkok minus ten hours is eleven o'clock tonight, twelve hours from now. At least.

* * *

Two days before Christmas they are in a hotel in Bangkok waiting for their children. When the children were little, it was always hard to figure out what to do with them at Christmas. You didn't want them to forget about being Jewish, even if you weren't really doing anything to make them remember their heritage. Alice liked to think of them as double-negative Jews: as long as they didn't seem not-Jewish, it was fine. She and Jeff had come up with different possibilities—the movies (more Jewish), ice-skating at Rockefeller Center (almost not-Jewish because of the angel), skiing or Hawaii (nonsectarian)—but meeting the children in Bangkok to tell them about a divorce had never been an option. Jews don't get divorced, her grandfather used to say, when he was alive.

Alice's friends said that it was insane to go on a trip with Jeff. The problem was that when she talked to Jeff—they didn't see each other, but they talked about practical things on the phone—nothing was different. Sometimes, if it had been weeks without any contact, she would start to agree with her friends, and then Jeff would call, with some news about Mandy or Josh, or something to do with taxes or insurance, or she would have a question about the house, or her investments, and within ten minutes they would be making the same kinds of jokes they had always made together. She wasn't dumb enough to think that this meant they should *be* together, but it was hard to believe that he was any kind of threat. He was Jeff. It was hard to believe that there was some abstract, hidden danger bigger than the two of them.

Her impression of Bangkok, from the taxi ride the night before, is of a city underwater, a sea of snaky red and yellow lights in the murk. It is like Los Angeles, with the concrete overpasses and the palm trees, but with surreal details, like a dream of Los Angeles: the billboards in the strange alphabet, vendors with glass carts—red, yellow, and pale green fruits jewellike in illuminated boxes—three-wheeled open taxis, like motorcycles with hoods, extravagantly decorated with streamers and decals in a way that reminds her of the Mexican Day of the Dead.

The first thing Jeff noticed when he saw her was her hair. Then he asked if she was seeing someone. She liked the way his eyes snapped over her when she said, "Not really." She didn't want it to seem like she'd colored her hair right away after he'd left, but she also didn't want him to think she'd decided to do it out of desperation, for example, on the day that he told her about the Mexican woman.

"When are we going to see the AIDS babies?" Jeff asks.

They are waiting in the breakfast lounge. Jeff's hair is the same, grayish white but not thinning, and he is wearing the same gold-framed glasses. The skin on his arms is obscenely dry, even flaking a little. She is glad that the Mexican woman hasn't prevailed on him to use moisturizer, hasn't succeeded where she failed. On the other hand, it is possible that Mexican women who travel the world practicing environmental law don't have time to think about whether their married lovers are using moisturizer.

"There's not a fixed itinerary," she tells Jeff. This sounds more defensive than she intended. "They aren't going anywhere," she adds.

"Who isn't?"

"The AIDS babies."

Jeff gives her a funny look. He has brought his briefcase to breakfast.

"If you need to work," she says.

As it turns out, the briefcase isn't work but software for Mandy's computer so that she can connect to the Internet. Alice knows that Mandy will never read the instructions or install the software, that the briefcase will sit in the corner of her bedroom for the rest of the year, until she is finished working with AIDS babies and finally comes home.

"I thought we could have our confab at dinner tonight," Jeff says.

"Our confab?" She is looking at Jeff's mouth.

"I made a reservation," says her husband, whose mouth is now being used on someone who smells different, who washes with different soap, eats different cereal or doesn't eat cereal, maybe doesn't eat breakfast at all, sleeps naked or with the windows open, listens to opera or salsa or bluegrass: a stranger.

They bounced one of the phone lines to Jeff's new apartment so that the children get him half the time. It's a small, temporary deception. She hasn't told him about the conversation in October, or the second one, not eleven hours later but sixteen, a period of time in which she bought an airline ticket, packed a suitcase, took a codeine pill, and made espresso and then threw it away because how could you drink espresso when your daughter may or may not have been raped in a city famous for pollution, prostitution, and AIDS?

"I just wanted to let you know that everything is fine now," Mandy said when she finally called at three in the morning New York time. As if it just occurred to her to call, as if she might not have called, but was passing the phone and thought her mother might want to hear that although she had been raped and hit, probably, the night before, everything was now fine. "It was a misunderstanding," her daughter said. "It was a cultural thing, actually." And when Alice expressed skepticism about the need for cross-cultural understanding with rapists, Mandy said, "He's not a rapist."

"I'm sorry," she said, "but if he raped you, he is a rapist."

And Mandy said, "Don't call him that, Mom. He's my boyfriend."

She had not been angry in that furious, helpless way since Mandy was a teenager. She remembered one incident in particular, when Mandy had gone somewhere that was not allowed—she couldn't remember now what hadn't been allowed—and lied about it, and then listened to her mother's lecture about lying, about how it was the lie rather than the dance club or the bar or the party under the bridge, with a tiny smile, as if honesty were a kitschy fad from her parents' generation, like spider plants or macramé. And she thought now that it was as if Mandy had known, while she and Jeff were busy drawing up rules and lists of instructions, that this whole nonsensical era of unbelievable things was coming, and she was smiling at it, like a collaborator, over her mother's left shoulder.

"I want you to know that I'm going to tell them," Jeff says. "It's my responsibility—you just have to be there."

She is going to say something about the patronizing and controlling nature of that remark, and how this tone is even more offensive now than it was when they were together, when something makes them both turn, like puppets on the same string, and look at the door. A second later their son walks into the lobby.

Josh looks like someone coming out of trench warfare in the Balkans, rather than college in Maine. He's wearing some kind of heavy canvas work pants, rolled up to expose shockingly white ankles, a pair of New Balance running shoes with, for some reason, the toes cut out, and a T-shirt, which she read as "KFC" but is actually "KRC," or really "CRK," since the T-shirt is inside out. He stops in the center of the white marble floor, between the cocktail area, with the piano, and the breakfast lounge, and takes off his sunglasses. His eyes are shadowed with tired, purple half-moons.

"Josh," she says. Josh allows himself to be recognized and kissed, and then falls into the red silk armchair, staring at them as if he's trying to place who they are.

"This is so *urban*," he marvels.

"Do you mean Bangkok is urban, compared to Colby College?"

Ever since Josh was accepted by Colby, Jeff has called it "Colby College," as if he has to remind himself that Colby is a college. Mandy, like her father, went to Yale.

"He means Bangkok is more urban than American cities. Even more urban than New York in some ways," she says. "It's probably just the number of people—didn't that strike you on the way in—the number of people?" She knows she's babbling, but she is just enjoying looking at her son, who seems so obviously depleted, so clearly in need of care. "Is that what you meant?"

Josh raises his eyebrows and shakes his head just slightly, as if he expected to deal with lunatics but has found his parents even crazier than he anticipated. "Just, urban," he says.

Jeff hands Josh a menu. "We thought we could have breakfast here now, while we wait for your sister, and then go see one of the sights in the afternoon." A waitress in a silk sarong comes and kneels at Josh's feet.

"Do you know what you'd like, sir?" The kneeling makes Alice uncomfortable, and probably Josh too, for different reasons, because he blushes. She looks at Jeff, but Jeff isn't paying attention, because their daughter is standing hesitantly just inside the door.

Mandy is his favorite. There has been no competition since she was born. She looks like him, with the same straight nose, small, determined mouth, and heavy eyelashes, but it's the controlled intensity, the stubbornness, that is most strikingly similar. She walks across the lobby with her head down; he stands up so that she can identify them. It's only in the second before she hugs him that the reserve slips and they look at each other with this incredible recognition: secretly, they think they're the only two completely sensible people in the world.

Her daughter is at least ten pounds thinner than she was in September, and her clothes are stiff and folded, as if they were handed to her in a brown paper package this morning: an ankle-length skirt, a neat white blouse, and sandals. She sits down on the edge of the armchair and looks around the big atrium.

"Wow," she says, but it's a combination of wonder and skepticism.

"What are you two having for breakfast?" Jeff asks.

"Breakfast," Josh says.

"Aren't you hungry?" Alice asks.

"It's just a trip," says Josh. "It's been a while since I was up for breakfast."

"That doesn't instill in me a great deal of confidence about your career at Colby College," Jeff says, signaling the waitress, who has been standing at a polite distance.

Mandy smiles knowingly at the waitress, in a way she has not yet smiled at her mother. *"Mee goy teow arai na kha?"*

"Cool," says Josh.

"That's wonderful, sweetheart," Alice says. But there is something different about her daughter's speech, even in English.

"It's weird that they don't have *goy teow*," Mandy says.

"What's that?" Jeff asks. If it's remotely possible, he will try to arrange *goy teow*.

"It's like, noodles and broth I guess," Mandy says. "It doesn't really have a translation."

Alice can't help it. "You want noodles now?"

Mandy's smile is pitying. "It's what most people have for breakfast here, Mom."

"I thought we could go to the Grand Palace and Wat Pra Keo this afternoon," Jeff says.

"The Grand Palace?" Mandy makes a face.

"The book says that it's better not to go on the weekends," Jeff says. "But if you don't want to do it today we could go early next week."

Alice knows that he has planned not only today but every day of the upcoming week, and she knows how much it costs him now to rearrange it, to pretend to be flexible. At this age, she is finding that it's easier to indulge her own compulsions than try to conceal them from other people. The fact that marriages can be ruined by this kind of self-indulgence is something she's thought a lot about recently.

She notices that Mandy is hugging herself. "Do you want my sweater?"

"I'm fine," Mandy says sweetly. "I think it's just not being used to the air-conditioning."

You would think that her children had never been given breakfast, or stayed in an air-conditioned hotel. When the food comes, however, Mandy and Josh finish two orders of bacon and eggs, fruit salad, and a Danish each from their parents' continental breakfast baskets.

"I guess I might not have time to see the—whatever it is," Josh says when they're finished.

Jeff looks up from the bill. "Why's that?"

"I'd really like to get to this party on Tuesday."

"Is that a joke?" Jeff asks. "We're here for a week to see your sister, and you want to go back three days early for a party?"

"Dad, I don't mind," Mandy says.

"It's kind of an important party," says Josh. "It's more like a meeting. I might not get another chance to go."

"A meeting of what?"

"This group I'm in at school."

"You want to go to a meeting in Maine."

"It's not in Maine," Josh says.

"Well unless it's in Bangkok, you're not going," Jeff says.

"It's in Brunei."

Jeff smiles tightly. "Brunei, as in the sultanate on the northwest coast of Borneo?"

"I guess," says Josh.

"Who's throwing the bash—the sultan?"

"*Bash,*" Josh says, incredulous.

"I wouldn't think anyone but the sultan would be allowed to throw parties in Brunei," Jeff continues.

"Well, it's his son," Josh says. "I guess he lets his son throw parties too."

•   •   •

They wind up going to see the Jim Thompson house, which is Mandy's suggestion. It's still morning when they leave the hotel, but the cab ride across the city takes an hour and fifteen minutes, and by the time they arrive at the sight, there are low, dark clouds. The cab goes down an alley and into a red gravel parking lot surrounded by black trees. The air is humid but not totally unpleasant, because of a perfumy smell, like jasmine. The only other car in the parking lot is a teal Mercedes-Benz, which seems out of place in a Third World country. She knows better than to comment on this, but she notices her daughter looking at the car and wonders if Mandy is thinking the same thing.

The house is made of teak and the doors and windows narrow at the top, giving the whole building an upward sweep, like a candle. Inside is cool and dank, and they wait in an inner courtyard, lushly planted around the edges with purple and yellow orchids, white flowering shrubs with waxy dark green leaves, and young bamboo in clusters. A stone Buddha without a head holds one hand up in a gesture that could be "Stop," or "Peace." The only other people waiting for the tour are a pair of elderly German tourists, and a couple of American teenagers leaning against their backpacks, holding hands. The girl is wearing army fatigues with a tiny Indian-print tank top, an outfit that seems inappropriate given the formal atmosphere of the house. The girl must sense Alice's disapproval; she kicks off her sandals and, smiling superiorly, points and flexes her dirty feet. Mandy and Josh have moved to the other side of the courtyard so as not to be associated with their parents any more than necessary. When the tour starts, it turns out that the teenagers already know all about the owner of the house, Jim Thompson, a silk magnate who disappeared in the Malaysian jungle on Easter Sunday of 1967.

"Wasn't he with his girlfriend when he disappeared?" the American girl asks.

The guide is a young Thai woman with a perfect round face, dressed in green silk.

"She was not his girlfriend, only a friend," the guide says.

The girl is skeptical. "But why did he come to Bangkok?"

"Jim Thompson came to Thailand in World War II. He loves Thailand and the Thai people so much that he leaves his home and his family to come and help the Thai people."

Listening to this woman, whose English is clear and almost grammatical, Alice thinks she recognizes what's different about Mandy's speech. She isn't swallowing her words, exactly, but seems to be pulling them up from her throat like a string, as if she is being coaxed and is surprised to find them coming out at all.

"Her English is very good," she says to Mandy, who nods.

"See how she mixes up her tenses, though," Mandy whispers. "That's because Thai doesn't have them."

"How's that possible?"

Mandy shrugs. "I don't know—I guess you just don't notice after a while."

She likes hearing about the language from her daughter; it reminds her of when Mandy was little and she would come home with bits of information, about volcanoes, or the California gold rush. Still, she doesn't see how you could have a conversation without tenses. She wonders if it has something to do with the tones, if you might pitch a word higher to talk about the future, for example, and lower for the past—some system that Mandy hasn't learned yet.

The guide leads them through the rooms on the ground floor of the house, some of which have been turned into galleries. In one, the walls have been fitted with glass cases to hold a collection of Chinese ceramics: blue and white vases spiderwebbed with yellow hairline cracks.

"Jim Thompson is the first man to recognize the potential of a worldwide market for Thai silk," she says.

The backpackers won't give up. "But he didn't know about the silk when he came to Bangkok," the girl insists. "He must have had a Thai girlfriend, if he left his wife in America."

"Das ist verboten!" Jeff yells in his college German. The Germans are trying to ascend the staircase to the second floor, where you aren't allowed to go without the guide.

"God," says Mandy.

"Classic," Josh agrees.

Alice's head hurts, and she's starting to feel that jet-lagged lightness in her stomach. The Germans apologize in a way that makes her think that they read the sign in English and chose to ignore it.

"Maybe we should have a cup of coffee," she suggests.

Jeff has already thought of this. "There's a café."

"Please, just finish the tour," Mandy says. "We can have coffee in, like, ten minutes, OK?"

They go upstairs in single file, sandwiched between the Germans and the teenagers, to see a table set with crystal and green porcelain dishes. The chairs are upholstered in dark red and green silk, and the tall windows that look out on the canal (the *klong,* Mandy and the guide correct them) have shutters instead of panes. They close like boxes with little wooden knobs. The guide tells them that at the time of his disappearance Jim Thompson was unhappy about the modernization of Bangkok; that he refused to have a refrigerator in his traditional kitchen; and that he liked to host dinner parties by candlelight, which the silk weavers watched through the windows, standing outside in the dark by the *klong.*

When the tour is over, they go down to the café—a few wrought-iron tables and a coffee bar selling pastries wrapped in plastic. The one table big enough for the four of them is taken by a young Thai man drinking an espresso.

"Should we ask him to move?" Jeff asks.

"Dad," Mandy says. "I want to introduce you to my friend. Mom?"

The young man stands up. He's been waiting for them. He is square-jawed, and his face is puffy around the eyes, like a fighter. He's solidly built, but not much taller than Mandy; Jeff and Josh both have several inches on him, a fact of which she is glad, since she knows, of course, who this is.

"You guys, this is Joo," Mandy says. "Joo, this is my father, Jeff"—Jeff and Joo shake hands—"and my brother, Josh."

"Hey," says Josh.

"And this is my mother, Alice." Up until now Joo's face has been expressionless; when he holds out his hand to Alice, he smiles.

"Very nice to meet you," he says in an accent that horrifies her. It is much less attractive than the guide's, garbled, as if his tongue is wrapped in gauze. She notices that he is wearing some kind of gel in his hair, which falls in a heavy fringe over his forehead, like Elvis. "I'm very glad that you could come visit Mandy in Bangkok," the Thai Elvis says, as if Mandy is another one of the sights in the book, which he and the Thai people are graciously making available to the foreign public.

Jeff has chosen this moment to be hip and relaxed. "What can I get for everybody?" he says. Mandy asks for something unpronounceable, which Joo assures her that they won't have. She tells him about the failure of the hotel at breakfast in a breathy, incredulous voice; he laughs at her indulgently and, right in front of them, puts his hand on her daughter's back and rubs it. It lasts only a second, but Alice is dizzy. The air in the courtyard is steamy, like a kitchen, and she smells something underneath Jim Thompson's flowers, the sour musk of cooking from the street.

"Are you OK, Mom?" Josh asks.

"It's the heat." She feels like some colonial woman out of the nineteenth century. "And the jet lag."

But Mandy is watching her. Her daughter's mouth is set in a recognizable way, and her eyes are bright under their dark lashes. Mandy's eyes are her best feature; they aren't any special color, but they are deep-set, especially in her too-thin face, mobile and more expressive, probably, than she would like.

Jeff returns with five espressos and five bottles of water, more than anybody is going to drink. Alice sees them as time, minutes in liquid form that she's going to have to consume before she can stand up and walk out into better air.

"Joo, what kind of work do you do?" Jeff asks. "Or are you in school?"

Joo laughs. "I'm too old for school." There is a silence in which everyone would like to know how old Joo is.

"Joo is thirty-one," Mandy says.

Ten years difference, Alice thinks. Nine or ten, she remembers: sixteen hours.

"I'm working for my father now. In business."

"What kind of business is it?" Jeff's doing the lawyer thing, focusing on Joo as if he were a client whose case the firm was considering.

"Seafood," Joo says. He laughs in a manner both self-deprecating and insinuating, that presumes their condescension and expresses it for them at the same time. "We export seafood to Europe. Shrimp, squid, crab." He ticks these off on his fingers, which are soft and white.

"Joo wants to go into government," Mandy says.

"I will go into government," Joo says. "It's in my family."

"That's interesting," Jeff says. She can see him drawing satisfying conclusions about the relative integrity of American politics. She wants to scream at him—you are sitting next to a man who raped your daughter. Who walked in the street with her in those grandma clothes, then took her inside and forced himself into her. Who hit her (with his fist, the flat of his hand?) when she resisted.

"Could you pass the sugar?" the rapist asks.

"How exactly does it work?" Jeff says. "I mean, do you run for a seat in the legislature?"

"It does not work," Joo says. "Without the king, it would be . . ." He looks for the word.

"Catastrophe," Mandy supplies.

"The government is not important. Now is the time for business." Joo inclines his head toward the courtyard, where another group is gathering in front of the woman in green. "I admire this man very much. He comes, he finds something, he sells it. He takes what he wants."

"Well, but they say he revitalized the whole industry," Jeff says. "That he kept all the manufacturing here."

"It's cheap here," Joo says.

Josh laughs. "News flash, Dad."

Jeff gives him a look that doesn't seem to bother Josh, but Alice hates it. Even in this situation, she can't help trying to defuse things. "The house is just beautiful," she says. "I love the architecture. And his art collection is phenomenal."

Joo nods as if he is agreeing with her. "He is also a very good thief."

"Mom," Mandy says. "You're staring at me."

She doesn't mean to kick the table, but when she stands up, the table jumps forward, Jeff spills his coffee, a bottle hits the ground and rolls.

"I'm sorry," she says. "I think I just need some air. I'm going to go out there and just get some air. I'm sorry."

She is walking away from her family, through the claustrophobic gift shop, tripping over the old-fashioned lintel. She walks out to the edge of the gravel and stands at the entrance to the parking lot, looking into the alley and just breathing. The sky is still dark, but the sun has come through the clouds and the direct sunlight is unpleasantly intense. In the alley there are several locked storefronts, and a stand where a woman is cooking something, noodles on a griddle. A dog sticks close to the shadowed side of the buildings, which end abruptly at the gray canal.

"Mom." Mandy has followed her out; she looks around, but no one else is with her. A small blessing. "What's *wrong*?" Mandy knows what's wrong, of course—she just wants to hear Alice say it.

"You might have warned me," Alice says. "It didn't need to be a surprise."

Mandy's voice is wounded and self-righteous. "I thought you actually might give him a chance this way. I thought you actually might *like* him."

"I'm sorry."

"You're saying you don't like him."

"I find him unappealing, yes."

"Physically."

"Not physically," Alice says, although, of course, she does. "Or yes, because I know what he did to you. I find him repulsive, because of that."

Mandy snorts a contemptuous little breath. "This is exactly—I knew you would say that. I remember you saying it before." She raises her voice in what is supposed to be an imitation of Alice: "'I just don't find Asian men *appealing.*' Just admit it. He disgusts you because he's Thai. You can't stand the thought of me in bed with him."

"I can't stand the thought of you in bed with him because he raped you." The expression on her daughter's face makes Alice think for a second that she might've said the right thing.

Mandy shakes her head. "I should never talk to you. I just shouldn't. One little thing—when I'm upset—and it's over. You've already closed your mind to the possibility."

"Of liking someone who raped you," Alice says. "Yes. I've closed my mind."

She feels a weird sense of calm as Mandy gets upset, as if the two of them can support a fixed quantity of anger, and Mandy is acting, just now, as a siphon. Behind the shuttered pharmacy directly across from them, someone is flying a square orange kite.

"Maybe I kind of liked it," Mandy said. "Have you thought of that?"

Alice doesn't say anything.

"Have you even heard of rape fantasies?"

"They're something I read about in college. Not something I believe in."

"You *believe* in? Jesus, Mom, it's not something you believe in or don't believe in. It just is." There are footsteps on the gravel. "Maybe I *wanted* to get fucked like that." Mandy says this under her breath, and then turns and smiles at her father, who is coming out of the house. She points to one of the hooded motorcycles with the seat in the back, and asks, in her normal voice, "Why don't you take that?"

"We're taking a cab," Jeff says.

There is no question that Jeff will find a cab. Alice watches him walking toward the main road in his Brooks Brothers loafers and wants to tell him that she loves him.

"I'm getting a ride," Mandy tells her brother, or at least she's looking at Josh when she says it. Josh gives her a melodramatic hug. Alice remembers a time when had she suggested that he hug his sister, she would have been met with sworn protests, squeals of disgust.

"Thanks," Mandy says, then crosses the lot in front of the teal Mercedes, which Joo has already started, and climbs into the car. The car slides past them into the alley without stopping, the gravel rattling in the wheels. She can only see the outline of Joo through the tinted window, and her daughter not at all. Josh knows enough to be quiet. They stand there in the alley, waiting for the cab.

● ● ●

At seven-thirty Mandy is still not back at the hotel. Jeff goes into the restaurant every six or seven minutes while they're waiting, to confirm the reservation. The third time, Josh rolls his eyes at her, which makes her feel favored, until she looks up and sees that this time Jeff is not in the restaurant but at the desk. They had planned, after tonight, that Mandy would move into their room, and Jeff in with Josh. Now that it looks like they aren't going to have the talk, Jeff is keeping the extra room—three rooms for four people.

They eat at eight without Mandy. There is almost no one in the restaurant. Alice sits on the same side of the table as Jeff, across from Josh, whose T-shirt is still inside out.

"Is that a band?" she asks. She asks because she can tell that Jeff, who has been preparing for the confab, has nothing in reserve.

"It's a club," Josh says.

"A dance club?" She's pleased that she remembered it's now "dance" as opposed to "night."

"A school club," Josh says. "Like the glee club. It's called CRK—Cool Rich Kids. It has ties to the Anarchist Collective, but it's a totally different thing."

Jeff stops what he's doing, which is eating a piece of salmon sushi. "What do the Cool Rich Kids do?" he asks, with the sharp-edged politeness that she thinks of as his courtroom voice, although he rarely goes to court anymore.

Josh explains to his father that the Cool Rich Kids are a nationwide club of college students who donate money—from trust funds; inheritances; the proceeds from sold stereo components, computers, cars—to a variety of grassroots organizations endorsed by the group.

"It's funny that anarchists would even have a collective, isn't it?" Alice remarks, and is ignored.

"You're a part of this group?" Jeff confirms. The salmon sushi is suspended between Jeff's black chopsticks; it hovers over the table like a cherub, escaped from some revelatory Renaissance painting to save them.

"Yes."

"We're not rich," Jeff tells him.

Josh looks pointedly around the restaurant, at the glazed wooden screens that separate one table from the next, the battalion of waiters, the enamel boxes on which their orders are sculpturally arranged.

"We're comfortable," Jeff says.

"Could we not talk about this, please," she says.

"I'm just curious," Jeff says. "I would think it would be up to the person who made the money to give it away."

"Not necessarily," says Josh. "We're pretty excited about it, actually, because it's this chance to endorse the more radical causes that people your age wouldn't support. Like prison abolition, for example. Or resistance to the World Bank." Josh pauses and serves himself more soba noodles from the platter in the center of the table. "A lot of us feel that even though we grew up with this incredible privilege, there weren't any real examples of charity."

"Are you saying that you feel that way?"

For a moment, Josh's neck and shoulders stiffen and she can see him at fourteen, unhappy in his own body. "Well, Dad, I mean—where did we give money?"

"Yale," Jeff says. "We give to Yale."

Josh looks at his mother, raises his thumbs in a little gesture of helplessness. "If you insist on giving to an institution, there are some that may need the money more than Yale."

She refrains from saying that he has a point, mostly because she feels implicated. "Would you like some dessert?" she asks Josh instead.

"I'm not a big dessert eater," her son informs her. "Would you mind if I went back upstairs?"

After he's gone to the room that he was supposed to be sharing with Jeff, Alice and Jeff decide to share another Sapporo. Then they decide to share a tumbler of cold sake.

"This is very unusual for me," Jeff says, as if it's their first date.

"I don't even keep it in the house anymore," she counters.

Her husband is holding the tiny cup between his thumb and finger, examining it with a worried expression, as if someone has accidentally served him from a doll's tea set. His shoulders, relaxed, are narrow for a man his height and inspire in her a kind of protectiveness.

"The Cool Rich Kids?" he says finally.

She laughs, but she's glad she's not the only one who can't talk to their children. She's also glad that Josh's T-shirt doesn't have anything to do with crack. She decides it would be OK to tell Jeff a little bit about her conversation with Mandy, as long as she omits certain details.

"Mandy thinks I'm a racist."

"She said that?"

"She said I don't like Joo because he's Thai."

"You don't like him for the same reason I don't like him," Jeff says. "He's an arrogant little shit."

"Didn't you think he was greasy?"

Jeff laughs. "On the other hand . . ."

"What?"

"I'm just kidding," Jeff says.

"Yes, but I don't know what you're kidding about."

Jeff smiles down at his cup in a way that makes her want to kill him. "It's just, 'greasy'—you know."

"I meant his hair," Alice says, which is what she meant, but somehow it doesn't sound believable.

"You don't like him because of his hair?" He's looking at her affection-ately, as if he knows her, and has the right to laugh at her. He looks re-laxed, from the drinking and the fucking. She hasn't been fucked for months, not since two months before they broke up, and he is looking at her as if they're friends.

"I don't like him because he raped our daughter," she says. "And hit her—I don't like that either."

Jeff checks her face to see whether there's some chance that he has mis-understood. He looks away immediately, at the door, as if he's suddenly remembered that he's meeting someone else. The door has a beaded cur-tain and is empty.

"I'm going to kill him," Jeff says.

For a second, she thinks he means it.

"It's going to be harder here. The system makes it more complicated."

She likes the simple version better. She would like it to be even sim-pler: she would like Jeff to cut Joo's throat with a knife. He means, of course, that he'll kill Joo in court, have him put away for years. Questions of international law aside, there is another complication, one that she's reluctant to explain to Jeff. Now that she's gone this far, however, she doesn't have a choice.

"Except that she thinks he didn't."

"What?"

"She said that he raped her, and now she says that he didn't."

Jeff coughs and visibly swallows, and his voice comes out scratchy: "What do you mean?" He grimaces and puts a hand on his throat.

Alice shrugs. "That."

Bizarrely, she feels beautiful. She feels like she sometimes does when she's looking at her upper arms in the mirror. Every once in a while, she allows herself to just look at this part of her, her triceps, which are thin and hard from the gym. Other women envy them. She goes to the gym almost every day; she isn't one of these women who let themselves go to hell. Or, rather, she doesn't let the exterior go to hell.

When the waiter comes back with Jeff's card, she smiles at him gracefully, the way a young woman might smile at the waiter while her date is paying for dinner, as if the two of them have pulled something off.

This waiter is a young man, probably in his early twenties. He looks apologetic. "There is a problem with the card."

"What?" Jeff almost whispers.

"We are—dialing—but there is no accepting the United States."

"I have no idea what you're talking about," Jeff says. He is getting to that point, the kind of frustration where he loses control, and Alice braces herself for it. She curls her toes in her espadrilles. "Can I speak to your manager? Is there anybody here who speaks English?"

"Sir, they do not accept the card."

"Give them the Visa," Alice says.

Jeff pauses, and then relents. He takes out his Visa. When the waiter sees it, he turns slightly to the side, as if willing himself somewhere else. "I am sorry, sir. But it is only American Express here."

Jeff stands up. He has at least five inches on the waiter and looks almost freakishly tall. He's holding his wallet in both hands as if it were something fragile, like an egg. "How do you want me to pay? How the fuck do you want me to pay. I have two cards, three bank accounts, or a checkbook. Do you want a personal check? Or would you rather I didn't pay? We could just walk out of here and not pay. Because I am trying to pay you—and there is not a fucking thing wrong with my card."

"I'm sorry, sir."

If he were not so well trained, so libel-conscious, this is the point at which he would grab the waiter. She can see the wild blue veins in his wrists.

"*You're* sorry—so why is this my problem? Can you tell me that?" The waiter looks for help, but there are only the two cocktail waitresses in kimonos at the bar. "What do you want me to do here? What do you *want*?"

Alice finds the Amex card in her own wallet, which she certainly should have done sooner, if only for the sake of the young man. "Try this one," she says to the waiter, who snaps out of their nightmare, in which he's been momentarily entangled, bows to both of them, and takes her card. Jeff stands above the sunken table like a man on stilts.

"What the fuck do you do?"

• • •

She prays that they will find both of their children in the hotel room, and miraculously, they do. Mandy and Josh are watching Thai MTV with the sound off and drinking airline-sized bottles of Tanqueray from the mini-bar. It's strange how happy this makes her, the sight of her children in their pajamas together, getting drunk.

"Can I talk with you in our room?" Jeff says.

Josh starts to get up off the bed. "This is what democracy looks like," he says for some reason, and Mandy giggles.

"Just Mandy," Jeff says.

Mandy tries to hide her surprise. She's wearing an undershirt and a pair of flannel pajama pants that are ripped at the bottom. She sits up on the bed, looks at Jeff, and tips her head back to finish the Tanqueray.

"Are there any more of these?" she asks Josh, without taking her eyes off her father.

"Absolutely, let me get you one," Josh says. "This is a very fine hotel."

"Let's go into the other room now," Jeff says.

"I don't mind if Josh hears," Mandy says.

There's a straight-backed chair next to the television, and Jeff has to close the television cabinet in order to sit down. He looks like a student getting ready for an oral exam.

"We want you to come home with us. Your mother and I think it's very important." Alice thinks about whether or not she thinks it's important. If there's only a possibility that it's important, is that enough reason to force Mandy to come home?

"Why?" Mandy asks. There are perhaps thirty seconds of silence in which Alice can hear the crackling electricity of the muted television.

"Because of what happened to you."

"What happened to me?"

Jeff's shoulders are rounded but his chin is thrust forward, as if he's struggling to read a screen. She thinks he might not be able to say anything, and then he finds the language he wants. "You were assaulted."

Alice waits for the accusation, but Mandy doesn't even look at her. She smiles at her father in a sympathetic way. "That didn't happen."

Behind his sister, Josh's eyes keep shifting back to the half-hidden TV screen. Alice thinks of the incredible frustration of not knowing things, and of knowing that they can't be known—the incredible privacy of people's experience. She wonders why they fight it at all, why they don't just allow each other to spiral off into their own interpretations: four people watching a movie about a family like themselves.

"You can come back and talk to someone," Jeff coaxes. "It doesn't have to be us."

Mandy gets up off the bed and goes to the cabinet. She takes out a sweatshirt with a hood and zips it over the tank top. Then she looks around for her jeans, which are draped over the back of her father's chair.

"Excuse me," she says. Flustered, Jeff gets up and moves to the other side of the room. Mandy goes into the bathroom and they hear the water running. When she comes out, she's dressed, and her hair is in a ponytail. She's wearing rubber flip-flops with cartoon frogs over the toes.

"We can all stay the week," Jeff says from across the room, but Mandy isn't listening.

"You're coming to my work in the morning?"

Alice nods.

"I'll see you then," Mandy says brightly, and heads for the door.

Alice has never seen Jeff cross a room so fast. He's behind Mandy in a second, before she can touch the door. His arms are around her, and he's leaning over her shoulder. He whispers something. Alice looks at Josh, who's embarrassed too, playing with the label on the little green bottle.

"No," Mandy says. She starts to struggle, but Jeff is pinning her arms at her sides. She kicks and it's only the rubber shoe, but he has to step back, still holding her—she's twisting quietly, and now Alice can see her face and her eyes are shut.

What would the night manager think if he were to come into their room right now? Would he focus on the man and the girl fighting in front of the door, or the others staying still? Would he recognize the struggle as something that happens in every home—in his own home— or would he back out of the room, in his neat suit, disgusted by their ugly, foreign habits?

As soon as Mandy stops fighting, Jeff lets go.

She drops onto the bed. "OK."

"You'll come home with us?" Jeff says. It occurs to both of them at the same time; he looks at Alice automatically and with shame. And maybe this unexpected sensation disconcerts him for a moment, breaking his usually perfect concentration, because when Mandy says, very firmly, "Good night," he doesn't protest but just steps toward the door, looking at her hopefully but as if he's forfeited his right to speak.

"Good night," she says, and he puts his hand on the knob. "Good night." Each one is like a little shove.

"We'll see you in the morning," Alice says.

Mandy doesn't change the pleasant intonation. "Good night."

They stand for a minute outside the room. They know that they'll pay for this room as long as their children want it, as many rooms as Josh and Mandy demand, forever and ever, whether they use them or not, whether they go out and leave the beds made in the middle of the night. She and Jeff are like people pretending to bargain with kidnappers and knowing all the time that they will give up everything, the minute they are asked.

* * *

The AIDS babies live in a better neighborhood than Alice expected, near an enormous new shopping mall. Across the street is a vacant lot, but the houses on the babies' side all have gardens with lush vegetation: berries and hanging flowers and palms spilling over locked wooden gates. The home is called Tarn Nam Jai, which means "flowing heart." A broken fountain stands in the middle of the courtyard, thick with algae. Orange and white carp glide just under the green surface, like pale, fat feet floating in a lake.

A young woman is sitting on a bench in the sun with one foot up on a plastic Big Wheel, smoking a cigarette. Mandy says hello in that sugary voice and puts her hands together; the attendant extinguishes her cigarette on the bench in order to return the gesture. Then she takes a pack of matches from a bag next to her on the bench and relights it.

Before they go inside, they put their shoes in a wooden rack, already half filled with flip-flops like Mandy's, soft flowered house slippers, and a few pairs of conservative flats. All of the shoes belong to women. They enter the house through a screened-in porch, into a kind of vestibule, where Mandy stops and asks them to wash their hands. When Alice hears the first cries, they surprise her, and she realizes she didn't expect to find live babies here. She didn't expect to find dead ones, but when she pictured Mandy working in a home for AIDS babies, it was always empty beds and abandoned toys, scared young women with silent bundles.

Instead the baby home is like an aviary. Three sides of the main room are screened, to let in the air; giant ferns press up against the screens from outside. Alice is surprised that the home isn't more strictly quarantined, but perhaps there isn't any point. Mandy says that all of the babies are orphans, but that some have contracted HIV from their mothers and some haven't. Sometimes you can't tell for several years.

The babies are sitting or lying on blue plastic matting. It seems absurd that they could be orphans, and babies, and AIDS patients at once—that anything their size could support all these deficiencies. They look like worms, dropped, or about to be snatched up, by enormous birds. She can hear birds calling all around, just outside the screen. She looks at the worm-babies and is horrified by an absence of sympathy, especially when Jeff kneels down on the mat and extends his finger to a toddler playing with a squeaking plastic hammer.

"Mom?" says Mandy. It's the first thing she's said directly to Alice since yesterday. She's holding a baby. "This is Esmerelda."

"Esmerelda?"

"They give them English names, to tell the visitors. They get a lot of missionary groups and stuff."

Alice has heard people describe skin as "gray" before, but she has never seen anyone with skin like Esmerelda's, the color of smoke. She has very little hair, and her head is dusted with fine white powder. Mandy has put a piece of flannel over her shoulder, and when Esmerelda starts to cough, she transfers her to the cloth, where the baby spits up a clear wet stain.

"I'm going to go help with lunch," Mandy says. "Do you want to hold her?"

Alice does not want to hold Esmerelda. She wants to turn around and walk out into the road, down the alley to the main street, with the concrete tramway, over the pedestrian flyover, into the gleaming new mall, the Emporium. She wants to ride the escalator. Certainly the mall has escalators. She wants to ride it all the way to the top—at least six floors—and then take it down to the bottom again, just once. Then she thinks she would be capable of coming back here and doing all the things she has to do.

She takes the baby from her daughter, who says, "Her Thai name is

Bun." Esmerelda/Bun is wrapped tightly in several layers of blankets, under which she feels hard, like a doll. Her hands are covered with blue knit booties, to keep her from scratching the scabby, bruise-colored marks on her neck and arms. She relaxes into Alice without struggling, like no baby she's ever held. She knows it's hokey, but she thinks that this baby, this Bun, knows what's going on. There are eyes like this in old master paintings, lace-bonneted infants who stare out of dark Dutch interiors, their monkey faces the only ones turned toward the painter. Esmerelda's eyes stay open, and fixed on Alice, as if she knows which one of them needs to be reassured.

"He's really smart," Jeff says to Josh, who's standing a few feet from the blue mat in his sweat socks. Jeff is on his hands and knees next to the toddler who is hitting pop-up Disney characters with a musical hammer. Each time Mickey gets slapped down, Donald or Goofy pops up. "Watch," Jeff says. "Look at that." Before he hits Mickey, the baby puts his hand over the hole where Goofy should appear, so Mickey descends halfway and only Goofy's head comes up out of the hole.

"Noum," says a fat attendant, pointing to Jeff's baby. She is sitting against the screen, giving one of the infants a bottle of formula.

"His name is Noum?" Jeff asks.

"Name," the girl says.

"Noum," says Jeff. Noum hits Jeff's knee with the hammer.

"English," the girl says.

"Actually, we're American," Jeff says, as if she will understand if only he speaks politely enough.

"English," she repeats sharply, and Noum looks up. "English!"

Noum sticks his hand straight out in front of him, then opens and closes his fist. "Good-bye," he says.

"Oh." Jeff cups one hand around each of the baby's small shoulders. "See," he tells Josh, "he's the smartest one."

All of a sudden, the lights go out. One of the babies whimpers but doesn't cry, and then Mandy appears in the doorway of the dim kitchen, her face lit by candlelight. She is carrying a cake and leading the singing of "Happy Birthday" in English to the fat attendant. The attendant's name is Pi Oi, and they sing to her, for some reason, three times. When they turn on the lights again, Jeff is holding Noum on his hip. Mandy goes over and puts a green foil party hat on Noum, who takes it off and pushes it into Jeff's chest. Jeff puts on the hat obediently, fixing the elastic band underneath his chin.

"Let me take a picture, Dad," Mandy says, but Alice takes it. She wants to get all three of them in the same frame. Jeff puts his cheek next to Noum's and points to the camera.

"Say Christopher Columbus," he says. It's a family tradition, one that has led to a lot of family pictures in which they all seem to be chewing something. There's a reason why people say "cheese" as opposed to making up another word; often, when you try to step around the conventional way of doing things, you end up with something worse. She's thinking this when she lifts the camera and sees something incredible: Jeff's eyes, wet behind his glasses. It's the second time in thirty years that she's seen him cry.

"Take the picture, Mom," Josh says. Even after she takes it, Jeff continues to hold Noum, walking him around the room and talking to him so that the baby won't get bored.

Maybe it's because his head is too big, but Alice doesn't like this baby. When she tries to imagine him grown up, she pictures a dwarf, like the one who works for the florist in their neighborhood and walks as if his knees didn't bend, swinging his stumpy arms. This isn't the baby she would choose, if she were going to choose a baby, but he's the one Jeff has chosen, and the idea she's been having—crazy—is that it could be enough.

She remembers sitting at the dining room table in their first apartment, pregnant, with her head down on her arms, listening to Jeff doing the dishes in the kitchen and thinking: I don't want to have this baby. And it was much worse than she'd expected. They didn't tell you that.

Of course she knew that they would make mistakes; she just hadn't understood how each mistake would come out of the last one, narrowing their choices, as if they were trying to solve a maze in ink. By the time she had Josh she understood this, but she still arranged the absurd miniature clothes—socks and hats and sweatpants—in perfect piles underneath the changing table, as if this would give her some kind of early advantage.

The best thing about Noum is that he is already born. He's already working at such a disadvantage that their mistakes wouldn't matter so much. There is probably a lot of paperwork, but who is going to turn them down? They could take Noum home and buy him new clothes so that he wouldn't smell like the AIDS home—not that the home smells bad, exactly, but there is something metallic about the air, mixed with the heavy odors from the kitchen. She wonders if this baby would start to smell the way Mandy and Josh did if they were to bring him back to the house on Sixty-sixth Street. She pictures too much food in the refrigerator, piles of things on the stairs that no one ever takes up, broken crayons at the bottom of her purse. She looks at Jeff looking at the baby and can see him thinking, "Yale."

Afterward, they cross the street to the Emporium, where they ride the escalators up six floors of the same sparsely decorated shops that you find in Soho, accompanied by the sound of throbbing, heartbroken Asian pop, to the top of the mall, where there is a long food court overlooking the park. While Jeff is in the bathroom, she and Mandy and Josh sit making fun of a man and a woman being professionally photographed on the steps of a hotel on the other side of the park. The man is in black tie, standing just behind the woman without touching her. The woman is wearing a V-necked crimson dress with long sleeves and a fishtail train, and holding a violin. Mandy admits that she comes here almost every day after work, and she says that the hotel is a popular place for pictures, although it's more often a wedding.

Jeff is gone for a long time. Finally she sees him coming back, carrying a ridiculous shiny pink bag.

"What happened to you?" Mandy asks. "What's that?"

"I had to get something," Jeff says. "It was hard to make the cretin in the store understand."

If Alice said that, Mandy would spend another twenty-four hours not speaking to her. Instead all she says is, "You should've let me do it." Then she takes the bag and looks inside. *"Dad."* She rustles around in the tissue and pulls out a toy race car, painted red. It's the kind you drag backward across the floor, that it shoots forward when you release it until a spring unwinds inside.

Jeff seems embarrassed. "It's for Noum, the next time you go." Then he looks at Alice significantly, as if he is confirming something. She has a pleasant, nervous feeling, like a teenager on a date. When they get up to leave, Jeff takes their trays back to the counter, allowing Mandy and Josh to get a little bit ahead.

"That's quite something," he says.

"The home?" She wants to be absolutely sure that she knows what he's talking about.

"It's hard to believe it's her, working there."

"Yes." Alice is careful to match her step to his. Now their children are laughing at something, probably at them.

"So we'll try again?" Jeff says.

"What?"

"We'll tell them at dinner tonight—if everybody can manage to get along until then?" Across the atrium, people are waiting to see *Titanic* in Thai. The line curves all the way around the central atrium, so shoppers getting off the escalator have to push their way through the crowd.

"I can manage," Alice just barely manages to say.

● ● ●

In the center of the restaurant, the Spice Route, a woman is sitting on a raised round dais.

"Oh, good," says Josh. "There's a floor show." The woman is dressed in traditional clothes, made of gaudy red silk, and her mouth is painted on like a geisha's. Her feet are tucked underneath her skirt, and she's peeling vegetables. On the plate in front of her are a series of roses, fruits, and pinecones carved out of radishes and carrots.

"I feel like we're on the Jungle Cruise," Josh says. "You know, at Disneyland?"

The restaurant is a little kitschy. They have to walk underneath a kind of bamboo trellis to get to the hostess stand, which is flanked by two large decorative clay water pots.

"Should we go somewhere else?" Jeff asks. "If you don't want to go here, I'm happy to take other suggestions."

"It's fine," Alice says.

"It's fine," says Mandy. "The food is supposed to be good." Then she giggles: "Look at the tiki torches."

Their waiter is dressed in a sarong and an unbleached cotton pullover with a hood. He has a bandana knotted around his head and there is no question that he's wearing eyeliner. "Hiya," he says. "My name's Chai, I'll be your waiter tonight." Chai's voice rises and falls in a way that doesn't have to do with tones. "Now what are we having to drink?"

"I don't think we need any drinks," Jeff says.

Chai weathers this news calmly. "I am going to bring you some of our famous cashews, anyway," he says. "They're only supposed to come with the drinks, but they are so *yummy.*"

"Do you have any tropical cocktails?" Josh asks. "Like a Hurricane, by any chance? I'm really feeling like a tropical cocktail right now."

Alice looks at Jeff, who has something wrong with his face. He's smiling, but he's only using his mouth; no other part of him is moving.

"Maybe Mandy should order for us," she says. They are seated unfortunately near the vegetable artist, who smiles demurely like—now that Josh has suggested Disneyland—one of the mechanical dolls in "It's a small world."

When Chai comes back with the drinks menu, Mandy orders dinner. After every dish, Chai gives a little exclamation at her pronunciation.

When she says a couple of sentences—Alice notices that she rarely wastes an opportunity to do this, even when it's completely unnecessary—Chai puts his hand over his heart, rolls his eyes to the ceiling, and tells them that their daughter must have been Thai in another life.

"I am really glad we could take this trip together," Jeff says when they have finally ordered.

"Uh-oh," Mandy says.

"This is what democracy looks like," says Josh.

Jeff looks at him. "What is that?"

"Nothing."

"What did you just say?"

Josh sighs. "I said, 'This is what democracy looks like.'"

"That's what I thought you said," Jeff says. "I just wanted to know what you meant by that."

"It's just a slogan. Forget it."

"I'm interested in what it has to do with our conversation."

It occurs to Alice that he's procrastinating.

"It's not so much our conversation." Josh removes a pineapple and strawberry skewer from his Hurricane and sets it carefully on the cocktail napkin. "It's more like the ambiance of the restaurant."

"Your father is trying to tell you something," Alice says.

"You're getting a divorce," Mandy says.

Everyone at the table looks at Mandy. Only Jeff seems not to realize that she was kidding. He's very relieved. She can tell because of the way he rearranges his napkin in his lap.

"We're getting separated," he says. "We're not sure about the divorce."

"Are you serious?" Mandy says.

"Yes?" He asks it like a question, but Alice knows by now that it isn't. He's using that inflection because he's afraid of his daughter, who is getting the fierce look that means she's about to cry.

"Where are you going to live?" Josh asks.

Jeff tells him about the Union Square apartment.

"But you're not living there yet?"

Jeff looks at her: a question they should have anticipated.

"How long have you been living there?" Josh demands.

"Six months."

"Here we go," says Chai. He begins unloading platters onto the table. The food looks as if it's been shellacked, like ornamental plastic food. Hot red peppers are spaced artistically through the meat. A brilliant carrot peacock is poised at the edge of a field of beef, mint, and peanuts.

"Enjoy," says Chai.

The food glistens.

"You can ask us any questions you want," Alice says.

"How come you're home when I call?" Josh asks his father.

This time Jeff doesn't even bother to look at Alice. "We bounced the phone line," he says. Alice thinks that his choice of pronoun is unfair and is glad to see that Josh's disgust is entirely focused on his father.

"It made sense for a number of reasons," Jeff says. "We didn't want to talk with you about this over the phone. We're all so far-flung." Jeff tries to make a joke: "New York, Bangkok, Waterville."

Josh looks at Mandy. "It's not the divorce we mind," he says. "It's the lying."

"Are you seeing someone else?" Mandy asks.

"It's not that," Jeff says.

A noise comes out of Alice, a snort. She didn't mean to do it, or at least she didn't think about it before she did it.

"You are?" Josh says.

"It isn't about that," says Jeff.

"It's just a coincidence," Josh says.

Alice is interested to know what Jeff will say about this, really interested, except that Mandy is crying, or preparing to cry: her eyes are full and brown, like a horse's eyes. She has always had this ability to prolong the dramatic moment.

"Sweetheart," Alice says.

Josh stands up.

"Where are you going?" Jeff asks.

"Brunei."

Jeff smiles, as if this answer pleases him. "Your friend must be the coolest of the Cool Rich Kids."

"He's the richest," Josh says, not getting it.

"Could we stop this," she says. "I would like for us to stop this."

"I wonder how the sultan feels about his son giving away his money?"

"I doubt he even notices," Josh says. "He's so preoccupied with his harem." There's a moment when they can hear the other tables. Josh looks around, as if someone else may have spoken, and then seems to realize that he isn't going to do any better than this. He starts to walk toward the door.

Mandy extracts herself from the table. "Josh!" It would have been touching, in another circumstance, to watch the two of them leaving the restaurant together, Josh's arm in a surprising place just above his sister's elbow, as if he were holding her together. They don't look at the vegetable carver on her platform but just proceed, like the walking wounded—beyond the tiki lights, underneath the thatched canopy, into the paths and waterfalls of the traditional garden.

•   •   •

The first time she went to bed with Jeff was in 1967. They were in college, and they went to a hotel so that it wouldn't have happened in a dorm room. At the time, the hotel looked very modern, but she thinks that if they saw it now every single thing would seem like an artifact: the glazed moss-green ashtray on the imitation-wood bedside table, the nubbly white spread on the bed that matched the textured wallpaper, the twin lamps with their enormous tubular shades. She had a lot of time to look at the things in the bathroom too. She can remember the plastic mat on the floor of the shower and the bare spot on the back of the hand towel, but not the way her face looked, what could have been wrong to make her stay in there and stare at herself in the mirror for so long.

When she came out he had lit candles, one on each night table, and the fact that he had brought them seemed mortifying. She remembers wishing that they were in the back of his car, or in the back of the van where she had done it the first time, with Rob Mednick, on a wool blanket on the corrugated metal floor, where it was not pleasant but at least free of mortifying details like candles and lampshades, at least just the thing, with no pressure for it to be anything else. She remembers that it was difficult for Jeff, that he almost lost it before she got on her hands and knees and let him do it that way, something she'd hated when Rob Mednick did it. But she knew it would be easier for Jeff not looking at her face. She felt, as she did it, that it was a kind of gift, and so she was surprised to find that it was better for her that way too.

She is thinking about this now, taking a bath in another hotel room, in a city that she couldn't have imagined she would ever visit, a place that, if she'd thought about it at all, she would have associated with a series of initials: LBJ, R&R, and the CIA.

"Should we get another room?" Jeff asked when they came in from the restaurant. The key to Mandy and Josh's room was gone, which was reassuring.

"I'm glad they're together," she said, which was true, mostly because she dreaded asking Mandy to share a room with her.

Jeff seemed to feel the same way, because he said, "I don't mind if you don't."

"No," she said, although she knew she should have minded. It was too hard to go back to a hotel room alone, on this particular night, but she knew at the same time that you paid for things later, and that two beds in the same room were not right, even after twenty-two years. There were reasons for these formalities, and she should have protected herself a little bit, because when she comes out of the bathroom he is reading in bed, in his glasses and a T-shirt and boxers. Always before this he has worn pajamas, which she bought for him at Brooks Brothers, blue cotton with white piping or white with blue, slightly different each year.

She is suddenly embarrassed about her old nightshirt, but he doesn't look up from what he's reading—a biography of Earl Warren—until she has walked all the way around her bed and gotten in on the side closest to the window. Then he puts his finger in the book.

"I bought Mandy a ticket," he says.

"Do you think she's going to use it?"

"We can talk to her," he says.

She tries to take this seriously. She doesn't want to hurt his feelings, even now.

"Thank you for tonight," he says.

He's looking at her and in the lamplight he's so familiar, heartbreaking really, exactly the way he was in 1967 when the completely obvious fact that they would get married—the real reason they had done it in a hotel—made it too difficult to look each other in the face.

"Are you ready?" he says, and turns out the light. A minute later he says: "Things will work themselves out."

That possibility never seemed less likely. You relaxed for a second and things tangled themselves up in thick wet knots that could never be undone.

Don't, she thinks when she hears him getting out of his bed, coming and sitting down on hers. This "don't" is very loud, but it's only in her head, which he is stroking, perfectly rhythmically, in a way that makes it important for her to close her eyes. When he climbs in behind her and puts his arm around her waist, she squeezes her eyes so tightly that she sees stars, which are really the optical nerves firing.

"I don't know," he says.

They know what each other likes, and they've never been so considerate: it's almost choreographed. When it's finished, he prepares to hold her and she thoughtfully absolves him of this responsibility. He expresses his gratitude by staying in this bed, and she moves as far from him as possible, although it's not necessary. There's already enough sheet between them, and the mattress is firm enough that you wouldn't know there was another person in the bed except for the irregular, wakeful breathing. She lies absolutely still anyway, and after a while it begins to feel as if there is something there, something delicate in the space between them, which they must be careful not to roll over and crush.

Outside the Eastern Gate

I was supposed to be born in Delhi, but when the doctors at AIIMS discovered that my blood was O negative, different from that of my mother and my father, they insisted that we return to Boston, where I was born at Peter Bent Brigham Hospital with no complications. This was a great disappointment to my mother, who wanted to have her second child in India, if she was going to have a second child at all. She used to say that going back to America was like waking up out of the most beautiful dream you'd ever had, which gives you a sense of how my mother thought about her life.

I was seven when she decided to drive to Istanbul by way of Afghanistan, over the Khyber Pass. Some children know when their parents are fighting, but it wasn't that way in our house. I think this is because my mother's moods were so overwhelming that they obscured the fluctuations in her relationship with my father. Her depression seemed to affect the barometer; we would wake up feeling heavy-headed, tired, and sore. Not that we wanted to stay home on those days. If the housekeeper,

Nandani, noticed that my sister's eyes looked cloudy, or that I couldn't finish my toast, one of us would start a fight on purpose so that we would be declared healthy enough to go to school.

In the same way, there were periods of clear days when my mother was awake first, playing her Spanish records. Then we would beg her to let us stay home. Nandani was more difficult to fool at these times, once even forcing us to go to school on a day when an elephant in Sunder Nagar was giving rides to the children around the park.

"I can't watch you all day," she would say, looking at me and raising her eyebrows. I knew she was thinking of the bogeyman.

The bogeyman appears in the first forty seconds after nightfall. He slides down the trunk of a tree as soon as the sun has set. Once, at that hour, Nandani and I were coming back from the market when she stopped just inside the gate and said: "Listen." I listened; the clouds had just begun massing seriously, as if they'd been waiting for the sun to go down. The sky was dark gray and dramatic, and the wind whizzed in the leaves. I could hear another sound, the squeaking of wheels outside the wall.

Nandani took my hand. "That's him," she said. "I hope you'll never see him." Then she said, "He has a small body and long arms and his ears are pointy, like arrows." Nandani put her fingers by her temples, like horns, but she wasn't playing. "If you see him, you stand very still and quiet: he has bad red eyes, but he'll see you if you run. He can smell you if you get too close."

If I had to play alone, I liked a lot of open space around me. I would check behind me with vigilance, especially if I heard the milkman or the rag seller on his rusty bike. I played outside a lot that spring, in the months my mother spent preparing for the journey.

*   *   *

It was my mother's friend Vivian, the photographer, who came up with the idea of driving to Istanbul. Almost immediately, my mother's mood lifted and she started singing—a startling sound, like a radio in a vacant apartment. My father began coming home from the lab later in the evenings and retreating to his study right after dinner. He and Vivian seemed to switch places, like the soldiers in Nandani's Czechoslovakian clock. As soon as he'd left in the mornings Vivian would appear, and she and my mother would spread out their maps on the coffee table in the living room. The maps weren't from the same years—some were separated by centuries—and the game was to figure out which roads still existed and connect them from Pakistan to Afghanistan to Iran to Turkey. It would have been easy enough to get a current map of the route, but that wasn't the way my mother and Vivian did things. I also think that a current map would have shown them how limited their options really were: this was in 1969, and the idea of two American women traveling over the Khyber Pass in a GM station wagon sounds like the setup for one of those stories that travelers repeat to each other, about people who perish in exotic ways.

The date they chose was the fifteenth of April. My sister, Penny, and I were ready a week early, with our suitcases packed. The idea was to do the trip in a leisurely way, but to arrive well before September in Istanbul, where my father was going to be a visiting scholar at Robert College. My mother would find a house and get us settled before he arrived. I think even I knew that the trip wouldn't work out this way, because it was obvious that my mother couldn't have found a house or made the necessary arrangements for our new life. These were the kinds of things that Nandani ordinarily did for us. She had lost her parents during Partition; had they escaped, she would certainly have been married with a family of her own instead of taking care of us in Sunder Nagar.

Nandani loved disaster stories, particularly train wrecks, and would read them out loud from *The Times of India* while we were having breakfast.

These stories stepped up as we prepared for the trip to Istanbul.

"But we're not going on the train," Penny reminded her.

"Traveling is for people who don't know how to be happy," Nandani said, but we ignored her. My mother sat in the dusty living room, with the blackened bronze Buddha that Vivian had brought from Srinagar, the shelves of my father's chemistry books, and the nineteenth-century pencil drawings—colonial fantasies of Rajput palaces and the hidden temples of Khajaraho, old photographs of the tiger hunts of the Maharaja of Scindia, the mahouts on their elephants in the tea plantations of Darjeeling—and she looked happy. With her head close to Vivian's in the geometric sunlight, she made lists with a fountain pen on one of the pads that she ordered from Paris, which came wrapped in white paper with the seal of a stationer on the Quai Voltaire.

One morning I got up to find Vivian already at our house. She had brought fresh yogurt and longans and was taking over breakfast, standing at the counter and peeling the delicate fruit. Nandani hovered nearby, making my father's toast and fuming. My mother, who was ordinarily in bed at that hour, was sitting on a high stool by the window, reading to Vivian from a travelogue about Afghanistan:

"'They rise up into strange knife-cut shapes of brilliant reds and greens, the colours rising from the stream bed to the very peak.'" My mother paused when I came into the room. "That's about the famous mountains in Afghanistan, the Hindu Kush," she told me. "The Koran calls them the 'tent pegs of heaven'—isn't that beautiful?"

"The Koran," Nandani exclaimed. "At breakfast!"

"'It is as if one were passing through a rainbow, the first slope red, the next orange, another green and the next purple, then back to blue again.'"

"Especially purple," Vivian observed. "This author has a weakness for it." She handed me a bowl of longans. Nandani indicated the toast rack, wrapped in a cloth napkin, and watched to see which I would choose. I looked at my mother, who glanced from Nandani to Vivian in mock fear and grinned at me.

I alternated judiciously between fruit and toast, stretching breakfast out as long as possible. When my mother was in this kind of mood it was almost impossible to leave her. You felt that she might not be there when you got home from school, and as it turned out, that was not such an unreasonable fear.

. . .

Vivian's orange station wagon pulled up outside the house at seven-thirty in the morning. I didn't believe that we were really going until I saw Nandani carrying the crates from the kitchen to the car. My mother's clothes were in our ordinary suitcases—navy blue canvas with yellow straps, a wedding present from her to my father—but the rest of the things for the trip were packed in orange crates. One crate contained Vivian's photographic supplies: Kodak paper and film and lenses in the leather cases with velvet linings that I was not allowed to touch. My mother's aquarelle paper, her Sennelier watercolors, oil pastels, and colored pencils filled another. She was planning a book about the journey, with watercolor illustrations. There were also several crates full of packaged food, because it would sometimes be difficult, or unsafe, to eat. This included the thin slices of sugary white bread, intended for tea sandwiches, which my mother liked to toast in the morning, cans of tomato paste and packaged spaghetti from a shop in Khan Market, boxes of muesli, imported from Turkey and now headed back toward the same place over treacherous roads, and great quantities of Cadbury's chocolate. We were usually not allowed to have candy, imported or otherwise, and the sight of the purple-and-gold-wrapped fifteen-ounce bars, stockpiled as if they were rice or lentils, promised a trip on which the greatest luxuries would become necessities.

I knew something was wrong when Penny gave me a kiss. I was standing on the green flagstone path in the front garden, with my red Mighty Mouse suitcase that I had packed myself. Vivian was resting her arms on the roof of the car, her Leica dangling from an embroidered strap around her neck—the only colored thing I ever saw her wear. Penny and I were wearing our salwar-kameez, clothing ordinarily intended for holidays, and then only if we were visiting the houses of Indian friends. I had put mine on that morning when I saw Penny wearing hers, although there had been no instructions about it. I think Vivian and even my mother were realistic enough to know that it didn't matter; nothing they wore would've allowed them to travel this route unobtrusively.

It was seven-thirty in the morning and most of the people in the street were servants, but the lack of a proper audience didn't inhibit my mother. When my father came out of the house she saw an opportunity for a performance. She was wearing a pair of loose beige linen pants and a long-sleeved cotton top with a round neck, and her hair was in two low ponytails, one under each ear. Her sandals, which tied with ribbons around her ankles, slapped on the concrete when she ran to embrace my father. She threw her arms around his neck in a way that forced him to pick her up, like a child, because of the difference in their heights. It is unlikely that my father was carried away by the emotion of the moment; he was always acutely conscious of etiquette in India, and the sight of a couple embracing on the street in Delhi is a spectacle. He almost certainly released my mother first, but not before Vivian had raised her camera and captured several shots of the farewell on film.

Penny refused to hug our father. She was thirteen and no longer hugged anyone. When I asked why, she rolled her eyes and said, "Because I'm developing." At that time Penny was very concerned about her breasts. She looked at them constantly; I would come into the bedroom we shared and find her at the mirror, with her tank top up around her neck, her hands gingerly on her shoulders. Once, when we were sitting on the bed, she lifted her shirt and giggled: "They're so pointy," she said, pressing one of them lightly with her finger, as if she might cajole it into a more acceptable shape. I reached out and touched the other the same way, to help.

"Stop it," Penny hissed. "Or I'll tell everyone you're a dyke."

The morning of our departure I watched my sister climb into the backseat, her *chuni* trailing out the door like a tail. I wanted to follow her, but I was worried about my suitcase. When my father crouched down next to me, I asked him if he could please put it on the roof. Instead he took my whole body in his arms, and then turned me around, so we were both facing the car. When my mother kissed me, I couldn't move my arms and I was sandwiched for a moment between the two of them, a heaven of attention both perfect and fleeting.

"How would you like not to go to school today?" my father asked.

"I'm not going to school," I told him. "I'm going to Afghanistan."

"You take care of Daddy," my mother said, but they had orchestrated it carefully, because she was in the car, and the car was pulling away before I understood what was happening.

"How would you like to go to the Red Fort?" my father asked.

I remember thinking that they were coming back around the block, that they were just testing the car and would return for me when they were certain that it worked. Still, there was this incredible anxiety about my suitcase, which was not yet on the roof with the others. "My suitcase," I said to my father, who was pinning my arms at my sides.

"I'm going to buy you a coconut ice cream. But you have to promise not to tell Nandani."

I think I knew what was going on then, but I kept pretending. "They forgot my suitcase," I said, as I watched Vivian stealing my mother and my sister, driving them off to Afghanistan, where they would draw their own map in watercolors, live on white toast and milk chocolate, and climb very carefully through a range of glinting colored knives.

•   •   •

I don't have a memory of going to the fort that day, but my father said we did. He said that when I asked, he told me I was too young to go to Afghanistan, and that half an hour later, when he thought I had forgotten, I looked at him—we were on the lawn, where you could watch the women in pink and yellow saris cutting the grass with machetes—and said, "What about Afghanistan children?" "Even at that age your logical powers were astonishing," my father said. He had hoped for a long time that I would become a scientist.

I think my father may have misremembered. "Afghanistan children" sounds invented, like something a child would say in a Hollywood movie; in addition, and probably more importantly, I had never had the same status as a brown child, couldn't do the things I saw them doing right in Sunder Nagar—playing cricket, flying kites, or, outside the gates, selling corn, touching the mangy dogs in the market, carrying smaller children on their backs. I knew that just because it wasn't safe for me to be seven in Afghanistan, that didn't mean there wasn't a whole class of Afghan seven-year-olds for whom it was.

* * *

I told myself that it was my father's memory that was taking me back to India. I was at home in my apartment in New York when Nandani called. It was strange to hear her voice coming through my answering machine, as if suddenly it was possible to receive calls across decades as well as continents:

"He mistakes the bedroom for the kitchen. He put the groceries away in the armoire!"

I was lying on the couch, listening to the Brahms Requiem and watching the snow on channel three. A movie had finished, but I hadn't turned off the television.

"Every morning he clips his trousers and tries to bicycle to work."

Nandani's problem didn't seem particularly pressing to me, which was the reason I picked up the phone. It seemed like something I could handle.

"Hold on," I said, searching for the remote to the stereo, which was too loud: *Selig sind, die da Leid tragen.*

"Sometimes I have to go out to the street and bring him home. Where everyone can *see.*"

I found the remote and turned down the volume, but there was so much variation in the music that certain phrases still surged from the speakers: *denn sie sollen getröstet werden.*

"He likes to go to the lab," I said. This was a fact Nandani should have known after living in our house for more than thirty years. It was exhausting to have to explain it to her. It was four in the afternoon in New York, which meant that it was eleven-thirty at night in Delhi. Nandani would be sitting at the glossy table in the hall, underneath the black and green Japanese print of snow falling into a canyon. There would be a light on in the kitchen, and she would be holding the receiver in both hands, the way she had ever since we'd gotten a long-distance line in the house, as if she might combat the fragility of the connection that way. My father used to tease her about it.

"This is different." Nandani paused, and then her voice became soft and wheedling: "I didn't think of calling your sister."

I was flattered, but only for a second. "You should call Penny," I told her. As soon as I got off the phone, I could lower the shades. I could take a bath, and a pill with scalded milk. I could read in bed until nighttime, and then I could sleep overnight. The possibility was deeply sweet.

"Your father is dying," Nandani whispered.

This melodrama was characteristic of her. More unsettling was the idea of Nandani's voice being carried through thousands of miles of cold black pressure, snaking across the Atlantic with the faith that it could be recombined at some numbered station in New Jersey; and Nandani's faith that I would hear her and call up and book a ticket to Delhi, and remember the right clothes for a different season in a different climate, and find my way from the chain-link holding pen at Indira Gandhi's airport home to Sunder Nagar, where I would somehow be able to solve a problem involving bicycle clips and an armoire.

"I don't think I can come now," I said.

"Will you call me back?" Nandani asked. "The connection from America is better." I said that I would: I would have told her anything to get her off the phone. But after I hung up I turned on the lights and went into the kitchen. For the first time in days, I felt hungry for something other than cereal or toast. When the phone rang again in my hand I answered it reflexively, without waiting for the machine to pick up.

"Are you lying on the couch?" my sister asked. I could picture her in her office with the phone tucked between her shoulder and her ear, scrolling through a screen full of messages. Whenever she called me, she was either typing or eating lunch.

"I just finished with that," I told her. "Now I'm thinking about whether to make a sandwich."

"I'm worried about you," Penny said. She'd been calling at around this time every day for the last few weeks. It was nice of her, but not especially comforting, because I knew that Penny didn't understand. I wasn't lying on the couch for any particular reason; it was the same problem I'd been having on and off since I was fourteen. When I had tried to explain this to Penny, she'd suggested that I take up yoga.

This time I told her I was packing.

"Packing for what?"

It occurred to me that my behavior of the last three weeks could suddenly become appropriate. Nobody could blame me for lying on the couch if my father was really dying.

"Nandani called," I said.

"Oh yeah," said Penny. "She called me too."

Nandani was the kind of liar who never actually believed that she was lying. It was just like her to tell me that she wasn't going to call Penny, hang up the phone, and then call Penny.

"She said he was dying."

Penny was a line producer for one of the big morning news shows, and no matter what you told her, she pretended she had heard it from someone else already. "Nandani exaggerates," she said. "Still, it's a relief to me that you're going." I could hear her other line, or lines, ringing in the background. "I think it's going to be good for both of you."

"For both of who?"

"What?" said Penny, to someone else. Then she said: "For you and Dad. He still misses her, you know."

"You sound busy," I said.

"It's crazy here. As usual."

"I'll let you go."

"You should see about her journals," my sister said, as if it had just occurred to her. "As long as you're there."

"I don't think there are any more journals," I said carefully. Our mother's journals were a topic I had resolved not to discuss with Penny.

"You should ask," Penny said. "They would be interesting for you."

"Not really." I was disappointed to hear the edge in my voice; Penny got to me the same way she always had.

"He might have put them somewhere."

"You mean hidden them."

I thought I could hear her sighing and rearranging the little yellow notes on her desk. "You never know."

* * *

I was six when I learned what I had inherited from my mother. We were putting on a play in the garden. The garden was more like a town square, surrounded by well-kept shops that sold mostly jewelry—you could buy emeralds and rubies there at prices my mother called "astonishing." On the north side, there were a few apartment houses. You were only supposed to use the garden if you lived in one of the Sunder Nagar apartments, but as long as you were rich and well dressed, you were welcome. It was a popular place for couples to come for the day, to look in the shops, eat at the restaurant, and then take a turn around the garden: that was where Penny nabbed them.

Once Penny had collected an audience, we would begin the play. One of us always wore our mother's wedding clothes—made by her friend, a theatrical costume designer. The dress was sheer purple gauze, embroidered with violets, and hemmed two inches above her knees. A high collar of the same stiff gauze had made her look like one of the duchesses in Penny's book about the Victorian age, where the solemn royal children were always holding a fan, or a rose, or a dog. When she got married, our mother weighed less than a hundred pounds; by the time Penny was fourteen, she could no longer zip the wedding dress in the back. The dress fell, blissfully, to me, but my glory was short-lived. Although I had imagined I would now play starring roles in the dramatic entertainments Penny organized in the Sunder Nagar garden, I did not. Often Penny and her friends would banish me on some impossible errand, so when I returned, after searching the apartment for whatever Penny wanted—a hula hoop, a torch (that really lit), a black lace mantilla—Penny would say, "Oh, we thought you weren't coming—there's no time to rehearse you now."

Our mother loved these performances and would often make us repeat them for our father.

"Let me get the camera and old stick-in-the-mud," she would say, and return, ten minutes later, with instructions for an encore in the house. Our father, who had endless patience for homework, and my painful efforts on the violin, could rarely be persuaded to watch his children cavorting in front of a crowd of strangers; he felt that it was inappropriate—as a foreigner and perhaps just in general—to draw unnecessary attention to yourself.

The day my mother found me in the study was humid and dark, at the beginning of the rainy season. I'd been sent there, minutes before what Penny called "curtain" (although there was no curtain or stage), to look up the name of the English manor house in *The Secret Garden*. Penny was performing her own adaptation of the story, set to *filmi* songs. I still remember the name of the house on the Yorkshire moors (Misselthwaite Manor) and that I was replacing the book when I heard the opening bars of "Mera Naam (Chin, Chin, Chu)," and knew I was too late. I sat down on the floor and cried. When I heard footsteps outside the study, I cried louder. I hoped it was my father but expected Nandani, come to tell me to leave my poor father's books alone.

But it was my mother, in black silk pajamas. She hadn't bathed, and her hair held its twist, like an oiled black snake against her fine, sharp collarbone. She swooped down on me in one passionate motion.

I was so surprised that I stopped crying. But it was easy to begin again when my mother wrapped me in her arms and said, "Sweet, sweet— what's wrong?" She smelled like the Chinese resin Nandani rubbed on her temples for a headache, medicinal and a little sour. Her hands felt hot on my skin. "Why are you crying?"

Since there was no reason for me to be crying, now that she was with me, I said: "I don't know." She'd given me the same answer more than once, when I'd found her on the chaise longue in her bedroom—keeping her place in a book with one hand, drawing the other index finger beneath each eye, blinking to keep her makeup from smearing. Sometimes I would sit on the upholstered arm, with my feet down underneath the cushion, and she would twist around so that I could rub her neck, until my father came in and told me to let my mother get some rest.

Nobody asked my mother anymore what was wrong, but I would sometimes hear her telling him, as I slowly left the room, that she was sorry; she was tired; she just didn't know what it was.

It was nice now to be in the other position, although it didn't feel real—it felt as if I had the child's role in a play.

"I don't know what it is," I sobbed. "I can't stop."

"Oh God," my mother said. She pulled away and looked at me. I imagine that she was looking for herself in my face and not finding it. But she smoothed my too curly hair out of my eyes anyway.

"You too," she said. "Not you too."

I took it as a diagnosis. I had never been so happy in my life.

It was different when it happened to me for real. This was after my mother was dead. I was living with three other people in a house in Brooklyn, working in a restaurant at night. During the days, I was supposed to be writing a novel. It wasn't going very well. Often, at ten or eleven in the morning, I found myself staring out the window and thinking about India.

It had been a few days of gloom, and then suddenly it hit me so hard that I had to sit down on the wooden floor. I didn't cry. It was more like being outside myself watching what was happening: a piece of my mother coming alive inside me. I sat on the floor and rocked back and forth. I thought of going to bed, but what I really wanted was to be inside the bed—inside the mattress, where it was warm and dense and silent, with the stuffing packed around my arms and legs. When I heard a key in the door, I felt a detached kind of pity, because I hadn't turned on the lights and I knew whoever it was would be startled either way, if I said something in the dark or stood up suddenly. In fact it didn't matter, because I found that I couldn't move.

I had three roommates at the time, but I knew it was Carolyn because of the way she put her coat and bag carefully on the chair, screamed, and then apologized. She bent down and said, "What's wrong?"

For the first time I understood viscerally what was wrong with my mother. It was like learning to read a language that I already spoke: a lovely free sound congealing into a string of letters.

"I don't know," I said, but I did. I felt that a layer of myself had come off, invisible to other people—that I was getting even smaller, like a bar of soap.

• • •

My mother had read all the tragedies. She admired the Greek heroines, with their rough, formless sorrow, and she liked to attend the open rehearsals at the theater, where she had worked in the box office. At lunchtime she would take her sandwich into the theater and watch them do the scenes again and again: tearing their hair, cajoling the gods, dying. It was there, when she was twenty-one, that she met my father. My father, a graduate student in chemistry, would come to the city on the weekends to go to the jazz clubs. He was not the kind of person to ask a woman out just because they were both sitting in a dark theater in the middle of the afternoon. As he tells it, he saw her; he watched her eating a sandwich instead of watching the play; he followed her into the lobby and stood at the pay phone for twenty minutes, trying to place his urgent, invented call, before managing to ask her out.

My father used to say that it was the only time he'd ever done anything like that, and even that he'd known right then they would get married. My mother was beautiful enough to inspire this kind of gesture on a regular basis. She was always talking about men who asked her out in elevators, slipped her notes in restaurants (while she was with my father!), and sent her anonymous gifts. After she died, Penny and I found a cream-colored shearling coat from Lord & Taylor—never worn, but obviously never returned. Sometimes I think my mother chose my father on a whim; and if he was capable of objectivity, I think my father, who does not believe in fate, would agree with me.

Penny was named, of course, for Penelope, and I would have been Cassandra if my father hadn't intervened (instead I am named after his great-aunt, a spinster who lived all her life in a one-street Kentucky town). My mother's name was Jean. She was from a working-class family in New York, and she didn't go to college. She kept a journal; she used to encourage us to do the same. She sometimes said that the trick in life was to record each of your ambitions at the moment it occurred to you, and then to stick to them, even if they later seemed foolish or strange.

It was the basement clubs where my father took her that convinced her to marry him, although she had conditions. I don't think my father had ever thought of going to India, any more than my mother had thought of marrying a chemist. She encouraged him to apply for the job there, rather than the one with Dupont in Delaware; when my father applied for both, she teetered at the edge of misery until he accepted the right one.

* * *

My mother met Vivian in Benares a few years after I was born. They were each in the city alone; my father had stayed in Delhi to work, and Nandani was taking care of Penny and me. It was early in the morning, when men take tourists out in boats on the Ganges. My mother wasn't going for a boat ride and she didn't have a camera, which Vivian thought was interesting. As they walked the length of the ghats, my mother described the place where she was staying—a pension run by a Japanese woman who had married a sadhu. The Japanese woman believed there were freshwater crocodiles in the Ganges, among other dangers, and the walls of her reception were papered with newspaper clippings about disappearances and kidnappings of foreigners. Vivian was interested in seeing that, and so my mother took her back to the pension.

Vivian also lived in Delhi and she and my mother came back from Benares together, with pictures. In one, my mother sits on the yellow steps by the river with the red, saffron, and white cloths of the sadhus drying behind her. In the foreground women in patterned saris perform ablutions with narrow-lipped copper pitchers, while a thin brown boy leaps from the stone edifice of the ghat. His knees are bent as if he's sitting in a chair, and his red lungi blurs at his back, so he almost could be ascending, like a small helicopter, instead of on his way down. On the matting underneath the photograph, which she framed and hung in her apartment, Vivian wrote in cursive: "Jean and Winged Boy: Benares, 1964."

* * *

I didn't expect to see Vivian waiting for me in the throng outside the barrier. I recognized her right away. Vivian at sixty was essentially the same person she had been at thirty: the Roman nose, like a general on a coin, the gray hair with blond streaks, braided and pulled back from her sharp cheekbones, the faint brown freckles that would have become more pronounced as she and my mother negotiated the high rock roads of the Hindu Kush. She was standing among the drivers and relatives and loiterers, wearing an expensive and obviously imported black linen shift over narrow trousers.

I had known Vivian was still in Delhi; my father often mentioned her on the phone. I thought he did it on purpose so that Penny and I wouldn't worry about him being alone. I didn't buy the idea that he and Vivian had suddenly made up and were palling around the city together; but I imagined he was happy, going into the lab and talking to the students, reading in his study. He didn't want us to come and bring him back to America, to some facility for "assisted living." He wanted to stay with Nandani in the sunny apartment in Sunder Nagar, and I didn't blame him. I thought Nandani had called me first, instead of responsible, efficient Penny, because she knew I was the one less likely to bring him home.

Vivian and I looked at each other. I kissed her on the cheek, something that made her start backwards and give a little laugh.

"I haven't seen you since you were eleven," she said.

"I'll be forty next year."

Vivian didn't acknowledge the significance of the number. She led me up an embankment to the parking lot, which was really just a dirt field above the terminal. We had to walk at the edge of the paved road (there was no walkway), amid a confusion of people, many of whom didn't seem to be traveling or meeting anyone. These people looked to me like figures in a movie that I might criticize for its romantic view of India. Women in technicolor saris were carrying what looked like trash in baskets on their heads. Little boys with shoeshine kits attached themselves to us immediately, entreating, "Madam, yes please, madam," until they were banished by a man in a red Rajasthani turban who stuck close to my right side, whispering silkily, "Hashish, hashish." The air smelled toxic, like burning plastic, and I could taste the grit between my teeth.

I had almost expected the orange station wagon, or even one of the gleaming Ambassadors, and I was surprised when Vivian led me to a Toyota hatchback, the color of sand. The seats inside were perforated to keep them cool, but the air-conditioning was broken. I purposely didn't complain about the heat. I didn't want Vivian to think I was some kind of tourist.

"It's too bad your first trip back had to be at this time of year," Vivian said.

"I would have come before. He always wanted to come to us."

Vivian glanced in the mirror and then roared skillfully out of the car park. The professionals, many of them Sikhs, glanced at her and then looked again to confirm what they were seeing—a white woman driving herself around New Delhi. Vivian used this to her advantage and cut them off.

I had not been to Delhi for almost thirty years, and I couldn't believe how ugly it was. As we crept toward India Gate, it seemed that the broad-leaved pipal trees that once hung above the avenues and made a sound like water had been replaced with scrawny, soot-coated yearlings. The avenues themselves seemed to have been pried apart to make room for wedge-shaped concrete islands, painted with cautionary stripes, where the familiar starved cows nosed a new kind of manufactured garbage: cartons and bags that wouldn't have been classified as garbage when I was a child. Not that people weren't equally poor; as soon as we left the airport, we began passing the black, plastic-roofed cities.

"Penny would have come too," I said. "She's so busy." On the plane I'd concluded that Penny had tricked me into doing an unpleasant and inconvenient thing, but somehow around Vivian I felt differently. I wanted to protect my family. It was the same impulse I'd had as a child when Vivian showed up at the door—as if I wanted to lower the blinds and pretend we weren't home.

"She has a really important job now."

Vivian looked at me skeptically, as if she knew what I thought of Penny's job. It made me uncomfortable to think we might have something in common.

"We thought she might have upset your father," Vivian said.

"Upset him?"

"Confused him," Vivian said. "The way she looks. If she still looks the same?"

I looked at Vivian. "He couldn't be that bad," I said.

"Well, you talked to Nandani."

"Nandani exaggerates," I said.

Vivian raised her eyebrows but kept her eyes on the road. We had gotten off the overpass and were jerking through a street dense with auto rickshaws, buses, and bicycles, none of which seemed to be staying inside any kind of lane. Signs hung one above the other—Gold Flake, Radhika Internet, Kodak—and were obscured by clusters of limp black wires, surely too many for the shabby businesses beneath them.

"She wants me to ask about the journals," I said. "From Afghanistan and Iran."

"She wants more!"

I looked at the road.

"Your mother didn't keep journals then," Vivian said. "Penny knows that."

"That's what I told her."

Vivian slammed on the breaks. "Fucking Biharis."

"It's gotten worse," I said, about the traffic.

"It gets worse every year," Vivian said. "You have no idea."

•　•　•

In contrast to the world outside, Sunder Nagar seemed both more verdant and more modern than I remembered it, with expensive-looking boutiques around the park, and a new, glass-fronted dosa restaurant with a red and yellow awning. I saw Nandani on the balcony, shading her eyes; she must have been standing out there all afternoon. When she saw the car, she clutched her hands over her heart and looked from left to right, as if she were searching for a way down directly from the balcony to the street. "I'm coming!" she shouted.

Vivian stopped the car and took off her glasses. Without them, her face was more visibly lined, deeply creased and spotted along her hairline from the sun. I remembered that my father sometimes used to call her "the spider."

"Are you coming in?" I asked her.

She hesitated for a moment and then said, "No."

I tried not to sound relieved. "I'll see you again before I leave, I'm sure."

Vivian smiled. "I'll be here later for dinner." As she pulled away, I could hear the first few chords of "Street Fighting Man," just as loud as she had played it in our living room in the spring of 1969.

"I'm glad you got here safely," Nandani said, squinting after the car.

"You look good," I said.

"Fat," said Nandani, her eyes gleaming. She must've known that it was no longer desirable to be fat, but she still prided herself on it. She smelled like the tamarind concoction she rubbed on the wooden furniture; hugging her was like entering the house before we'd even gone inside.

"You're the same," Nandani whispered, and I felt, unexpectedly, my eyes filling up.

* * *

Although it was Nandani who told me about the bogeyman, and my mother who took me to the slum, I blamed Vivian. All Vivian did was give me the intellectual context. She had come to India the first time with her former husband, a Sanskrit professor at City College in New York. Nandani, Vivian informed me, was using an imported English word for a much older kind of demon, called *rakshas,* or *rakshasas,* who appear in the *Ramayana* as well as the *Mahabharata.* In backward places, people took all kinds of precautions to keep the *rakshasas* away from their children, dressing them in rags, giving female names to the boys and other names to the girls: Half-Cowry, Broomstick, Rubbish, Dirt, or Pot. Vivian said that in Orissa there was a ceremony in which a child who was particularly at risk would be "sold" to a poor woman, who anointed the child and gave her a lower-caste name in order to further confuse the demons.

Vivian had a book of Hindu myths, from which she read to me about snake- and elephant-headed creatures, and something called "the ugly Vartikas of dreadful sight." The *vartikas* were known for vomiting blood (in the direction of the sun) to predict disaster. According to the book, people who died violent or unnatural deaths—murder, suicide, hanging, or accident—became evil spirits, wandering around and terrorizing ordi-

nary people. This isn't the kind of book anyone would read to a child today, but I don't think Vivian meant to scare me. Women at that time—
Vivian, and to some extent my mother—thought of themselves as part of
the vanguard, instructing their daughters by their own rigorous example.
Vivian had no children, and so, on occasion, she instructed me.

Vivian was interested in religion and what she called "the everyday."
Her favorite subjects were people going about their daily lives in holy
places, as if they were gods themselves. She had taken a famous picture
that you still see reprinted in books about India: a rich old woman at a
temple, furtively removing something from her shoe, while behind her a
pink stone apsara plucks a thorn from the flesh of one shapely foot. Vivian
had a fancy dealer at a gallery in New York, and extra money to spend on
things; she was constantly going on trips with her camera and coming
back with valuable gifts for my mother: the bronze Buddha, for example,
or a Tibetan silk tanka. My father resented the gifts as well as the religion.
He refused to go inside the temples where Vivian and my mother took us,
where we had to take off our shoes and walk around an icon in the crush of
a holy day, with the wailing and the bells. I didn't like the rotting offerings, the sweet soft things underneath my feet, but I liked to throw the
ball of rice at the god, to watch my little bit stick with all the others.

•   •   •

It was this kind of excursion that Nandani thought would eventually kill
me, which was probably why my mother didn't tell anyone the morning
that she took me to the slum. It was Saturday, and I was awake before anyone else. On my way to the kitchen, where I was allowed to mix powdered
milk with bottled water for cereal, I passed the balcony and started. I
thought there was a burglar out there. But it was my mother, dressed in
jeans and a sweater and black sunglasses, drinking tea. She had probably
been awake all night, but I didn't know that then. I thought I was incredibly lucky, to come upon her all alone.

I approached her carefully. My mother looked up as if she were surprised to see me, but then she picked me up and carried me into the kitchen, sat me on the counter, and, still wearing her sunglasses, asked me what I wanted for breakfast. This was so unusual that I was not able to think of anything.

"Aren't you hungry?" my mother asked.

I shook my head.

"I'm not hungry either," she admitted. "Maybe we should go somewhere." I got my sweater and shoes with the urgency of someone leaving a burning building, and was relieved to find her waiting for me on the landing of the outside stairs: a thin, black figure against the milky green stone. It was a bright, crisp morning, the coldest season. I could have been six, or just seven.

We took a cycle rickshaw all the way across the city, something you would never do now. I don't remember the scenery until the point when we got off the paved road, onto a dirt track. There were black pigs nosing around in the mud from a rainstorm; in the distance, beyond a field, you could see the low concrete buildings of a prosperous gated enclave. The rickshaw let us off at a two-story row of new shops, almost all of them untenanted. Particularly on the second floor, many of the windows were still missing glass. In the paved square in front of these shops, people had camped out, selling roasted corn and miniature bananas. I was hungry, but I didn't say anything. My mother had a plan for the two of us, and I wanted to follow it exactly.

"Hold my hand," she said.

Around the back of the shops was another track, even smaller than the first, which became a bridge; ahead of us was a small dump, maybe twenty square meters. The road that passed through it was filled with large chunks of rock. It was very difficult to walk. Along the side of the road, men in dhotis broke more stone with hammers; they looked up, but casually, as if they'd seen people like my mother here before.

You didn't notice the hutment colony among the heaps of trash until you were right there: shelters that shared two walls with their neighbors, with roofs made of tin or cloth or, occasionally, the black treads of tires. A boy a few years younger than I was stood facing the road and screaming at intervals; I looked away, shocked because he was naked beneath his T-shirt and I could see the tiny penis, like the nib of my mother's fountain pen.

We heard the chanting before we turned the corner, first one voice and then the collective reply. The temple was a new, white building, the same style as the empty shops in the market, but its windows were sealed with saffron cloth and there was a saffron curtain across the door. My mother parted the curtain and pushed me gently inside. A sadhu sat on the floor with a book, reading to an audience of Indians and a few foreigners, mostly younger than my mother and dressed in bright cotton clothes.

As soon as we were inside, a tall, clean-shaven man in a white kurta got to his feet and crossed the room. He took my mother's shoulders in his hands and kissed her forehead.

"You brought your daughter," said the man. "What a gift."

My mother bent down and we looked up at the man from my level. "This is Vimal," she said. "This festival is because of him."

"Do you know the story of the *Bhagavad-Gita*?" Vimal asked me. I was feeling light-headed from the incense. I was glad that the reading was so loud, because I was afraid he would hear my stomach rumbling.

"She knows it," my mother said, although I didn't.

"This reading will continue for seven days and seven nights," Vimal said. "Sometimes our sadhu will change, but the reading will never stop."

I wondered how long my mother meant to stay.

Vimal touched the side of my face; his palm smelled like something sweet. "Come and have an offering," he said.

We climbed over the hands and feet. My mother took off my sweater, so I was wearing just my undershirt. People in the room were looking at us, but she didn't seem to mind. She knelt down, and Vimal poured cloudy liquid from a brass pitcher into her open palms. She dripped some of it over her head, then took my hands and guided them through the same motion.

"Milk from a coconut," she whispered, as the sticky liquid ran down the side of my face and into my ears.

On the walls around us, the gods appeared the way they did in Vivian's book: fighting from the back of a Chinese lion, or with hands and feet flexed, performing a dance in a cloud of red and blue and gray flames. Little heads peered out from the stomach of a god who lifted to his mouth a shiny pink body, with legs or a forked tail.

"This is Vimal's temple," my mother said. "Isn't it beautiful?"

"This is Shiva's temple," Vimal said. "Shiva is beautiful."

The sadhu's eyes were closed. I sat in my mother's lap, and Vimal sat next to us. The two of them didn't participate in the chanting but whispered to each other. I thought that people might tell them to be quiet, but no one did.

"Have you been sleeping?" Vimal asked.

"In the afternoons sometimes," my mother said. "Never at night."

"What is the energy like?"

There was a loud response, so I couldn't hear her answer.

"Your suffering is suffering too," Vimal said.

Then the two of them got up and went down a hallway toward the back of the temple, Vimal guiding my mother with a hand just below her waist. I could feel my neck and my ears and the back of my shoulders getting hot, the way they did before I got hives. The audience started to clap. The blond man next to me clapped right in front of my face, as if he thought I wasn't joining in because I didn't know how. I looked at the ceiling and began to say the ABCs, but that was too easy. I tried to remember a Chinese poem my mother had taught us, which began: "Outside the eastern gate are girls as many as the clouds," but after the first two lines I got stuck; the poem kept turning into the pledge of allegiance. We hadn't said the Pledge of Allegiance at my school in Boston, but we said it every morning at the American Embassy School, standing up at our desks with our hands over our hearts. Now I said it over and over, in rhythm with the sadhu, making a dot in the dust on the floor each time I got to "liberty and justice for all." By the time my mother reappeared, alone this time, the dots had blurred into one clean space on the floor in front of me and I had lost count.

On our way out to the highway to get a taxi, we passed the dump again.

"Those poor children," my mother said.

"I'm hungry," I told her.

"We'll get you something." She looked around. "How about pancakes?" I knew she meant the *aloo tikki* they sold in every street market, but I pretended I was going to eat real pancakes, with bubbles on the doughy underside, a stack separated by pats of warm butter and crisscrossed with maple syrup.

My mother was buying the potato cakes when I heard the wheels scraping inside the covered market. I was standing in the sun, and my mother was in the shade underneath the canvas, where a legless man was coming through the market on a makeshift wheelchair. I thought the ragged white patches on his face were made by sunlight coming through the canvas, but the marks didn't change as he rolled up next to my mother. His lungi modestly covered his stumps, with the extra cloth looped over one bare shoulder. The discoloration affected his neck and his face only; the skin on the rest of his body was smooth and brown. Unlike any Indian person I had ever seen, his hair and his beard were red. I wasn't deceived by his black eyes or ordinary ears, since I knew from Nandani that his kind could change their shape. I held my breath and stood very still. It was only the middle of the morning, but this man was already turning into a *rakshasa*.

It was true that there were beggars with tin pots who fluttered their fingers at the ankles of the people going to make offerings at the temples, and true that I had seen a legless man at our market, reaping more than his associates because of the extreme nature of his deformity. This wasn't the worst thing I saw as a child in India. Once, at the Agra train station, a man with bumps growing underneath his skin smiled right at me; not only his arms and legs but the flesh up to his neck, behind his ears, and along the sides of his face had bubbled with smooth growths, as hard as fruits. I looked quickly at my shoes, to reassure whichever adult I was with that I hadn't seen it.

The bogeyman was terrible, but he was not disgusting. He held out his hand to my mother, who crouched down and spoke to him. When she took one of his hands in hers, some men playing cards at a table turned to look at them. My mother reached into her bag, from which, to my horror, I saw her take a wad of rupees and hand them to the demon.

In my memory he looks at me and even turns his wheels in my direction as my mother accepts the yellow cakes and pays the vendor. It doesn't matter that the *rakshasa* then disappears back into the market, or that the men go back to their game, or that my mother returns to me with the fried cakes in their grease-stained newspaper cone. There are at least eight hours until twilight, but I have already been sold.

•   •   •

When I asked Nandani about the bogeyman, she denied it.

"I'm sure I never frightened you," she said. "Of course I remember your mother taking you there. And eating at the market! I took your temperature every day for a month." Nandani looked darkly toward the living room, where Vivian was sitting with my father. "That was one of *her* things, you know."

I was surprised: the excursion had had such an air of separateness, of being outside my mother's relationship with Vivian or my father. "Do you think so?"

"Of course," Nandani said. "Your mother would not have known a place like that on her own."

I realized almost as soon as I arrived in Delhi that there was a war going on in the apartment.

"Sit down and eat," my father instructed Nandani, who had prepared enough food for the reunion of a real family. The plates were garnished with parsley and lemon, and she had made the dishes I had liked as a child: black butter dal, lamb saag, baskets of bread, and fried pappadams. There were only three pieces of each kind of bread; in the past, Nandani always had sat in the kitchen, reading a movie magazine, so that she could bring hot bread at intervals throughout the meal.

"Please eat with us," I said.

"I've eaten already," Nandani said. "I have to eat early or I have night-mares."

A smile flicked the corners of Vivian's elegant lips. She looked at Nan-dani as if she were thinking of taking a photograph.

"Because we're so boring," my father said mournfully.

My father had become dashing in his old age. His reddish hair had turned white, adding some contrast to his face and making his blue eyes bluer. He was wearing new wire-framed glasses, and a very pale lavender shirt. I had never known my father to take pains like that with his cloth-ing, and it touched me that he might have done it for my visit.

At first I saw no signs of his disease. My father described a student at the lab and the molecule he was studying, a six-sided isomer of benzene. He said that the boy looked exactly like Apu from the Satyajit Ray movies, remembering the director's name as well as the character's. Vivian said that *Aparajito,* the second film in the trilogy, was the most challeng-ing, which meant that she liked it best. When we went to the living room for a brandy after dinner, my father chose the music: *Sketches of Spain.* Peri-odically, Nandani would appear and ask him if he needed anything: if he was tired, or if he wanted a sweater.

"He's fine," Vivian finally snapped.

"Excuse me, ma'am," Nandani said, a locution so absurd, given their relationship, that Vivian stood up suddenly and went to the bookshelf, where she stayed for several minutes with her back to us, looking at a book. Vivian had the kind of temper that could go from zero to a hundred in an instant. Once, in Istanbul, I saw her bring her hand down hard above the hood of a taxi, stopping just before it hit the windshield. She laughed when the driver cringed, but she hadn't been faking; she'd come that close to breaking her hand on the glass.

Nandani retreated in triumph, shooting me a significant look, and then one at the clock on the wall. I was relieved when Vivian finally put her glass down on the coffee table and said she was going home. My father stood up gallantly.

"I can see myself out," Vivian said.

"Now where did my sweater get to?" my father asked me.

"Are you cold?"

"It gets chilly now at night," he said. "Or I'm an old man."

I looked at Vivian, who was watching him with a wary expression.

"And my shoes," said my father, who was wearing running shoes, as usual. He looked down thoughtfully: "My boots."

"I'll see you in the morning," Vivian said to me. "I can drive you, if there's anything you want to see."

My father put his glass down on the table next to Vivian's and turned to me. "See you in the morning," he said.

I felt my body temperature change, as if I'd missed a step on a steep flight of stairs. My father crossed the room and stopped next to Vivian.

"You're staying here," she said.

"All right," said my father cheerfully. "That's fine."

Nandani was standing in the kitchen doorway, like the witness to a car accident. I wished that both of these women would leave my father and me in private, and, as if she knew what I was thinking, Vivian took her jacket from the bench by the door and went out. But as soon as she was gone it was worse; for the first time since she had picked me up at the airport, I felt as if I were really in a foreign country. My father had sat down on the couch and was methodically removing the laces from his shoes. When Nandani said she would help him, I didn't protest, nor did I ask how long it had been that my father needed assistance getting undressed for bed.

• • •

Vivian came over every day and took my father for his walk. I'd been surprised the first morning she arrived; I remembered things he had said about her—the way he had called her "the spider"—and I had a horror of putting him in a situation that he wouldn't be able to control. But the prospect of walking with Vivian made my father cheerful, as if he were flattered by her attention.

"I think he remembers he had strong feelings for me," Vivian told me, with an embarrassed half-laugh. "He's just confused about their nature."

I discovered by accident that he still remembered how to play ping-pong. The table was in a junk room that my mother had once used for meditation. The room was now filled simply with things: paperback novels, old suitcases, empty glass jars. There were two recorders crowded into one case, sitting on top of a stack of piano scores, and a tin pot filled with dirty rags. A stick broom was in one corner, leaning against boxes of Christmas ornaments from my mother's childhood: globes made of silvered glass, hollowed out and striped with paint and glitter, excessively breakable and beautiful in their tarty, candy-colored skins.

My father appeared in the doorway while I was sifting systematically through the boxes. I felt I had been caught.

"What do you need?" he asked.

I thought about lying, but of course it didn't matter what my father saw me doing.

"Mom's journals," I said.

My father nodded, as if this were what he'd expected. "Any luck?"

"No," I said. "Do you know where they are?"

"Sure," said my father. "Sure." He put his hands in his pockets and glanced around the room. "What a mess," he said finally.

I had been in Delhi only a week, but my father had asked me three times to remind him of the names of Penny's children. Occasionally he called her Penny, but more often he would begin the sentence and then re-phrase it to eliminate the need for her name: "What are my grandchildren called now?" he asked, as if this might have changed in the last forty-eight hours.

"Caitlin and Meredith are the girls," I told him. "Reuben's the youngest."

Once he said: "My grandson is named after a sandwich," in the same deadpan voice he had always used, but when I laughed, he looked genuinely angry and left the room. Another time he asked whether any of them were smart.

"They're like Penny," I said. "They're very bright."

"Quick," said my father scornfully.

He was the one who picked up the paddle and found a ball on the windowsill, behind a row of misshapen yellow candles. We rallied gently for several minutes, correcting each other's errors, allowing the ball to bounce twice, or catching it and beginning again if it threatened to sail off the back of the table. I'd come close to beating him three or four times among thousands of games, but he'd never allowed it, even when I was a child. Even now, his eye-hand coordination remained intact. All of a sudden he flicked a topspin backhand; the ball made a snapping sound on the table and hit the back window. Bright light was coming into the room.

"Ha!" my father exclaimed, and then looked chastened, as if he were unsure of what he had done.

"Should we play a game?" I said.

My father narrowed his eyes. "To twenty-one," he said. "My service."

It was eighteen-eighteen when he put down his paddle.

"Well, that's it," he said. "I have to go to the toilet."

"I'll wait for you," I said. "I'm not letting you get out of it that easily."

My father picked up the paddle and looked at it unhappily. "I really have to go," he said.

"Go," I said.

"OK." He nodded, staying where he was. I led my father to the toilet in the hall and stood outside. I heard sounds in there and prayed he wouldn't need help. I wasn't generally squeamish, but I had to force myself to remain in the hall. The front hall hadn't changed since we had bought the apartment. It seemed incredible to me that these were the same objects I had handled as a child. Was the flat green rotary phone really sturdier than my father? I could accept that things made of wood, picture frames, might outlast him, but wallpaper? An umbrella?

•   •   •

My father and I had joined my mother and Penny, along with Vivian, in Istanbul a year later, but we spent only a few months with her there before she disappeared, this time alone—or not really alone, but with someone we didn't know, a film director from Los Angeles.

After she left for Los Angeles, my father took my sister and me back to Boston, where his life was as closely regulated as it had been in Delhi. He had a new job at a lab at MIT; in the mornings, he woke up at five to run six miles at the high school track, come home and shower, and be at work by seven-thirty. On the weekends you would find him standing in the kitchen at exactly one o'clock, eating a peanut butter and jelly sandwich and staring out the window. Ordinarily he would last until about two, when he would remember a mimeographed article or a notepad he'd left at the lab and go back to his office until dinnertime.

I remember him bringing up the subject of my mother only once. We were in the car, on the way to Penny's dance class.

"I find it incredible how some people change," he said, almost as if he were continuing an earlier conversation.

"What?" said Penny warily. I looked out the window. It was as if he had suddenly decided to talk to us about sex.

"Well, your mother, for example. She's completely different from the way she was when I met her."

"Everybody changes," Penny said.

"Not me," my father said. "I'm still the same person I always was."

Penny snorted.

"He's so blind," she said later, when I came into her bedroom as I always did to watch her getting ready to go out. "Everyone else changes, but he stays exactly the same!" She had a way of flipping her hair that I admired. Her hair was waist length, and there was always a space of white skin between the bottom of her blouse and her hip-hugger jeans. She didn't tan like other girls; like our mother, she had that way of making the things that were different about her seem stylish and new.

"Seriously," she said, "he's the least introspective person I've ever met."

I was grateful for the confidence, but privately I didn't agree. I think that some people don't change, and that my father was one of them. I think my mother changed more than most people, and that was what scared her so badly as soon as she got back to America.

•　•　•

Penny wore yellow to the funeral. It was a floor-length smock dress, and her hair was pulled back from her face in a barrette with a yellow flower in it. She was carrying a leather patchwork bag with a long strap. When she got up to speak the effect was startling, particularly since some of the mourners hadn't seen our mother since she was Penny's age. In the group that had come to comfort our father, there were people who would've had strong things to say about our mother under different circumstances; simply by standing there, Penny went some way toward redeeming the deceased.

Unlike everyone who had come before her, she was absolutely calm. She swept her eyes over all of us in front of the plain wooden cross (the church was Methodist because of our father's parents) and paused, not because she was mastering her emotions but for dramatic effect. Then she reached into her purse and pulled out our mother's journal, which she had stolen from the safe under the floor.

"My mother wrote this when she was seventeen."

The journal was bound in red leather. It looked like a hymnal, only slimmer. Our father wouldn't have known she had it until that moment.

"I have always wanted to visit the East," Penny read. "I want to stand on the deck of a Yangtze junk, early in the morning; to travel the Grand Trunk Road all the way to Benares; to wander through the bazaars of Esfahan and Damascus, where you can find saffron from Madagascar, and

Burmese rubies as big as crabapples, and powerful aphrodisiacs made from the testicles of elephants." There was some gentle laughter. "I sometimes think I was meant to be born somewhere else, to different parents, and that there is a girl somewhere—in a village on the slopes of the high Himalaya—who would be happy to exchange her life for mine." At this, people whispered and gave one another significant looks, as if they were trying to prove how well they knew our mother. But the next thing Penny said made everyone quiet.

"I think the air is going out of this room a little bit at a time. I think that if I don't leave here soon, I might not even notice."

Penny made a point of reading the sentences, although she must have known them by heart.

"I want to go before I'm forty." She looked up. "I don't want to be an old lady." Again, like a swimmer breathing. "Life after forty wouldn't be life."

Sitting next to me, my father grunted. It was an unusual, spontaneous, and private sound, almost sexual, and the people around us pretended they hadn't heard it. Penny came down out of the nave, holding her skirt to avoid tripping on the steps. The organist started playing, as planned, the hymn that my father had chosen—something without Jesus—and the three of us walked out in a line.

* * *

Vivian wasn't at my mother's funeral; neither was my mother, who died in a house in the Hollywood Hills and was cremated there. She had described to Penny and me the house on Coldwater Canyon: there was a pool, a garden (bamboo, birds of paradise, rare Egyptian date palms), and a turquoise bathroom, with a Jacuzzi tub and a skylight right above the shower. Both times that she visited us in the year before she died, our mother talked about the day soon when we would come to visit her in California (as soon as she was feeling better), and the party that the director would host for us outside on the deck by his pool.

It was at one of the director's parties, supposedly, that she came in from the pool to the bathroom with the skylight and swallowed too many of her pills. I can see her in her black tank suit with her hair wet and slicked back, setting the paper cup down on the counter, checking her face in the mirror, and arranging herself carefully on the turquoise tiles beneath the window. I like to imagine her falling asleep with only the birds of paradise for an audience, showing their curious orange heads above the sill. It was three and a half months after her fortieth birthday.

* * *

"She was received by the royal family."

"Who was?" I asked.

My father waved his arm impatiently: "In Afghan."

"Afghanistan," I said. You were supposed to give him a few minutes to think of the answer himself, and then help. You weren't supposed to limit your conversation, in scope or vocabulary. Penny had found a pamphlet called "Living with Alzheimer's" and mailed it to me express.

"Did Vivian tell you that?" I asked my father.

He shook his head. "I saw it in a newspaper."

My father did, in fact, still read the newspaper. I thought it was amazing, and I remarked on it to Nandani and Vivian.

"Who knows how much he understands," Nandani said sorrowfully.

"More than most people, I imagine," Vivian said. "And not just the newspaper."

She was arranging the pages of a photo book on Bollywood: portraits of the actors, men perched on a bamboo scaffold hand-painting an advertisement for a film called *Campus Love,* the crowd outside a Calcutta theater being beaten back from the ticket cage by a policeman with a *lathi.* Vivian said that she liked to work at our house because of the big table on the sunny screened-in porch.

"Is she always here this much?" I asked Nandani, who pursed her lips as if she were experiencing some kind of inner struggle.

"I can't lie to you," she said. "It's shocking."

I laughed. "I don't know if it's shocking."

Nandani conceded that much. "Of course, nothing can happen any-more."

"What could happen before?"

"If it could happen, it did happen," Nandani said. "I am only glad that you and Penelope had gone by then."

It was irrational to be angry with Vivian. While Penny and I went about our lives eight thousand miles away, she had been here taking care of our father. Of course, that had started before he'd gotten sick. Clearly she'd been here for years, shopping and eating with him, listening to his records and drinking brandy, showing him her photographs—maybe even photographing my father too.

Nandani was watching me closely.

"What are you making for dinner?" I asked.

"Chicken makhani."

"And for a vegetable?"

"Peas paneer."

"What else do they have at the market now?"

"Tomatoes," Nandani said. "Ladyfingers are fresh, but expensive now."

"We'll have those," I said. "No peas."

Nandani smiled and nodded her approval. "It's good that you're home," she said.

•   •   •

In addition to taking his walks with Vivian, my father would go out with me several times during the day. Sometimes we would get halfway around the enclave, and he would turn around and go back toward the house. An hour or two later he might say, "Are we going for our walk?" and I would put on my shoes and go out again. All of the neighbors said hello to my father, and occasionally we would meet an old person who remembered me too. A tall, elegant neighbor, named Prem, whom Penny and I had once observed doing yoga in his underwear on the roof very early in the morning, stopped us and asked whether I was planning to see any sights.

"The Blue Mosque," my father said.

"Which mosque?" Prem asked.

"With the tomb of the Prophet," my father said. "The largest and most gorgeous tomb of solid silver."

"Very interesting," Prem said, smiling at me in a way I hoped my father didn't see. But my father wasn't paying attention to Prem. He was looking at me as if we were playing a guessing game and it was my turn to give the answer.

"Which mosque?" I said when Prem was gone.

My father nodded.

"In Afghanistan? Or Iran?"

"Maybe in the book room," my father said. "It's possible." This time, I was the one who turned us around. As soon as we got home, I began to take apart his library.

The period I wanted to know about lasted from April of 1969 until March of 1970. If I had wanted the details of the trip itself, its route or hardships, I could have gotten them from Vivian. Although she didn't publish the photographs from that trip, she has them; it occurred to me that by establishing herself so accessibly on the sun porch, she might be making me an offer. But talking to Vivian about the trip would have ruined it, the way a book can be ruined by a movie, or a child's game by an adult walking past the door. I felt that I had to hear it directly from the source.

* * *

I was apart from my mother for less than nine months, but it felt as if I had been living without her for years. After she'd arrived in Istanbul, my father would call and put me on the phone, and she would come up with similes about the extent to which she missed me:

"I miss you as much as monkeys miss bananas."

Then it would be my turn. "I miss you as much as fish miss water."

"Oh, really? I miss you as much as a camel misses water, after he walked a hundred miles in the desert."

"Camels don't need water," I told her.

"They do when their hump runs out," my mother said. "I miss you as much as a humpless camel."

I liked that one, and I heard it again and again as the months went by and my father and I did not make preparations to leave for Istanbul.

According to the information Penny had sent me, patients often remember events from the deep past, while forgetting what happened yesterday or an hour ago. I didn't think my father was reading my mother's journals now. I thought he knew I was looking for them, and that this fact had triggered descriptions—overwrought descriptions of the most gorgeous tombs of solid silver—that he had read years before, perhaps when he first returned to the house in Sunder Nagar and found himself alone with all of her familiar things.

*　　•　　•　　•*

I was opening the books one at a time because I didn't trust the spines. I thought the journals might not be a bound book, just pages stuck inside something else. I also thought they might be hidden, in the space between the books and the back of the shelf. I was flipping through a pale blue chapbook called *Principles of Solid State Matter* when I heard Vivian and Nandani arguing in the hall. Vivian knocked and entered at the same time.

"You should open the curtains," she said. "How can you read?" She crossed the room and opened the drapes. Light revealed the dust settling into the rug. Vivian glanced at the book in my hand.

"I thought I would learn something about what he did," I said. She was standing in front of the window, and I could see the shadow of her body in the white shirt she was wearing, like an X ray. She was still thin, but her bones gave her the appearance of a bigger person: a broad back; thick wrists and ankles; wide, solid hips.

"You won't find anything," she said.

"They're somewhere here. He remembers them."

"Do you keep a journal?" she asked me.

I didn't understand what that had to do with it. "Yes."

"Regularly?"

"Why?"

"That must require a certain amount of discipline."

I thought she might be making fun of me; it had always been difficult to tell what she was thinking from her expression. "I guess so."

Vivian nodded. "Discipline wasn't one of your mother's strong suits."

She picked up a framed reproduction of a Mughal miniature from my father's desk and looked at it. I had a sharp sense of déjà vu, of having been in exactly this position in this room with her and my mother before. Vivian's lips were not old-lady lips yet; they stood out against her tan, freckled skin. I thought of her kissing my mother and it seemed to me that some kind of biological record, like a fingerprint, must have been left on her mouth.

"I'm not going to do anything with them," I said. "I'm not even going to tell Penny I found them. I just need to know what she was thinking."

Vivian drew back a little: she didn't like confessions or pleas of any kind. She frowned at the picture in her hand—a princess and a musician in a garden—as if she'd never seen it before.

"Look in the drawer by his bed."

*　　*　　*

I had been looking at *The Secret Garden;* my mother had appeared in her black pajamas; and then someone had taken her away from me. It was Vivian who had led her away, her arm around my mother's waist, my mother's head resting in the hollow between Vivian's shoulder and her neck. I was crying.

"Stop that," Vivian said.

"She can't," my mother said.

Vivian looked back at me, not meanly. "Yes she can."

And I found that once there was no one in the room, I could.

• • •

I stayed in my father's room, reading for a long time, while it got hazy and brown outside, the way it does in the hot weather, and then suddenly dark, as if the light had collapsed under the weight of the air. My father was downstairs in the kitchen with Nandani, but the sheets on his side of the bed were still disturbed from his nap; a smell came off of them, powdery and intimate. I turned on the Tiffany lamp on the nightstand, which had been brought from New York, packed in newspaper. It illuminated a print of an American street, the tiny people nicked in with charcoal, just a vertical dash to indicate a figure underneath an eyebrow of umbrella, with a river and the smokestacks of a factory in the background, its exhaust blurry in the wet atmosphere. "That's Boston," my mother used to say. On her writing table, there was the purple glass paperweight with ragged purple iceberg shapes inside. The armoire was painted with blue and green peacocks. Behind the peacocks was an imaginary Mughal palace.

The book had been borrowed from a library and never returned. The title, *The Tent Pegs of Heaven,* was from the Koran and referred to the legendarily dangerous mountains of the Hindu Kush. Published under the auspices of something called the Travel Book Club on Charing Cross Road, it was written by a woman named Lucie Street, who had taken a trip through Afghanistan two years before my mother did. Lucie Street had traveled in great style from the moment she arrived in Kabul, where she was received by the royal family. A whole chapter is devoted to the blue mosque at Mazar-i-Sharif, which is described in all its fantastic range: blue ice, periwinkle, anchusa, the darkest delphinium, the blackest blue of the lupin, primrose, aquamarine, turquoise, lapis lazuli. Lucie Street shares with my mother a penchant for superlatives, a weakness for seeing each thing as the most intense in a chain of inevitably fading impressions. Alone in the bedroom I indulged in a habit of my mother's—

saying the names of foreign places out loud for the sound of them: "Bamiyan, Pul-i-Kumri, Baghlan, Samargan, Mazar-i-Sharif, Balkh."

My father was drawn to my voice, or the light.

"You found your book." He was smiling with the dumb excitement of a child who has made a fantastic mess and knows it. I had an impulse to grab his arm and twist it hard, to replace his reflex smile with actual pain. I could see myself doing it.

"No."

"Well, I don't know why you'd want to know about something like that."

"You don't?"

He nodded as if he'd understood, and didn't say anything.

"You know." It was the humiliating feeling of negotiating with a child. "Now you're the only one who knows."

"Yes."

"People don't just go off and leave one of their children. They don't."

"Yes."

"So why didn't she take me?"

"You didn't fit in the car." My father pressed his hands together in front of his mouth—a professorial gesture to conceal a smile. But he couldn't control himself. The joke burst past his fingertips. He laughed as he delivered the punch line: "You were too big!"

The house was so lonely to me that I had the delusion, for a moment, that my father's illness wasn't biological, that he had caught it from the nightstands and the lamps and the malignant purple globe, winking like a live thing on the table.

•   •   •

In 1972, my father's grief only made him more desirable to the ladies of Cambridge, Massachusetts. After an appropriate interval, they began to invite him to traveling exhibitions at the Museum of Fine Arts. My father made polite excuses.

"He should say yes," Penny told me, but I knew she was pleased. I was twelve when she went away to college, in Michigan, and was still waiting to go away myself when she graduated four years later. She got a job right away at a television network, answering the phones and running errands for the anchors. When I talked to her, she always mentioned someone she had spoken to at a party, or a restaurant where she had been taken by a man. If I didn't know the name of the person or the restaurant, she became curt and exasperated.

On the rare weekends when she visited from New York, my father and I would meet her Friday night at the station. She would come toward us at a tilt, a small bag with everything neatly packed over one shoulder, her hair loose, her lips slightly open, as if she couldn't wait to begin the story of whatever crazy thing had happened to her on the train. My father held back and let me hug her first, as if he needed those few seconds to prepare.

Some people said Penny was our mother all over again, but that is wrong. Penny is our mother cleaned up, with all her faults corrected—a miracle, with the gloom washed out like dust.

●　　●　　●

The Saturday before I went home, Vivian, my father, and I took a walk in the old part of the city. We had to get there by auto rickshaw, and Vivian and I were worried that the bumps and turns would scare my father. She kept one hand on his knee the whole time, something that seemed to please him. He would smile and say, "That's fine," each time he noticed it. The driver thought we were tourists and let us off at the Jama Masjid.

We went around the back of the mosque, past the old Muslim tailors, to the main street of the bazaar, where Vivian browsed through the stalls, examining porcelain doorknobs arranged by size in cardboard cartons, allowing perfumes to be brought out and opened for her, and finally stopping at a stall that sold fruit and nuts, where she bought a kilo of yellow longans.

My father and I waited in the street behind her, the bicycles and children and rickshaws going around us like any other obstacle. In the confusion, we didn't see the man coming until he was upon us. You don't find them so much anymore. Even Vivian, who prides herself on not being surprised by anything in India, looked twice at the cripple, which was enough to make him roll up and stop at our feet. He would have been a small man anyway, but he wasn't old. He had black hair and handsome black eyes and his beard was well trimmed; obviously someone was taking care of him. He was wearing a laborer's white round-necked T-shirt, and a neat blue and green plaid lungi covered his stumps.

"Hello," he said. "My name is Mohammad Issan. Perhaps you have something to spare?" If these were the only English words he knew, he spoke them very well.

Vivian clicked her tongue and flicked her hand, palm down, a native gesture that might have deterred him if my father hadn't been staring with such frank, open admiration.

"Sir?"

A few people had turned to look. You never would have known my father was sick. Vivian had dressed him in fawn-colored pants, a short-sleeved shirt of white Egyptian cotton, and leather sandals that made him look almost fey. He was like a lingering colonial, except for his guilelessness, which seemed to promise some drama: either he would show his savvy by playing a little game with the beggar, or he was about to be spectacularly duped.

"That's something," my father said.

"Come on," I said.

Mohammad Issan inched a little closer and reached up, still smiling. He didn't touch us. You could tell that he knew his effect: he could feel the people slowing down around him, the vendors turning, the children pausing to see how much my father would give.

"He gets around," my father said.

Two women stood giggling by the fruit, their hands covering their mouths and their saris looped over their heads. I looked at Vivian, who ordinarily would have snapped something at them in Hindi, but she was staring at my father too.

"He's OK," my father announced to the assembled group. "Even without his . . ."

I took his arm, but he seemed unwilling to move until he had finished his thought. "His legs," I whispered.

"No," my father said, but encouragingly, as if I were getting warmer.

"One dollar," the beggar said.

I resented Vivian for not helping, but when my father put his hand over his heart, she was next to him in a second, squinting up into his eyes.

"Does it hurt?" she said. "Your arm, your heart?"

"Ah," he sighed. He smiled at her. "I'm fine now."

"Let's all go, then," Vivian said.

My father nodded, but then he turned to me, suddenly stern.

"It's not *legs*," he said.

The Tutor

She was an American girl, but one who apparently kept Bombay time, because it was three-thirty when she arrived for their one o'clock appointment. It was a luxury to be able to blame someone else for his wasted afternoon, and Zubin was prepared to take full advantage of it. Then the girl knocked on his bedroom door.

He had been in the preparation business for four years, but Julia was his first foreign student. She was dressed more like a Spanish or an Italian girl than an American, in a sheer white blouse and tight jeans that sat very low on her hips, perhaps to show off the tiny diamond in her belly button. Her hair was reddish brown—chestnut, you would call it—and she'd ruined hazel eyes with a heavy application of thick black eyeliner.

"I have to get into Berkeley," she told him.

It was typical for kids to fixate on one school. "Why Berkeley?"

"Because it's in San Francisco."

"Technically Berkeley's a separate city."

"I know that," Julia said. "I was born in San Francisco."

She glanced at the bookshelves that covered three walls of his room. He wanted the kids he tutored to see them, although he knew his pride was irrelevant: most didn't know the difference between Spender and Spenser, or care.

"Have you *read* all of these?"

"Actually that's the best way to improve your verbal. It's much better to see the words in context." He hated the idea of learning words from a list; it was like taking vitamin supplements in place of eating. But Julia looked discouraged, and so he added: "Your dad says you're a math whiz, so we don't need to do that."

"He said that?"

"You aren't?"

Julia shrugged. "I just can't believe he said 'whiz.'"

"I'm paraphrasing," Zubin said. "What were your scores?"

"Five-sixty verbal, seven-sixty math."

Zubin whistled. "You scored higher than I did on the math."

Julia smiled, as if she hadn't meant to, and looked down. "My college counselor says I need a really good essay. Then my verbal won't matter so much." She dumped out the contents of an expensive-looking black leather knapsack and handed him the application, which was loose and folded into squares. Her nails were bitten and decorated with half-moons of pale pink polish.

"I'm such a bad writer, though." She was standing expectantly in front of him. Each time she took a breath, the diamond in her stomach flashed.

"I usually do lessons in the dining room," Zubin said.

The only furniture in his parents' dining room was a polished mahogany table, covered with newspapers and magazines, and a matching sideboard—storage space for jars of pickle, bottles of Wild Turkey from his father's American friends, his mother's bridge trophies, and an enormous, very valuable Chinese porcelain vase, which the servants had filled with artificial flowers: red, yellow, and salmon-colored cloth roses beaded with artificial dew. On nights when he didn't go out, he preferred having his dinner served to him in his room; his parents did the same.

He sat down at the table, but Julia didn't join him. "'Which book that you've read in the last two years has influenced you most, and why?'"

Julia wandered over to the window.

"That sounds OK," he encouraged her.

"I hate reading."

"'Talk about the place where you live, and what it means to you.'" Zubin looked up from the application. "There you go. That one's made for you."

She'd been listening with her back to him, staring down Ridge Road toward the Hanging Garden. Now she turned around—did a little spin on the smooth tiles.

"Can we get coffee?"

"Do you want milk and sugar?"

Julia looked up, as if shyly. "I want to go to Barista."

"It's loud there."

"I'll pay," Julia said.

"Thanks. I can pay for my own coffee."

Julia shrugged. "Whatever—as long as I get my fix."

Zubin couldn't help smiling.

"I need it five times a day. And if I don't get espresso and a cigarette first thing in the morning, I have to go back to bed."

"Your parents know you smoke?"

"God, no. Our driver knows—he uses it as blackmail." She smiled. "No smoking is my dad's big rule."

"What about your mom?"

"She went back to the States to find herself. I decided to stay with my dad," Julia added, although he hadn't asked. "He lets me go out."

Zubin couldn't believe that any American father would let his teenage daughter go out at night in Bombay. "Go out where?"

"My friends have parties. Or sometimes clubs—there's that new place, Fire and Ice."

"You should be careful," Zubin told her.

Julia smiled. "That's so Indian."

"Anyone would tell you to be careful—it's not like the States."

"No," Julia said.

He was surprised by the bitterness in her voice. "You miss it."

"I am missing it."

"You mean now in particular?"

Julia was putting her things back into the knapsack haphazardly—phone, cigarettes, date book, lip gloss. She squinted at the window, as if the light were too bright. "I mean, I don't even know what I'm missing."

●　●　●

Homesickness was like any other illness: you couldn't remember it properly. You knew you'd had the flu, and that you'd suffered, but you didn't have access to the symptoms themselves: the chills, the swollen throat, the heavy ache in your arms and legs. He had been eighteen, and in America for only the second time. It was cold. The sweaters he'd bought in Bombay looked wrong—he saw that the first week—and they weren't warm enough anyway. He saw the same sweaters, of cheap, shiny wool, in too bright colors, at the "international" table in the Freshman Union. He would not sit there.

His roommate saw him go out in his T-shirt and windcheater, and offered to loan him one of what seemed like dozens of sweaters: brown or black or wheat-colored, the thickest, softest wool Zubin had ever seen. He went to the Harvard Coop, where they had a clothing section, and looked at the sweaters, which were at least unobtrusive. He did the calculation several times: they were "on sale" for eighty dollars, which worked out to roughly thirty-three hundred rupees. If it had been a question of just one, he might have managed, but you needed a minimum of three. When the salesperson came over, Zubin said that he was just looking around.

It snowed early that year.

"It gets like, how cold in the winter in India?" his roommate, Bennet, asked.

Zubin didn't feel like explaining the varied geography of India, the mountains and the coasts. "About sixty degrees Fahrenheit," he said.

"*Man,*" said Bennet. Jason Bennet was a nice guy, an athlete from Weston, Massachusetts. He took Zubin to eat at the lacrosse table, where he looked not just foreign but as if he were another species—he weighed at least ten kilos less than the smallest guy and felt hundreds of years older. He felt as if he were surrounded by enormous and powerful children. They were hungry, and then they were restless; they ran around and around in circles, and then they were tired. Five nights a week they'd pledged to keep sober; on the other two they drank systematically until they passed out.

He remembered the day in October that he'd accepted the sweater (it was raining) and how he'd waited until Jason left for practice before putting it on. He pulled the sweater over his head and saw, in the second of woolly darkness, his father. Or, rather, he saw his father's face, floating in his mind's eye like the Cheshire Cat. The face was making an expression that Zubin remembered from the time he was ten and had proudly revealed the thousand rupees he'd made by organizing a betting pool on the horse races among the boys in the fifth standard.

He'd resolved immediately to return the sweater, and then he had looked in the mirror. What he saw surprised him: someone small but good-looking, with fine features and dark, intense eyes, the kind of guy a girl—an American girl—might find attractive.

And he wanted one of those: there was no use pretending he didn't. He watched them from his first-floor window, as close as fish in an aquarium tank. They hurried past him, laughing and calling out to one another, in their boys' clothes: boots, T-shirts with cryptic messages, jeans worn low and tight across the hips. You thought of the panties underneath those jeans, and in the laundry room you often saw those panties: impossibly sheer, in incredible colors, occasionally, delightfully torn. The girls folding their laundry next to him were entirely different from the ones at home. They were clearly free to do whatever they wanted—a possibility that often hit him, in class or the library or on the historic brick walkways of the Radcliffe Quad, so intensely that he had to stop and take a deep breath, as if he were on the point of blacking out.

He wore Jason's sweater every day and was often too warm; the classrooms were overheated and dry as furnaces. He almost never ran into Jason, who had an active and effortless social schedule to complement his rigorous athletic one. And so it was a surprise, one day in late October, to come back to the room and find his roommate hunched miserably over a textbook at his desk.

"Midterms," Jason said, by way of an explanation. Zubin went over and looked at the problem set from an introductory physics class. He'd taken a similar class at Cathedral; now he laid out the equations and watched as Jason completed them, correcting his roommate's mistakes as they went along. After the third problem Jason looked up.

"Man, thanks." And then, as if it had just occurred to him. "Hey, if you want to keep that . . ."

He had managed so completely to forget about the sweater that he almost didn't know what Jason meant.

"It's too small for me anyway."

"No," Zubin said.

"Seriously. I may have a couple of others too. Coach has been making us eat like hogs."

"Thanks," Zubin said. "But I want something less preppy."

Jason looked at him.

"No offense," Zubin said. "I've just been too fucking lazy. I'll go tomorrow."

The next day he went back to the Coop with his almost new textbooks in a bag. These were for his required classes (what they called the core, or general knowledge), as well as organic chemistry. If you got to the reserve reading room at nine, the textbooks were almost always there. He told himself that the paperbacks for his nineteenth-century novel class weren't worth selling—he'd bought them used anyway—and when he took the rest of the books out and put them on the counter, he realized he had for-gotten *The Norton Anthology of American Literature* in his dorm room. But the books came to $477.80 without it. He took the T downtown to a mall where he bought a down jacket for three hundred dollars, as warm as a sleeping bag, the same thing the black kids wore. He got a wool watch-man's cap with a Nike swoosh.

When he got home, Jason laughed. "Dude, what happened? You're totally ghetto." But there was approval in it. Folding the brown sweater on Jason's bed, Zubin felt strong and relieved, as if he had narrowly avoided a terrible mistake.

• • •

Julia had been having a dream about losing it. There was no sex in the dream; she couldn't remember whom she'd slept with, or when. All she experienced was the frustrating impossibility of getting it back, like watching an earring drop and scatter in the bathroom sink, roll and clink down the drain before she could put her hand on it. The relief she felt on waking up every time was like a warning.

She had almost lost it in Paris, before they moved. He was German, not French, gangly but still handsome, with brown eyes and blondish hair. His name was Markus. He was a year ahead of her at the American School, but he already knew that he wanted to go back to Berlin for university, and then join the Peace Corps. On the phone at night, he tried to get her to come with him.

At dinner Julia mentioned this idea to her family.

"*You* in the Peace Corps?" said her sister, Claudia, who was visiting from New York. "I wonder if Agnès B. makes a safari line?"

When Claudia came home, she stayed with Julia upstairs in the *cham-bre de bonne,* where she had twin beds and her Radiohead poster, all her CDs organized by record label, and a very old stuffed monkey named Frank. The apartment was half a block from the Seine, in an old hotel on the Rue des Saint-Pères; in the living room were two antique chairs, upholstered in red-and-gold-striped brocade, and a porcelain clock with shepherdesses on it. The chairs and the clock were Louis XVI, the rugs were from Tehran, and everything else was beige linen.

Claudia, who now lived with her boyfriend in a railroad apartment on the Lower East Side, liked to pretend she was poor. She talked about erratic hot water and rent control and cockroaches, and when she came to visit them in Paris she acted surprised, as if the houses she'd grown up in—first San Francisco, then Delhi, then Dallas, Moscow, and Paris—hadn't been in the same of kind of neighborhood, with the same pair of Louis XVI chairs.

"I can't believe you have a Prada backpack," she said to Julia. Claudia had been sitting at the table in the kitchen, drinking espresso and eating an orange indifferently, section by section. "Mom's going crazy in her old age."

"I bought it," Julia said.

"Yeah, but, with what?"

"I've been selling my body on the side—after school."

Claudia rolled her eyes and took a sip of her espresso; she looked out the window into the little back garden. "It's so *peaceful* here," she said, proving something Julia already suspected: that her sister had no idea what was going on in their house.

*   *   *

It started when her father's best friend, Bernie, left Paris to take a job with a French wireless company in Bombay. For years Bernie and her father had talked about getting out of the oil business, but now that Bernie had decided to do it, her father wouldn't leave. Julia heard him telling her mother that he was in the middle of an important deal.

"This is the biggest thing we've done. I love Bernie—but he's afraid of being successful. He's afraid of a couple of fat Russians."

Somehow Bernie had managed to convince her mother that Bombay was a good idea. She would read the share price of the wireless company out loud from the newspaper in the mornings while her father was making eggs. It was a strange reversal; in the past, all her mother had wanted was for her father to stay at home. The places he traveled had been a family joke, as if he were trying to outdo himself with the strangeness of the cities—Istanbul and Muscat eventually became Tbilisi, Ashkhabad, Tashkent. Now, when Julia had heard the strained way that her mother talked about Bernie and wireless communication, she knew she was hearing part of a larger argument—enough to determine its size, if not its subject. It was like watching the exposed bit of a dangerous piece of driftwood, floating just above the surface of a river.

• • •

Soon after Claudia's visit, in the spring of Julia's freshman year, her mother took her to Galleries Lafayette, and then to lunch at her favorite crêperie on the Ile Saint-Louis, where, in between *galettes tomate-fromage* and *crêpes pomme-chantilly,* she told Julia about the divorce. She said she had found a two-bedroom apartment in the West Village: a "feat," she called it.

"New York will be a fresh start—psychologically," her mother said. "There's a bedroom that's just yours, and we'll be a five-minute train ride from Claudie. There are wonderful girls' schools—I know you were really happy at Hockaday—"

"No, I wasn't."

"Or we can look at some coed schools. And I'm *finally* going to go back for my master's . . ." She leaned forward confidentially. "We could both be graduating at the same time."

"I want to go back to San Francisco."

"We haven't lived in San Francisco since you were three."

"So?"

The sympathetic look her mother gave her made Julia want to yank the tablecloth out from underneath their dishes, just to hear the glass breaking on the rustic stone floor.

"For right now that isn't possible," her mother said. "But there's no reason we can't talk again in a year."

Julia had stopped being hungry, but she finished her mother's crêpe anyway. Recently her mother had stopped eating anything sweet; she said it "irritated her stomach," but Julia knew the real reason was Dr. Fabrol, who had an office on the Ile Saint-Louis very near the crêperie. Julia had been seeing Dr. Fabrol once a week during the two years they'd been in Paris; his office was dark and tiny, with a rough brown rug and tropical plants, which he misted from his chair with a plastic spritzer while Julia was talking. When he got excited he swallowed, making a clicking sound in the back of his throat.

In front of his desk Dr. Fabrol kept a sandbox full of little plastic figures: trolls with brightly colored hair, toy soldiers, and dollhouse people dressed in American clothes from the fifties. He said that adults could learn a lot about themselves by playing *les jeux des enfants*. In one session, when Julia couldn't think of anything to say, she'd made a ring of soldiers in the sand, and then without looking at him she put the mother doll in the center. She thought this might be over-the-top even for Dr. Fabrol, but he started arranging things on his desk, pretending he was less interested than he was so that she would continue. She could hear him clicking.

The mother doll had yellow floss hair and a full figure and a red and white polka-dotted dress with a belt, like something Lucy Ricardo would wear. She looked nothing like Julia's mother—a fact that Dr. Fabrol obviously knew, since Julia's mother came so often to pick her up. Sometimes she would be carrying bags from the nearby shops; once she told them she'd just come from an exhibit at the new Islamic cultural center. She brought Dr. Fabrol a postcard of a Phoenician sarcophagus.

"I think this was the piece you mentioned?" Her mother's voice was louder than necessary. "I think you must have told me about it—the last time I was here to pick Julia up?"

"Could be, could be," Dr. Fabrol said in his stupid accent. They both watched Julia as if she were a TV and they were waiting to find out about the weather. She couldn't believe how dumb they must have thought she was.

• • •

A few days later her father asked her if she wanted to go for an early-morning walk with their black Labrador, Baxter, in the Tuileries. She would've said no—she wasn't a morning person—if she hadn't known what was going on from the lunch with her mother. They put their coats on in the dark hall, with Baxter running around their legs, but by the time they left the apartment, the sun was coming up. The river threw off bright sparks. They crossed the bridge and went through the archway into the courtyard of the Louvre. There weren't many tourists that early, but a lot of people were walking or jogging on the paths above the fountain.

"Look at all these people," her father said. "A few years ago, they wouldn't have been awake. If they were awake they would've been having coffee and a cigarette. Which reminds me."

Julia held the leash while her father took out his cigarettes. He wasn't fat, but he was tall and pleasantly big. His eyes squeezed shut when he smiled, and he had a beard, mostly gray now, which he trimmed every evening before dinner with special scissors. When she was younger, she had looked at other fathers and felt sorry for their children; no one else's father looked like a father to her.

In the shade by the stone wall of the Tuileries, with his back to the flashing fountain, her father tapped the pack, lifted it to his mouth, and pulled a cigarette out between his lips. He rummaged in the pocket of his brown corduroys for a box of the tiny wax matches he always brought back from India, a white swan on a red box. He cupped his hand, lit the cigarette, and exhaled away from Julia. Then he took back Baxter's leash and said:

"Why San Francisco?"

She wasn't prepared. She could picture the broad stillness of the bay, like being inside a postcard. Was she remembering a postcard?

"It's quiet," she said.

"I didn't know quiet was high on your list."

She tried to think of something else.

"You know what I'd like?" her father said suddenly. "I'd like to watch the sunrise from the Golden Gate—do you remember doing that?"

"Yes," Julia lied.

"I think you were in your stroller." Her father grinned. "That was when you were an early riser."

"I could set my alarm."

"You could set it," he teased her.

"I'm awake now," she said.

Her father stopped to let Baxter nose around underneath one of the gray stone planters. He looked at the cigarette in his hand as if he didn't know what to do with it, dropped and stamped it out, half smoked.

"Can I have one?"

"Over my dead body."

"I'm not sure I want to go to New York."

"You want to stay here?" He said it lightly, as if it were a possibility.

"I want to go with you," she said. As she said it, she knew how much she wanted it.

She could see him trying to say no. Their shadows were very sharp on the clean paving stones; above the bridge, the gold Mercury was almost too bright to look at.

"Just for the year and a half."

"*Bombay,*" her father said.

"I liked India last time."

Her father looked at her. "You were six."

"Why are you going?"

"Because I hate oil and I hate oilmen. And I hate these goddamn *kommersants*. If I'd done it when Bernie first offered—" Her father stopped. "You do not need to hear about this."

Julia didn't need to hear about it; she already knew. Her father was taking the job in Bombay—doing exactly what her mother had wanted him to do—just as her parents were getting a divorce. The only explanation was that he'd found out about Dr. Fabrol. Even though her mother was going to New York (where she would have to find another psychologist to help her get over Julia's), Julia could see how her father wouldn't want to stay in Paris. He would want to get as far away as possible.

Julia steered the conversation safely toward business: "It's like, mobile phones, right?"

"It is mobile phones." Her father smiled at her. "Something you know about."

"I'm not *that* bad."

"No, you're not."

They'd walked a circle in the shade, on the promenade above the park. Her father stopped, as if he weren't sure whether he wanted to go around again.

"It's not even two years," Julia said. There was relief just in saying it, the same kind she'd felt certain mornings before grade school when her mother had touched her head and said "fever."

Her father looked at the Pont Neuf; he seemed to be fighting with himself.

"I'd rather start over in college—with everybody else," she added.

Her father was nodding slowly. "That's something we could explain to your mother."

●　●　●

As you got older, Zubin noticed, very occasionally a fantasy that you'd been having forever came true. It was disorienting, like waking up in a new and better apartment, remembering that you'd moved but not quite believing that you would never go back to the old place.

That was the way it was with Tessa. Their first conversation was about

William Gaddis; they had both read *Carpenter's Gothic,* and Zubin was halfway through *JR.* In fact he had never finished *JR,* but after the party he'd gone home and lay on his back in bed, semi-erect but postponing jerking off with the relaxed and pleasant anticipation of a sure thing, and turned fifty pages. He didn't retain much of the content of those pages the next morning, but he remembered having felt that Gaddis was an important part of what he'd called his "literary pedigree," as he and Tessa gulped cold red wine in the historic, unheated offices of the campus literary magazine. He even told her that he'd started writing poems himself.

"Can I read them?" she asked.

As if he could show those poems to anyone!

Tessa moved closer to him, until their shoulders and their hips and their knees were pressed together. She took a sip and looked at him over the rim of her plastic cup.

"Sure," he said. "If you want."

They had finished the bottle. Zubin told her that books were a kind of religion for him, that when things seemed unbearable, the only comfort he knew was to read. He did not tell her that he was more likely to read science fiction at those times than William Gaddis; he hardly remembered that himself.

"What do you want to do now?" he'd asked as they stepped out onto the narrow street, where the wind was colder than anything he could have imagined at home. He thought she would say she had class in the morning, or that it was late, or that she was meeting her roommate at eleven, and so it was a surprise to him when she turned and put her tongue in his mouth. The wind disappeared then, and everything was perfectly quiet. When she pulled away, her cheeks and the triangle of exposed skin between her scarf and her jacket were pink. Tessa hung her head, and in a whisper that was more exciting to him than any picture he had ever seen, print or film, said:

"Let's go back to your room for a bit."

• • •

He was still writing to Asha then. She was a year below him in school, and her parents had been lenient because they socialized with his parents (and because Zubin was going to Harvard). They had allowed him to come over and have a cup of tea, and then to take Asha for a walk along Marine Drive, as long as he brought her back well before dark. Once they had walked up the stairs from Hughes Road to Malabar Hill and sat on one of the benches, where the clerks and shopgirls whispered to one another behind screens of foliage. He had ignored her flicker of hesitation and pointed down at the sun setting over the city: the Spenta building with a pink foam of cloud behind it, like a second horizon. He said that he wouldn't change the worst of the concrete block apartments, with their exposed pipes and hanging laundry and water-stained, crumbling façades, because of the way they set off plain Babulnath Temple, made its tinseled orange flag and bulbous dome rise spectacularly from the dense vegetation, like a spaceship landed on Malabar Hill.

He was talking like that because he wanted to kiss her, but he sometimes got carried away. And when he noticed her again he saw that she was almost crying with the strain of how to tell him that she had to get home *right now.* He pointed to the still-blue sky over the bay (although the light was fading and the people coming up the path were already dark shapes) and took her hand, and together they climbed up to the streetlight and turned left toward her parents' apartment. They dropped each other's hand automatically when they got to the driveway, but Asha was so relieved that in the mirrored elevator on the way up, she closed her eyes and let him kiss her.

• • •

That kiss was the sum of Zubin's experience when he lost it with Tessa on Jason Bennet's green futon. He would remember forever the way she pushed him away, knelt in front of him, and, with her jeans unbuttoned, arched her back to unhook her bra and free what were still the breasts that

Zubin held in his mind's eye: buoyant and pale with surprising long, dark nipples.

Clothed, Tessa's primary feature was her amazing acceptability; there was absolutely nothing wrong with the way she looked or dressed or the things she said at the meetings of the literary magazine. But when he tried to remember her face now, he came up with a white oval into which eyes, a nose, and a pair of lips would surface only separately, like leftover Cheerios in a bowl of milk.

When he returned from the States the second time, Asha was married to a lawyer and living in Cusrow Baug. She had twin five-year-old boys and a three-year-old girl. She had edited a book of essays about Bombay by famous writers. The first time he'd run into her, at a wine tasting at the Taj President, he'd asked her what she was doing and she did not say, like so many Bombay women he knew, that she was married and had three children. She said: "Prostitution." And when he looked blank, she laughed and said, "I'm doing a book on prostitution now. Interviews and case histories of prostitutes in *Mumbai*."

When their city and its streets had been renamed overnight, in '95, Zubin had had long discussions with Indian friends in New York about the political implications of the change. Now that he was back, those debates seemed silly. The street signs were just something to notice once and shake your head at, like the sidewalks below them—constantly torn up and then abandoned for months.

● ● ●

His mother was delighted to have him back. "We won't bother you," she said. "It will be like you have your own artist's loft."

"Maybe I should start a salon," Zubin joked. He was standing in the living room, a few weeks after he'd gotten back, helping himself from a bottle of Rémy Martin.

"Or a saloon," his father remarked, passing through.

He didn't tell his parents that he was writing a book, mostly because only three of the thirty poems he'd begun were actually finished; that regrettable fact was not his fault, but the fault of the crow that lived on the sheet of tin that was patching the roof over his bedroom window. He'd learned to ignore the chain saw from the new apartment block that was going up under spindly bamboo scaffolding, the hammering across the road, the twenty-four-hour traffic, and the fishwallah who came through their apartment blocks between ten and ten-thirty every morning, carrying a steel case on his head and calling "Hell-o, hell-o, hell-o." These were routine sounds, but the crow was clever. It called at uneven intervals, so just as Zubin was convinced it had gone away, it began again. The sound was mournful and rough, as depressing as a baby wailing; it sounded to Zubin like despair.

When he'd first got back to Bombay, he'd been embarrassed about the way his students' parents introduced him: "BA from Harvard; Henry fellow at Oxford; PhD from Columbia." He would correct them and say that he hadn't finished the PhD (in fact, he'd barely started his dissertation) when he quit. That honesty had made everyone unhappy and had been bad for business. Now he said his dissertation was in progress. He told his students' parents that he wanted to spend a little time here, since he would probably end up in the States.

The parents assumed that he'd come back to get married. They pushed their children toward him, yelling at them: "Listen to Zubin; he's done three degrees—two on scholarship—not lazy and spoiled like you. Aren't I paying enough for this tutoring?" They said it in Hindi, as if he couldn't understand.

The kids were rapt and attentive. They did the practice tests he assigned them; they wrote the essays and read the books. They didn't care about Harvard, Oxford, or Columbia. They were thinking of Boston, London, and New York. He could read their minds. The girls asked about particular shops; the boys wanted to know how many girlfriends he had had, and how far they'd been willing to go.

None of his students could believe he'd come back voluntarily. They asked him about it again and again. How could he tell them that he'd missed his bedroom? He had felt that if he could just get back *there*—the dark wood floor, the brick walls of books, the ancient rolltop desk from Chor Bazaar—something would fall into place, not inside him but in front of him, like the lengths of replacement track you sometimes saw them fitting at night on dark sections of the Western Railway commuter line.

He had come home to write his book, but it wasn't going to be a book about Bombay. There were no mangoes in his poems, and no beggars, no cows or Hindu gods. What he wanted to write about was a moment of quiet. Sometimes, sitting alone in his room, there would be a few seconds, a silent pocket without the crow or the hammering or wheels on the macadam outside. Those were the moments he felt most himself; at the same time, he felt that he was paying for that peace very dearly—that life, his life, was rolling away outside.

"But why did you wait three years?" his mother asked. "Why didn't you come home right away?"

When he thought about it now, he was surprised that it had taken only three years to extract himself from graduate school. He counted it among the more efficient periods of his life so far.

•   •   •

He saw Julia twice a week, on Tuesdays and Thursdays. One afternoon when his mother was hosting a bridge tournament, he went to her house for the first time. A servant showed him into her room and purposefully shut the door, as if he'd had instructions not to disturb them. It was only four o'clock, but the blinds were drawn. The lights were on and the door to her bathroom was closed; he could hear the tap running. Zubin sat at a small, varnished desk. He might have been in any girl's room in America: tacked-up posters of bands he didn't know, shoes scattered across a pink rag rug, and pieces of pastel-colored clothing crumpled in with the sheets of the bed. A pair of jeans was on the floor where she'd stepped out of them, and the denim held her shape: open, round, and paler on the inside of the fabric.

Both doors opened at once. Zubin didn't know whether to look at the barefoot girl coming out of the bathroom or the massive, bearded white man who had appeared from the hall.

"Hi, Daddy," Julia said. "This is Zubin, my tutor."

"We spoke on the phone, sir," said Zubin, getting up.

Julia's father shook hands as if it were a quaint custom Zubin had insisted on. He sat down on his daughter's bed, and the springs protested. He looked at Zubin.

"What are you working on today?"

"Dad."

"Yes."

"He just got here."

Julia's father held up one hand in defense. "I'd be perfectly happy if you didn't get into college. Then you could just stay here."

Julia rolled her eyes, a habit that struck him as particularly American.

"We'll start working on her essay today." Zubin turned to Julia: "Did you do a draft?" He'd asked her the same thing twice a week for the past three, and he knew what the answer would be. He wouldn't have put her on the spot if he hadn't been so nervous himself. But Julia surprised him:

"I just finished."

"What did you write about?" her father asked eagerly.

"The difficulties of being from a broken home."

"Very interesting," he said, without missing a beat.

"I couldn't have done it without you."

"I try," he said casually, as if this were the kind of conversation they had all the time. "So maybe we don't even need Zubin—if you've already written your essay?"

Julia shook her head: "It isn't good."

Zubin felt he should say something. "The new format of the

SAT places much greater emphasis on writing skills." He felt like an idiot.

Julia's father considered Zubin. "You do this full-time?"

"Yes."

"Did you always want to be a teacher?"

"I wanted to be a poet," Zubin said. He could feel himself blushing, but mostly he was surprised, that he had told these two strangers something he hadn't even told his parents.

"Do you write poems now?"

"Sometimes," Zubin said.

"There are some good Marathi poets, aren't there?"

"That's not what I'm interested in." Zubin thought he'd spoken too forcefully, but it didn't seem to bother Julia's father.

"I'll leave you two to work now. If you want, come to dinner sometime—our cook makes terrible Continental food, because my daughter won't eat Indian."

Zubin smiled. "That sounds good—thank you, sir."

"Mark," Julia's father said, closing the door gently behind him.

"Your dad seems cool."

Julia was gathering up all of her clothes furiously from the bed and the floor. She opened her closet door—a light went on automatically—and threw them inside. Then she slammed it. He didn't know what he'd done wrong.

"Do you want me to take a look at what you have?"

"What?"

"Of the essay."

"I didn't write an essay."

"You said . . ."

Julia stared at him. "Yeah."

"How do you expect to get into Berkeley?"

"You're going to write it."

"I don't do that." He sounded prim.

"I'll pay you."

Zubin got up. "I think we're finished."

She took her hair out of the band and redid it, her arms above her head. He couldn't see any difference when she finished. "A hundred dollars."

"Why do you want me to write your essay?"

Suddenly Julia sank down onto the floor, hugging her knees. "I have to get out of here."

"You said that before." He wasn't falling for the melodrama. "I'll help you do it yourself."

"A thousand. On top of the regular fee."

Zubin stared. "Where are you going to get that much money?"

"Almost half a lakh."

"That calculation even I could have managed," Zubin said, but she wasn't paying attention. She picked up a magazine off her night table and flopped down on the bed. He had the feeling that she was giving him time to consider her offer, and he found himself—in that sealed-off corner of his brain where these things happened—considering it.

With two hundred dollars a week, plus the thousand-dollar bonus, he easily could stop all the tutoring except Julia's. And with all of that time, there would be no excuse not to finish his manuscript. Artists, he thought, did all kinds of things for their work. They made every kind of sacrifice—financial, personal, moral—so as not to compromise the only thing that was truly important.

"I'll make a deal with you," Zubin said.

Julia looked bored.

"You try it first. If you get really stuck—then maybe. And I'll help you think of the idea."

"They *give* you the idea," she said. "Remember?"

"I'll take you to a couple of places. We'll see which one strikes you." This, he told himself, was hands-on education. Thanks to him, Julia would finally see the city where she had been living for nearly a year.

"Great," said Julia sarcastically. "Can we go to Elephanta?"

"Better than Elephanta."

"To the Gateway of India? Will you buy me one of those big spotted balloons?"

"Just wait," said Zubin. "There's some stuff you don't know about yet."

• • •

They walked from his house past the Hanging Garden to the small vegetable market in the lane above the Walkeshwar Temple. They went down a flight of uneven steps, past small, open electronic shops where men clustered around televisions and waited for the cricket scores. The path wound between low houses, painted pink or green, a primary school, and a tiny, white temple with a marble courtyard and a black Nandi draped in marigolds. Two vegetable vendors moved to the side to let them pass, swiveling their heads to look, each with one hand lightly poised on the round basket balanced on her head. Inside the baskets, arranged in elegant multicolored whorls, were eggplants, mint, tomatoes, Chinese lettuces, okra, and the smooth white pumpkins called *dudhi*. Further on, a poster man had laid out his wares on a frayed blue tarpaulin: the usual movie stars and glossy deities, plus kittens, puppies, and an enormous white baby, in a diaper and pink headband. Across the bottom of a composite photo—an English cottage superimposed on a Thai beach, in the shadow of Swiss mountains dusted with yellow and purple wildflowers and bisected by a torrential Amazonian waterfall—were the words HOME IS WHERE. WHEN YOU GO THERE, THEY HAVE TO LET YOU IN. Punctuation aside, it was difficult for Zubin to imagine a more depressing sentiment.

"You know what I hate?"

Zubin had a strange urge to touch her. It wasn't a sexual thing, he didn't think. He just wanted to take her hand. "What?"

"Crows."

Zubin smiled.

"You probably think they're poetic or something."

"No."

"Like Edgar Allan Poe."

"That was a raven."

"Edgar Allan Po*etic.*" She giggled.

"This kind of verbal play is encouraging," Zubin said. "If only you would apply it to your practice tests."

"I can't concentrate at home," Julia said. "There are too many distractions."

"Like what?" Julia's room was the quietest place he'd been in Bombay.

"My father."

The steps opened suddenly onto the temple tank: a dark green square of water cut out of the stone. Below them, a schoolgirl in a purple jumper and a white blouse, her hair plaited with two red ribbons, was filling a brass jug. At the other end a laborer cleared muck from the bottom with an iron spade. His grandmother had brought him here when he was a kid. She had described the city as it once was: just the sea and the fishing villages clinging to the rocks, the lush, green hills, and in the hills these hive-shaped temples, surrounded by the tiny colored houses of the priests. The concrete block apartments were still visible on the Malabar side of the tank, but if you faced the sea you could ignore them.

"My father keeps me locked up in a cage," Julia said mournfully.

"Although he lets you out for Fire and Ice," Zubin observed.

"He doesn't. He ignores it when I go to Fire and Ice. All he'd have to do is look in at night. I don't put pillows in the bed or anything."

"He's probably trying to respect your privacy."

"I'm his *kid.* I'm not supposed to have privacy." She sat down suddenly on the steps, but she didn't seem upset. She shaded her eyes with her hand. He liked the way she looked, looking—more serious than he'd seen her before.

"Do you think it's beautiful here?" he asked.

The sun had gone behind the buildings and was setting over the sea and the slum on the rocks above the water. There was an orange glaze over half the tank; the other, shadowed half was green and cold. Shocked-looking white ducks with orange feet stood in the shade, each facing a different direction, and on the opposite side two boys played an impossibly old-fashioned game, whooping as they rolled a worn-out bicycle tire along the steps with a stick. All around them bells were ringing.

"I think lots of things are beautiful," Julia said slowly. "If you see them at the right time. But you come back and the light is different, or someone's left some trash, or you're in a bad mood—or whatever. Everything gets ugly."

"This is what your essay is about." He didn't think before he said it; it just came to him.

"The Banganga Tank?"

"Beauty," he said.

She frowned.

"It's your idea."

She was trying not to show she was pleased. Her mouth turned up at the corners, and she scowled to hide it. "I guess that's OK. I guess it doesn't really matter what you choose."

• • •

Julia was a virgin, but Anouk wasn't. Anouk was Bernie's daughter; she lived in a fancy house behind a carved wooden gate, on one of the winding lanes at Cumballa Hill. Julia liked the ornamental garden, with brushed-steel plaques that identified the plants in English and Latin, and the blue ceramic pool full of lumpy-headed white and orange goldfish. Behind the goldfish pond was a cedar sauna, and it was in the sauna that it had happened. The boy wasn't especially cute, but he was descended from the royal house of Jodhpur. They'd only done it once; according to Anouk, that was all it took before you could consider yourself ready for a real boyfriend at university.

"It's something to get over with," Anouk said. "You simply hold your breath." They were listening to the new Shakira album in Anouk's room, which was covered with pictures of models from magazines. There were even a few pictures of Anouk, who was tall enough for print ads, but not to go to Europe and be on runways. She was also in a Colgate commercial that you saw on the Hindi stations. Being Anouk's best friend was the thing that saved Julia at the American School, where the kids talked about their fathers' jobs and their vacation houses even more than they had in Paris. At least at the school in Paris they'd gotten to take a lot of trips—to museums, the Bibliothèque Nationale, and Monet's house at Giverny.

The school was at Breach Candy, near the consulate. The guard at the gate had a less impressive uniform than the guard in Paris, and a much more impressive gun. Not counting Anouk, there was only one other American in her class. Dwight was from Florida, although he'd been living in Taipei since he was five. He was always trying to start conversations with her after homeroom; she learned that he wanted to be a software engineer but that his "real passion" was military code.

"Did you know that the best code talkers in World War Two were Native American marines?"

"Yes," Julia said.

Dwight looked disappointed. "Do you know why?"

"Because no one could understand them," Julia said. "All their friends and relatives were dead."

Dwight gave her a pitying look. "It was because their languages were linguistically unrelated to *every other* living language."

Julia felt lucky to hang out with the French kids. She was surprised one day when her history teacher, Mr. Khan, asked her if she might like to do her end-of-term project on Simone de Beauvoir.

"You don't want me to do someone American?"

"It's up to you," Mr. Khan had said. "But I'd thought everyone would represent his or her own country."

"I was born in San Francisco."

"But your parents are French, aren't they?"

"No," Julia said.

Mr. Khan looked confused. "I was certain—well, never mind." He shuffled through his seating chart, checking her last name as if he thought she might be lying. "Dwight already has Roosevelt; how would you like to do his wife, Eleanor?"

Julia wondered why she hadn't just kept her mouth shut.

*　　•　•　•*

There was no question of losing her virginity to any of the boys at school. Everyone would know about it the next day.

"You should have done it with Markus," Anouk said, for the hundredth time, one afternoon when they were lying on the floor of her bedroom, flipping through magazines.

Julia sometimes thought the same thing; it was hard to describe why they hadn't done it. They'd talked about it, like they'd talked about everything, late at night on the phone, as if they were the only people awake in the city. Markus was her best friend—when she was sad, he was the one she wanted to talk to—but when they kissed he put his tongue too far into her mouth and moved it around in a way that made her want to gag. He was grateful when she took off her top and let him put his hand underneath her bra, and sometimes she thought he was relieved, too, when she said no to other things.

"You could write him," Anouk suggested.

"I'd love him to come visit," Julia allowed.

"Visit *and* come."

"Gross."

Anouk looked at her sternly. She had fair skin and short hair that flipped up underneath her ears. She had cat-shaped green eyes exactly like the ones in the picture of her French grandmother, who stared out of an ivory frame in the hall.

"What about your tutor?"

Julia pretended to be horrified. "Zubin?"

"He's cute, right?"

"He's about a million years older than us."

"How old?"

"Twenty-nine, I think."

Anouk went into her dresser and rummaged around. "Just in case," she said innocently, tossing Julia a little foil-wrapped packet.

This wasn't the way it was supposed to go—you weren't supposed to be the one who got the condom—but you weren't supposed to go to high school in Bombay, live alone with your father, or lose your virginity to your SAT tutor either. She wondered if Zubin would want to do it on the mattress in his room, or if he would press her up against the wall, like in *9½ Weeks*.

"You're crazy," Julia said.

"Uh-huh," said Anouk. "You better call me, like, the second after."

She almost told Anouk about the virginity dream, and then didn't. She didn't really want to hear her friend's interpretation.

It was unclear where she and Markus would've done it, since at that time boys weren't allowed in her room. There were a lot of rules, particularly after her mother left. When she was out, around eleven, her father would message her mobile, something like: WHAT TIME MISSY? or simply, ETA? If she didn't send one right back, he would call. She would roll her eyes, at the café or the party or the club, and say to Markus, "My dad."

"Well," Markus would say. "You're his daughter."

When she came home, her father would be waiting on the couch with a book. He read the same books over and over, especially the ones by Russians. She would have to come in and give him a kiss, and if he smelled cigarettes he would ask to see her bag.

"You can't look in my bag," she would say, and her father would hold out his hand. "Everybody else smokes," she told him. "I can't help smelling like it." She was always careful to give Markus her Dunhills before she went home.

"Don't you trust me?" she said sometimes (especially when she was drunk).

Her father smiled. "No. I love you too much for that."

• • •

In Paris, after her mother left, her father became a cook. He would go all the way to Les Frères Tang to buy rare vegetables for Thai soup. None of the roots and leaves and grasses in the Thai soup were edible, but the broth was fantastic. You poured it, garlicky and golden, over rice. It was so spicy that her eyes teared and her nose ran and her mouth burned so no drink could cool it.

"Is it too hot?" her father would ask. It was just the two of them at the table then; even with the leaves taken out and stored against the wall in the coat closet, they had to half-stand in order to pass the soup.

"It's delicious," she said. It was, but she liked it better when they ate in the kitchen. The kitchen was small and faced a concrete patio, where her mother had grown herbs in a desultory way. Now a few of the pots had turned over. It was winter, the last real winter they would see for a while, and it got dark before five. Her father wore an apron with the Dürer rabbit on the front, and he fogged the black windows with his soups and curries. In the morning you could taste the lemongrass and cumin in the bread that had been left out on the table.

The fact was that she knew it was a sad time for her father, but she liked having him to herself. She liked the quiet of the house without Claudia or her mother. Often, when her mother called, she would shake her head so that her father would have to lie and say that she'd gone out. She stopped seeing Dr. Fabrol.

She thought she was showing her father her loyalty; she misunderstood. In the mornings when she got up, she found him at the computer, wrapped in a red robe, reading the *New York Times* online. Sometimes his left eye fluttered a little at the corner when he looked at her; then she knew he'd been up for hours, maybe all night. There was a mug of tea with the teabag still in it (he never took them out) and, eventually, an ash-tray again.

"Dad!" she said, playing, really, because she'd never actually ex-pected him to stop. But the way he grimaced and half turned away was awful.

"It's OK," she said right away. "I don't care."

She felt so sorry for him! She didn't know you couldn't choose like that—decide that your father was right and your mother was wrong—be-cause people were all different things at the same time. They were like onions under fine layers of skin; you didn't ever peel away a last layer, be-cause the layers were what they were.

• • •

It was pouring and the rain almost shrieked on Zubin's tin roof, which still hadn't been repaired. They were working on reading comprehen-sion; a test two years ago had used Marvell's "To His Coy Mistress." Zu-bin preferred "The Garden," but he'd had more success teaching "To His Coy Mistress" to his students—they told him it seemed "modern." Many of his students seemed to think that sex was a relatively new in-vention.

"It's a persuasive poem," Zubin said. "In a way, it has something in common with an essay."

Julia narrowed her eyes. "What do you mean, persuasive?"

"He wants to sleep with her."

"And she doesn't want to."

"Right," Zubin said.

"Is she a virgin?"

"You tell me." Zubin remembered legions of teachers singsonging ex-actly those words. "Look at line twenty-eight."

"That's disgusting."

"Good," he said. "You understand it. That's what the poet wanted—to shock her a little."

"That's so manipulative!"

It was amazing, he thought, the way Americans embraced that kind of psychobabble. *Language* is manipulative, he wanted to tell her.

"I think it might have been very convincing," he said instead.

"*Vegetable* love?"

"It's strange, and that's what makes it vivid. The so-called metaphysical poets are known for this kind of conceit."

"That they were conceited?"

"Conceit," Zubin said. "Write this down." He gave her the definition; he sounded conceited.

"The sun is like a flower that blooms for just one hour," Julia said suddenly.

"That's the opposite," Zubin said. "A comparison so common that it doesn't mean anything—you see the difference?"

Julia nodded wearily. It was too hot in the room. Zubin got up and propped the window open with the wooden stop. Water sluiced off the dark, shiny leaves of the magnolia.

"What is that?"

"What?"

"That thing, about the sun."

She kicked her foot petulantly against his desk. The hammering outside was like an echo, miraculously persisting in spite of the rain. "Ray Bradbury," she said finally. "We read it in school."

"I know that story," Zubin said. "With the kids on Venus. It rains for seven years, and then the sun comes out and they lock the girl in the closet. Why do they lock her up?"

"Because she's from Earth. She's the only one who's seen it."

"The sun."

Julia nodded. "They're all jealous."

• • •

People thought she could go out all the time because she was American. She let them think it. One night she decided to stop bothering with the outside stairs. She was wearing new jeans that her mother had sent her, purple cowboy boots, and a sparkly silver halter top. She had a shawl for outside, but she didn't put it on right away. Her boots made a loud noise on the tiles.

"Hi," her father called. He was working in his study with the door cracked open.

"Hi."

"Where are you going?"

"A party."

"Where?"

"Juhu." She stepped into his study. "On the beach."

He put the book down and took off his glasses. "Do you find that many people are doing ecstasy—when you go to these parties?"

"Dad."

"I'm not being critical—I read an article about it in *Time*. My interest is purely anthropological."

"Yes," Julia said. "All the time. We're all on ecstasy from the moment we wake up in the morning."

"That's what I thought."

The clock in the hall chimed ten. "I have to go."

"I don't want to keep you." He smiled. "Well I do, but . . ." Her father was charming; it was like a reflex.

"See you in the morning," she said.

•   •   •

The worst thing was that her father *knew* she knew. He might have thought Julia knew even before she actually did; that was when he started letting her do things like go out at ten-thirty, and smoke on the staircase outside her bedroom. It was as if she'd entered into a kind of pact without knowing it; and by the time she found out why they were in Bombay for real, it was too late to change her mind.

It was Anouk who told her, one humid night when they were having their tennis lesson at Willingdon. The air was so hazy that Julia kept losing the ball in the sodium lights. They didn't notice who'd come in and taken the last court next to the parking lot until the lesson was over. Then Anouk said:

"Wow, look—*Papa!*" Bernie lobbed the ball and waved; as they walked toward the other court, Julia's father set up for an overhead and smashed the ball into the net. He raised his fist in mock anger and grinned at them.

"Good lesson?"

"Julia did well."

"I did not."

"Wait for Bernie to finish me off," Julia's father said. "Then we'll take you home."

"How much longer?"

"When we're finished," said Bernie sharply.

"On sort ce soir."

"On va voir," her father said. Anouk started to say something and stopped. She caught one ankle behind her back calmly, stretched, and shifted her attention to Julia's father. "How long?"

He smiled. "Not more than twenty."

They waited in the enclosure, behind a thin white net that was meant to keep out the balls but didn't, and ordered fresh lime sodas.

"We need an hour to get ready, at least."

"I'm not going."

"Yes, you are."

Anouk put her legs up on the table and Julia did the same and they compared: Anouk's were longer and thinner, but Julia's had a better shape. Julia's phone beeped.

"It's from Zubin."

Anouk took the phone.

"It's just about my lesson."

Anouk read Zubin's message in an English accent: CAN WE SHIFT FROM FIVE TO SIX ON THURSDAY?

"He doesn't talk like that," Julia said, but she knew what Anouk meant. Zubin was the only person she knew who wrote SMS in full sentences, without any abbreviations.

Anouk tipped her head back and shut her eyes. Her throat was smooth and brown, and underneath her sleeveless white top her breasts were outlined, the nipples pointing up. "Tell him I'm hot for him."

"You're a flirt."

Anouk sat up and looked at the court. Now Bernie was serving. Both men had long, dark stains down the fronts of their shirts. A little bit of a breeze was coming from the trees behind the courts; Julia felt the sweat between her shoulders. She thought she'd gone too far, and she was glad when Anouk said, "When are they going to be finished?"

"They'll be done in a second. I think they both just play 'cause the other one wants to."

"What do you mean?"

"I mean, my dad never played in Paris."

"Mine did," Anouk said.

"So maybe he just likes playing with your dad."

Anouk tilted her head to the side for a minute, as if she were thinking. "He would have to, though."

The adrenaline from the fight they'd almost had, defused a minute before, came flooding back. She could feel her pulse in her wrists. "What do you mean?"

Her friend opened her eyes wide. "I mean, your dad's probably grateful."

"Grateful for *what?*"

"The job."

"He had a good job before."

Anouk blinked incredulously. "Are you serious?"

"He was the operations manager in Central Asia."

"Was," Anouk said.

"Yeah, well," Julia said. "He didn't want to go back to the States after my mom did."

"My God," Anouk said. "That's what they told you?"

Julia looked at her. *Whatever you're going to say, don't say it.* But she didn't say anything.

"You have it backwards," Anouk said. "Your mother left because of what happened. She went to America because she knew your father couldn't. There was an article about it in *Nefke Compass*—I couldn't read it, because it was in Russian, but my dad read it." She lifted her beautiful eyes to Julia's. "My dad said it wasn't fair. He said they shouldn't've called your dad a crook."

"Four-five," her father called. "Your service."

"But I guess your mom didn't understand that."

Cars were inching out of the club. Julia could see the red brake lights between the purple blossoms of the hedge that separated the court from the drive.

"It doesn't matter," Anouk said. "You said he wouldn't have gone back anyway, so it doesn't matter whether he *could* have."

A car backed up, beeping. Someone was yelling directions in Hindi.

"And it didn't get reported in America or anything. My father says he's lucky he could still work in Europe—probably not in oil, but anything else. He doesn't want to go back to the States anyway—*alors, c'est pas grand chose.*"

The game had finished. Their fathers were collecting the balls from the corners of the court.

"Ready?" her father called, but Julia was already hurrying across the court. By the time she got out to the drive she was jogging, zigzagging through the cars clogging the lot, out into the hot nighttime haze of the road. She was lucky to find an empty taxi. They pulled out into the mass of traffic in front of Haji Ali and stopped. The driver looked at her in the mirror for instructions.

"Malabar Hill," she said. "Hanging Garden."

• • •

Zubin was actually working on the essay, sitting at his desk by the open window, when he heard his name. Or maybe hallucinated his name: a bad sign. But it wasn't his fault. His mother had given him a bottle of sambuca, which someone had brought her from the duty-free shop in the Frankfurt airport.

"I was thinking of giving it to the Mehtas but he's stopped drinking entirely. I could only think of you."

"You're the person she thought would get the most use out of it," his father contributed.

Now Zubin was having little drinks (really half-drinks) as he tried to apply to college. He had decided that there would be nothing wrong with writing a first draft for Julia, as long as she put it in her own words later. The only problem was getting started. He remembered his own essay perfectly, unfortunately on an unrelated subject. He had written, much to his English teacher's dismay, about comic books.

"Why don't you write about growing up in Bombay? That will distinguish you from the other applicants," she had suggested.

He hadn't wanted to distinguish himself from the other applicants, or, rather, he'd wanted to distinguish himself in a much more distinctive way. He had an alumni interview with an expatriate American consultant working for Arthur Andersen in Bombay; the interviewer, who was young, Jewish, and from New York, said it was the best college essay he'd ever read.

"Zu-*bin.*"

It was at least a relief that he wasn't hallucinating. She was standing below his window, holding a tennis racket. "Hey, Zubin—can I come up?"

"You have to come around the front," he said.

"Will you come down and get me?"

He put a shirt over his T-shirt and then took it off. He took the glass of sambuca to the bathroom sink to dump it, but he got distracted looking in the mirror (he should've shaved) and drained it instead.

He found Julia leaning against a tree, smoking. She held out the pack.

"I don't smoke."

She sighed. "Hardly anyone does anymore." She was wearing an extremely short white skirt. "Is this a bad time?"

"Well—"

"I can go."

"You can come up," he said, a little too quickly. "I'm not sure I can do antonyms now, though."

In his room Julia gravitated to the stereo. A Brahms Piano quartet had come on.

"You probably aren't a Brahms person."

She looked annoyed. "How do *you* know?"

"I don't," he said. "Sorry—are you?"

Julia pretended to examine his books. "I'm not very familiar with his work," she said finally. "So I couldn't really say."

He felt like hugging her. He poured himself another sambuca instead. "I'm sorry there's nowhere to sit."

"I'm sorry I'm all gross from tennis." She sat down on his mattress, which was at least covered with a blanket.

"Do you always smoke after tennis?" he couldn't help asking.

"It calms me down."

"Still, you shouldn't—"

"I've been having this dream," she said. She stretched her legs out in front of her, crossed her ankles. "Actually it's kind of a nightmare."

"Oh," said Zubin. Students' nightmares were certainly among the things that should be discussed in the living room.

"Have you ever been to New Hampshire?"

"What?"

"I've been having this dream that I'm in New Hampshire. There's a frozen pond where you can skate outside."

"That must be nice."

"I saw it in a movie," she admitted. "But I think they have them—anyway. In the dream I'm not wearing skates. I'm walking out onto the pond, near the woods, and it's snowing. I'm walking on the ice but I'm not afraid—everything's really beautiful. And then I look down and there's this thing—this dark spot on the ice. There are some mushrooms growing, on the dark spot. I'm worried that someone skating will trip on them, so I bend down to pick them."

Her head was bent now; she was peeling a bit of rubber from the sole of her sneaker.

"That's when I see the guy."

"The guy."

"The guy in the ice. He's alive, and even though he can't move, he sees me. He's looking up and reaching out his arms and just his fingers are coming up—just the tips of them through the ice. Like white mushrooms."

"Jesus," Zubin said.

She misunderstood. "No—just a regular guy."

"That's a bad dream."

"Yeah, well," she said proudly. "I thought maybe you could use it."

"Sorry?"

"In the essay."

Zubin poured himself another sambuca. "I don't know if I can write the essay."

"You have to." Her expression changed instantly. "I have the money—I could give you a check now even."

"It's not the money."

"Because it's dishonest?" she said in a small voice.

"I . . ." But he couldn't explain why he couldn't manage to write even a college essay, even to himself. "I'm sorry."

She looked as if she'd been about to say something else and then changed her mind. "OK," she said dejectedly. "I guess I'll think of something." She looked around for her racket, which she'd propped up against the bookshelf. He didn't want her to go yet.

"What kind of a guy is he?"

"Who?"

"The guy in the ice—is he your age?"

Julia shook her head. "He's old."

Zubin sat down on the bed, at what he judged was a companionable distance. "Like a senior citizen?"

"No, but older than you."

"Somewhere in that narrow window between me and senior citizen-ship."

"You're not old," she said seriously.

"Thank you." The sambuca was making him feel great. They could just sit here, and get drunk and do nothing, and it would be fun, and there would be no consequences; he could stop worrying for tonight and give himself a little break.

He was having that comforting thought when her head dropped lightly to his shoulder.

"Oh."

"Is this OK?"

"It's OK, but—"

"I get so tired."

"Because of the nightmares."

She paused for a second, as if surprised he'd been paying attention. "Yes," she said. "Exactly."

"You want to lie down a minute?"

She jerked her head up—nervous all of a sudden. He liked it better than the flirty stuff she'd been doing before.

"Or I could get someone to take you home."

She lay down and shut her eyes. He put his glass down carefully on the floor next to the bed. He stroked her head and moved her hair away from her face. He adjusted the glass beads she always wore and ran his hand lightly down her arm. He felt that he was in a position where there was no choice but to lift her up and kiss her very gently on the mouth.

"Julia."

She opened her eyes.

"I'm going to get someone to drive you home."

She got up very quickly and smoothed her hair with her hand.

"Not that I wouldn't like you to stay, but I think—"

"OK," she said.

"I'll just get someone." He yelled for the servant.

"I can get a taxi," Julia said.

"I know you *can*," he told her. For some reason, that made her smile.

●　●　●

In September she took the test. He woke up early that morning as if he were taking it, couldn't concentrate, and went to Barista, where he sat trying to read an *India Today* article about regional literature for two hours. She wasn't the only one of his students taking the SAT that day, but she was the one he thought of, at the 8:40 subject change, the 10:00 break, and at 11:25, when they would be warning them about the penalties for continuing to write after time was called. He thought she would ring him that afternoon to say how it had gone, but she didn't, and it wasn't until late that night that his phone beeped and her name came up:

JULIA: VERBAL IS LIKE S-SPEARE: PLAY

It wasn't a perfect analogy, but he knew what she meant.

●　●　●

He didn't see Julia while the scores were being processed. Without the bonus, he hadn't been able to give up his other clients, and the business was in one of its busy cycles; it seemed as if everyone in Bombay were dying to send their sixteen-year-old child halfway around the world to be educated. Each evening, he thought he might hear her calling up from the street, but she never did, and he didn't feel he could phone without some pretense.

One rainy Thursday he gave a group lesson in a small room on the first floor of the David Sassoon library. The library always reminded him of Oxford, with its cracked chalkboards and termite-riddled seminar tables, and today in particular the soft, steady rain made him feel as if he were somewhere else. They were doing triangles (isosceles, equilateral, scalene) when all of a sudden one of the students interrupted and said:

"It stopped."

Watery sun was gleaming through the lead glass windows. When he had dismissed the class, Zubin went upstairs to the reading room. He found Bradbury in a tattered ledger book and filled out a form. He waited while the librarian frowned at the call number, selected a key from a crowded ring, and, looking put-upon, sent an assistant into the reading room to collect the book from a locked glass case.

It had been raining for seven years; thousands upon thousands of days compounded and filled from one end to the other with rain, with the drum and gush of water, with the sweet crystal fall of showers and the concussion of storms so heavy they were tidal waves come over the islands.

He'd forgotten that the girl in the story was a poet. She was different from the other children, and because it was a science fiction story (this was what he loved about science fiction), it wasn't an abstract difference. Her special sensitivity was explained by the fact that she had come to Venus from Earth only recently, on a rocket ship, and remembered the sun—it was like a penny—while her classmates did not.

Zubin sat by the window in the old seminar room, emptied of students, and luxuriated in a feeling of potential he hadn't had in a long time. He remembered when a moment of heightened contrast in his physical surroundings could produce this kind of elation; he could feel the essay wound up in him like thread. He would combine the Bradbury story with the idea Julia had had, that day at the tank. Beauty was something that was new to you. That was why tourists and children could see it better than other people, and it was the poet's job to keep seeing it the way the children and the tourists did.

He was glad he'd told her he couldn't do it, because it would be that much more of a surprise when he handed her the pages. He felt noble. He was going to defraud the University of California for her gratis, as a gift.

* * *

He intended to be finished the day the scores came out, and, for perhaps the first time in his life, he finished on the day he'd intended. He waited all day, but Julia didn't call. He thought she would've gone out that night to celebrate, but she didn't call the next day, or the next, and he started to worry that she'd been wrong about her verbal. Or she'd lied. He started to get scared that she'd choked—something that could happen to the best students, you could never tell which. After ten days without hearing from her, he rang her mobile.

"Oh yeah," she said. "I was going to call."

"I have something for you," he said. He didn't want to ask about the scores right away.

She sighed. "My dad wants you to come to dinner anyway."

"OK," Zubin said. "I could bring it then."

There was a long pause, in which he could hear traffic. "Are you in the car?"

"Uh-huh," she said. "Hold on a second?" Her father said something and she groaned into the phone. "My dad wants me to tell you my SAT scores."

"Only if you want to."

"Eight hundred math."

"Wow."

"And six-ninety verbal."

"You're kidding."

"Nope."

"Is this the Julia who was too distracted to do her practice tests?"

"Maybe it was easy this year," Julia said, but he could tell she was smiling.

"I don't believe you."

"Zu*bin!*" (He loved the way she added the extra stress). "I *swear.*"

*   *   *

They ate *coquilles St. Jacques* by candlelight. Julia's father lit the candles himself, with a box of old-fashioned White Swan matches. Then he opened Zubin's wine and poured all three of them a full glass. Zubin took a sip; it seemed too sweet, especially with the seafood.

"A toast," said Julia's father. "To my daughter the genius."

Zubin raised his glass. All week he'd felt an urgent need to see her; now that he was here he had a contented, peaceful feeling, only partly related to the two salty dogs he'd mixed for himself just before going out.

"Scallops are weird," said Julia. "Do they even have heads?"

"Did any of your students do better?" her father asked.

"Only one, I think."

"Boy or girl?"

"Why does *that* matter?" Julia asked. She stood up suddenly; she was wearing a sundress made of blue and white printed cotton, and she was barefoot. "I'll be in my room if anyone needs me."

Zubin started to get up.

"Sit," Julia's father said. "Finish your meal. Then you can do whatever you have to do."

"I brought your essay—the revision of your essay," Zubin corrected himself, but she didn't turn around. He watched her disappear down the hall to her bedroom: a pair of tan shoulders under thin, cotton straps.

"I first came to India in '76," her father was saying. "I flew from Moscow to Paris to meet Julia's mom, and then we went to Italy and Greece. We were deciding between India and North Africa—finally we just tossed a coin."

"Wow," said Zubin. He was afraid Julia would go out before he could give her the essay.

"It was February and I'd been in Moscow for a year," Julia's father said. "So you can imagine what India was like for me. We were staying in this pension in Benares—Varanasi—and every night there were these incredible parties on the roof.

"One night we could see the burning ghats from where we were— hardly any electricity in the city, and then this big fire on the ghat, with the drums and the wailing. I'd never seen anything like that—the pieces of the body that they sent down the river, still burning." He stopped and refilled their glasses. He didn't seem to mind the wine. "Maybe they don't still do that?"

"I've never been to Benares."

Julia's father laughed. "Right," he said. "That's an old man's India now. And you're not writing about India, are you?"

Writing the essay, alone at night in his room, knowing she was out somewhere with her school friends, he'd had the feeling, the delusion really, that he could hear her. That while she was standing on the beach or dancing in a club, she was also telling him her life story: not the places she'd lived, which didn't matter, but the time in third grade when she was humiliated in front of the class; the boy who wrote his number on the inside of her wrist; the weather on the day her mother left for New York. He felt that her voice was coming in the open window with the noise of the motorbikes and the televisions and the crows, and all he was doing was hitting the keys.

Julia's father had asked a question about India.

"Sorry?" Zubin said.

He waved a hand dismissively in front of his face. "You don't have to tell me—writers are private about these things. It's just that business guys like me—we're curious how you do it."

"When I'm here, I want to write about America, and when I'm in America, I always want to write about being here." He wasn't slurring words, but he could hear himself emphasizing them: "It would have made *sense* to stay there."

"But you didn't."

"I was homesick, I guess."

"And now?"

Zubin didn't know what to say.

"Far be it from me. But I think it doesn't matter so much, whether you're here or there. You can bring your home with you." Julia's father smiled. "To some extent. And India's wonderful—even if it's not your first choice."

It was easy if you were Julia's father. He had chosen India because he remembered seeing some dead bodies in a river. He had found it "wonderful." And that was what it was to be an American. Americans could go all over the world and still be Americans; they could live just the way they did at home and nobody wondered who they were, or why they were doing things the way they did.

"I'm sure you're right," Zubin said politely.

Finally his host pressed a buzzer and a servant appeared to clear the dishes. Julia's father pushed back his chair and stood up. Before disappearing into his study, he nodded formally and said something—whether "good night" or "good luck," Zubin couldn't tell.

Zubin was left with a servant, about his age, with big, southern features and stooped shoulders. The servant was wearing the brown uniform from another job: short pants and a shirt that was tight across his chest. He moved as if he'd been compensating for his height his whole life, as if he'd never had clothes that fit him.

"Do you work here every day?" Zubin asked in his schoolbook Marathi.

The young man looked up as if talking to Zubin were the last in a series of obstacles that lay between him and the end of his day.

"Mangalwar ani guruwar."

Zubin smiled—they both worked on Tuesdays and Thursdays. "Me too," he said.

The servant didn't understand. He stood holding the plates, waiting to see if Zubin was finished and scratching his left ankle with his right foot. His toes were round and splayed, with cracked nails and a glaucous coating of dry, white skin.

"Okay," Zubin said. *"Bas."*

• • •

Julia's room was, as he'd expected, empty. The lights were burning and the stereo was on (the disk had finished), but she'd left the window open; the bamboo shade sucked in and out. The mirror in the bathroom was steamed around the edges—she must've taken a shower before going out; there was the smell of some kind of fragrant soap and cigarettes.

He put the essay on the desk where she would see it. There were two CDs, still in their plastic wrappers, and a detritus of pens and pencils, hair bands, fashion magazines—*French Vogue, Femina* and *YM*—gum wrappers, an OB tampon, and a miniature brass abacus with tiny ivory beads. There was also a diary with a pale blue paper cover.

The door to the hall was slightly open, but the house was absolutely quiet. It was not good to look at someone's journal, especially a teenage girl's. But there were things that would be worse—jerking off in her room, for example. It was a beautiful notebook, with a heavy cardboard cover that made a satisfying sound when he opened it on the desk.

"That's nothing."

He flipped the diary closed but it was too late. She was climbing in through the window, lifting the shade with her hand.

"That's where I smoke," she said. "You should've checked."

"I was just looking at the notebook," Zubin said. "I wouldn't have read what you'd written."

"My hopes, dreams, fantasies. It would've been good for the essay."

"I finished the essay."

She stopped and stared at him. Her hair was wet. "You wrote it?"

He pointed to the neatly stacked pages in the clutter of the desk. Julia examined them, as if she didn't believe it.

"I thought you weren't going to?"

"If you already wrote one—"

"No," she said. "I tried but . . ." She gave him a beautiful smile. "Do you want to stay while I read it?"

Zubin glanced at the door.

"My dad's in his study."

He pretended to look through her CDs, which were organized in a zippered binder, and snuck glances at her while she read. She sat down on her bed with her back against the wall, one foot underneath her. As she read, she lifted her necklace and put it in her mouth—unconsciously, he thought. She frowned at the page.

It was better if she didn't like it, Zubin thought. He knew it was good, but having written it was wrong. There were all these other kids who'd done the applications themselves.

Julia laughed.

"What?" he said, but she just shook her head and kept going.

"I'm just going to use your loo," Zubin said.

He used it almost blindly, without looking in the mirror. Her towel was hanging over the edge of the counter, but he dried his hands on his shirt. He was drunker than he'd thought. When he came out she had folded the three pages into a small square, as if she were getting ready to throw them away.

Julia shook her head. "You did it."

"It's OK?"

Julia shook her head. "It's perfect—it's spooky. How do you even know about this stuff?"

"I was a teenager—not a girl teenager, but you know."

She shook her head. "About being an American, I mean? How do you know about that?"

She asked the same way she might ask who wrote *The Faerie Queene* or the meaning of the word "synecdoche."

Because I am not any different, he wanted to tell her. He wanted to grab her shoulders: *If we are what we want, I am the same as you.*

But she wasn't looking at him. Her eyes were like marbles he'd had as a child, striated brown and gold. They moved over the pages he'd written as if they were hers, as if she wanted to tear one up and put it in her mouth.

"This part," Julia said. "About forgetting where you are? D'you know, that *happens* to me? Sometimes coming home I almost say the wrong street—the one in Paris, or in Moscow when we used to have to say 'Pushkinskaya.'"

Her skirt was all twisted around her legs.

"Keep it," he said.

"I'll write you a check."

"It's a present," Zubin told her.

"Really?"

He nodded. When she smiled she looked like a kid. "I wish I could do something for *you.*"

Zubin decided that it was time to leave.

Julia put on a CD—a female vocalist with a heavy baseline. "This is too sappy for daytime," she said. Then she started to dance. She was not a good dancer. He watched her fluttering her hands in front of her face, stamping her feet, and knew, the same way he always knew these things, that he wasn't going anywhere at all.

"You know what I hate?"

"What?"

"Boys who can't kiss."

"All right," Zubin said. "You come here."

Her bed smelled like the soap—lilac. It was amazing, the way girls smelled, and it was amazing to put his arm under her and take off each thin strap and push the dress down around her waist. She made him turn off the lamp, but there was a streetlamp outside; he touched her in the artificial light. She looked as if she were trying to remember something.

"Is everything OK?"

She nodded.

"Because we can stop."

"Do you have something?"

It took him a second to figure out what she meant. "Oh," he said. "No—that's good, I guess."

"I have one."

"You do?"

She nodded.

"Still. That doesn't mean we have to."

"I want to."

"Are you sure?"

"If you do."

"If I do—yes." He took a breath. "I want to."

She was looking at him very seriously.

"This isn't—" he said.

"Of course not."

"Because you seem a little nervous."

"I'm just thinking," she said. Her underwear was light blue, and it didn't quite cover her tan line.

"About what?"

"America."

"What about it?"

She had amazing gorgeous perfect new breasts. There was nothing else to say about them.

"I can't wait," she said, and he decided to pretend she was talking about this.

• • •

Julia was relieved when he left and she could lie in bed alone and think about it. Especially the beginning part of it: she didn't know kissing could be like that—sexy and calm at the same time, the way it was in movies that were not 9½ Weeks. She was surprised she didn't feel worse; she didn't feel regretful at all, except that she wished she'd thought of something to say afterward. "I wish I didn't have to go," was what he had said, but he put on his shoes very quickly. She hadn't been sure whether she should get up or not, and in the end she waited until she heard the front door shut behind him. Then she got up and put on a T-shirt and pajama bottoms, and went into the bathroom to wash her face. If she'd told him it was her first time, he would've stayed longer, probably, but she'd read enough magazines to know that you couldn't tell them that. Still, she wished he'd touched her hair the way he had the other night, when she'd gone over to his house and invented a nightmare.

Zubin had left the Ray Bradbury book on her desk. She'd thanked him, but she wasn't planning to read it again. Sometimes when you went back you were disappointed, and she liked the rocket ship the way she remembered it, with silver tailfins and a red lacquer shell. She could picture herself taking off in that ship—at first like an airplane, above the hill and the tank and the bay with its necklace of lights— and then straight up, beyond the sound barrier. People would stand on the beach to watch the launch: her father, Anouk and Bernie, everyone from school, and even Claudia and her mother and Dr. Fabrol. They would yell up to her, but the yells would be like the tails of comets, crusty blocks of ice and dust that rose and split in silent, white explosions.

She liked Zubin's essay too, although she wasn't sure about the way he'd combined the two topics; she hoped they weren't going to take points off. Or the part where he talked about all the different perspectives she'd gotten from living in different cities, and how she just needed one place where she could think about those things and articulate what they meant to her. She wasn't interested in "articulating." She just wanted to get moving.

* * *

Zubin walked all the way up Nepean Sea Road, but when he got to the top of the hill he wasn't tired. He turned right and passed his building, not quite ready to go in, and continued in the Walkeshwar direction. The market was empty. The electronics shops were shuttered and the JUST ORANGE advertisements twisted like kites in the dark. There was the rich, rotted smell of vegetable waste, but almost no other trash. Foreigners marveled at the way Indians didn't waste anything, but of course that wasn't by choice. Only a few useless things flapped and flattened themselves against the broad, stone steps: squares of folded newsprint from the vendors' baskets, and smashed matchbooks—extinct brands whose labels still appeared underfoot: "export quality premium safety matches" in fancy script.

At first he thought the tank was deserted, but then he saw a man in shorts, standing on the other side next to a small white dog with stand-up, triangular ears. Zubin picked a vantage point on the steps out of the moonlight, sat down, and looked out at the water. There was something different about the tank at night. It was partly the quiet; in between the traffic sounds a breeze crackled the leaves of a few, desiccated trees growing between the paving stones. The night intensified the contrast, so the stones took on a kind of sepia, sharpened the shadows, and gave the carved and whitewashed temple pillars an appropriate patina of magic. You could cheat for a moment in this light and see the old city, like taking a photograph with black-and-white film.

The dog barked, ran up two steps, and turned expectantly toward the tank. Zubin didn't see the man until his slick seal head surfaced in the black water. Each stroke broke the black glass; his hands made eddies of light in the disturbed surface. For just a moment, even the apartment blocks were beautiful.

Letter from the Last Bastion

....

Dear Sir or Madam:

I'm writing this letter to tell you some things you might not know about your Writer-in-Residence, Henry Marks. Some you may already know. If you've read *Private George Johnson,* his first novel, you know that Henry completed a tour of duty in Vietnam in November of '68. If you've read *The Birder* (and I guess everyone has), you also know what happened to him at the end of his tour. You might get this information just as easily from his *Collected Essays,* especially "Stalking the Birder," his meditation on writing, guilt, and the war, published in 1990, a year that marked Henry's return to form after the brief embarrassment of *The Accident* in '88. Critics have attributed the failure of *The Accident* to carelessness; they said that Henry had become sloppy as a result of his success.

On bad days Henry tells me that *The Accident* was a sign, and that he's through with novels because he can't find a way to finish his work-in-progress: *The Last Bastion.* (He has written the final chapter at least three times but hasn't shown me any of those efforts). On days when he's feeling optimistic, Henry says that *The Last Bastion* is sure to cement his reputation as a front-runner among American novelists of his generation. I would like to tell him that his reputation is already cemented; however, as of yet, I don't talk back to Henry.

I'll explain how it is that I know so much about Henry (and how I've read sections of *The Last Bastion* before it's been published), but first I should tell you something about myself. I am seventeen years old, and I'm going to be an optometrist. My mother and I live in a small apartment (second floor, rear) on West Lemon, above the mayor. That sounds fancy but it isn't; the mayor is also the owner of the drugstore. My mother doesn't make a lot of money, but there's an account at the Fulton Bank where my college tuition has been gaining interest since I was born. My mother would really like for me to use that money to go to a college like yours, but she says that even if I don't go, the account is mine anyway. So I guess that settles it: I'm going to stay here in Lancaster.

Although I don't feel the need to travel all over the world, I like hearing about foreign places. I was glad to get Henry's letters about a trip he took recently, back to Vietnam with four of his buddies from the war. This was three years ago, just after Henry's fifty-fourth birthday. In Saigon they had a beer on the roof of the remodeled Rex Hotel, and wandered through Cholon, the old Chinese district, shopping for souvenirs. Henry tried to visit a particular noodle shop in a nameless alley behind the Binh Tay market, but found in its place a store that sold parakeets. He stood for a long time among the blue, yellow, and green birds in their ornate bamboo cages, before rejoining his friends in the market.

From Saigon, the five of them went north, to Danang and finally Hanoi, where they chartered a Chinese junk and drifted through the karst formations of Halong Bay. They dove over the side and surfaced, one at a time, wiping water from their eyes. The young Vietnamese men to whom they'd trusted their safety (as well as the safety of five, bright-colored recreational backpacks bought in the "adventure travel" sections of sporting goods stores in major American cities, including New York, Los Angeles, Detroit, and, in Henry's case, the New England college town that you, Sir or Madam, know well) sat relaxing and smoking on the deck of the junk, while the five former soldiers bobbed naked (except for Gore-Tex swim trunks, waterproof watches, and one or two MedicAlert bracelets) as the day they were born in the warm, clear, and fantastically green waters of the Gulf of Tonkin. They had to laugh. Henry laughed so much that he had to flip on his back and float, which was easy in the calm, salty water. On his back he looked up at the junk's beautiful square sail, which he memorably describes in *The Accident* as: "thin and stiff as old paper, the color of dry blood, with light straining through the oily patches as if the sail were the shade of a dark, gigantic lamp."

* * *

In *The Accident,* a young man goes on a trip almost exactly like the one Henry told me about in his letter, in order to research his dead father's past. In Saigon the son meets his namesake, a Frenchman formerly associated with the CIA, who is living in a Cholon back alley above a parakeet shop. I like it when places Henry has described to me in his letters show up in his novels; in the same way, I enjoy matching the characters in the books with real people from Henry's life. Private George Johnson is always Henry; and although Henry wasn't a private—he was a second lieutenant—you can see how lowering his rank gives the title of the first book more impact. By the time he began writing *The Accident,* however, Henry was using his own name in all of his books. That might have contributed to his hesitation about the trip, which made him so nervous that he had to get two prescriptions: an antacid medication for his stomach, and for his insomnia, sleeping pills called Halcyon. In spite of the

Halcyon, he didn't shut his eyes for three days before his departure. Nevertheless, as a writer, Henry felt that the trip was an opportunity he couldn't pass up.

● ● ●

Henry's work is his first priority; he isn't shy about telling his students that he's organized his life around it. On the first day of each semester, he describes his routine: up and out the door by six-fifteen, to run a four-mile loop that starts on North Pleasant Street, skirts the campus, and joins a trail that runs in the bed of the abandoned railway, passing the reservoir. He likes to hear his footsteps echo on the old wooden bridge, which crosses the water at its narrowest point.

Henry is home by seven, showered and breakfasted—one poached egg on wheat toast, one glass of grapefruit juice, one black coffee—and at his desk by ten to eight, ten minutes earlier than the department secretary, whom he doesn't like to greet. It doesn't have anything to do with the secretary, a pleasant, efficient African-American woman named Renée, but with Henry, who has a strong superstition about speaking to anyone before he begins to write in the morning.

Renée is near retirement. When she started, in the late summer of 1984, the former department secretary, Maggie Straub (whom you probably don't remember) told her everything she needed to know about Henry's schedule. I imagine that Renée's attitude toward Henry's work is slightly less reverential than Maggie's was, but Renée has been with the department eighteen years as of this April and has never found a reason to knock on Henry's door. That would require a real emergency—specifically, it would require Henry's mother to die. He's told Renée that he can't think of any other situation with the potential to call him away unexpectedly.

At 11:05 Henry reluctantly reconnects the phone jack and settles down to read submissions from the students in his workshop, making notes in the margins. He's switched from blue to red ink over the years as the submissions have become more exasperating. At a quarter of one, with relief, Henry drives to the health food store, where his sandwich is waiting for him: roasted turkey on seven-grain, with tomato, sprouts, and a single slice of Swiss. (Because of a history of arteriosclerosis in his family, Henry is watching his heart.) Henry's undergraduate workshop and his graduate workshop each meet once a week, on Tuesdays and Thursdays respectively from two to four; he also teaches a class called "The Craft of the Short Story" on Mondays at the same time. On Wednesdays, Fridays, Saturdays, and Sundays, he follows the same schedule, but from home, where instead of teaching he puts in another three hours at his computer. If his mother were to die on one of those days, assuming it was not between eight and eleven or two and five, Henry would get the phone call himself.

Henry is sought after, as a friend or otherwise, by many members of your faculty and he accepts maybe three invitations a week; he often tells his students that Henry James would go to dinner parties in order to collect other peoples' stories. Nevertheless, Henry is happiest when he can make his own dinner. He does not like sweets, except in the summer, when blueberries, nectarines, and cherries are in season. On rare trips to New York to see his agent or his editor, Henry always picks up a case of very good wine.

But he doesn't drink the wine until after dinner, while he's reading the newspaper, which he can't do earlier in the day because it distracts him from his writing. He can listen to a symphony while he reads the paper; these vary, although Mahler's Ninth is his favorite. (I once checked Mahler's Ninth Symphony out of the library—our library has CDs now—and tried listening to it, but it made me feel silly; it didn't go with the view out my bedroom window, which is of the Fillings Men's Shop). Henry thinks that he likes symphonies because they are broad, expansive works, like novels. His friend Richard (your Composer-in-Residence) once speculated that the different characters must have to be heard in the head all at once, like instruments. Henry appreciated the comparison, although he finds that his own work often centers around a single character, at first called George Johnson, and later simply Henry. Henry has been lucky as a writer to have had discreet packets of experience, which are both personal and typical of his generation, so he's able to write about his own life and the century in America at the same time. As he gets older he finds the distinction between fiction and nonfiction to be increasingly meaningless; in his workshops, he wonders aloud whether there will even *be* novels in fifteen or twenty years.

Maybe it's this doubtfulness about fiction that encouraged Henry to befriend me in the first place. Because I'm exactly the age of the girl in his new novel, *The Last Bastion,* he may think that I'll teach him some lessons about seventeen-year-old girls in small towns, whom he may be in danger of misrepresenting. Maybe he thinks of it as a kind of research. Although writing from the perspective of a teenage girl is a stretch for him, Henry is confident; my contribution to his work, as he's told me over and over again, is purely voluntary. He's given me absolute freedom, to open these letters or throw them away unread, to read the bits of manuscript he sends me or discard them. He's told me that I don't have to write back, unless I feel like it.

. . .

On his trips home from New York, Henry always stops in Atlantic City, in order to spend an afternoon at the Sands Casino playing poker. Maybe it's a surprise to you that Henry's a poker player? Or maybe not—the students in his workshop know that he stays at the casino for an hour and a half, has one Jack and Coke at the table and another at the bar afterward, sometimes wins but more often loses, and even on his best days has never wanted to stay longer than the time he's allotted himself. Driving home, he likes to get off the Hutchinson River Parkway and take the smaller, wooded roads that curve through Greenwich and Stamford, shooting through the dappled tunnels of trees in his little silver car, past the stately white homes of people who would no sooner spend the afternoon playing poker in Atlantic City than they would sunbathe naked on the still expanses of their cropped and voluptuous lawns.

"What makes you want to be writers?" Henry asks his students angrily. (Lately he's been losing patience with them.)

The students smile shyly. They all dream of being exactly like him.

●   ●   ●

Another reason that I knew a lot about Henry, even before he started writing to me, is that we're from the same hometown: Lancaster, PA. Recently they've put his picture in the public library. It's an old picture, taken just after *The Birder* was published in 1975. Can you imagine the bachelor librarian with his suspenders and his moustache, and the children's librarian, a housewife who volunteers, as they received the photograph in the mail? The envelope was stamped with the name and address of Henry's agent in New York. Opening it up, the two librarians told each other again the things people in Lancaster always tell you about Henry: that he exchanged a scholarship at Oxford University for a tour in Saigon in '67, when so many young people from other places were making up excuses. Henry had an excuse, but he didn't use it. He went over there, and it wasn't what he'd expected, but he stuck it out and came home and made a success of himself. With unaccustomed energy, the two librarians looked around for the picture wire and some nails.

I guess Henry's handsome, although it's hard for me to say. In the picture he looks mostly young. He has very short hair (only a little longer than it was when he was Lieutenant Marks), and he hasn't yet grown the neatly trimmed, black and silver beard that is one of the distinctive things about his appearance now. He's wearing a beige, short-sleeved shirt that has something military about it, and you can't see the bronze amulet against his chest, although I know he's wearing it. His hair is dark, not yet gray. He's half looking over his shoulder, as if he'd just said good-bye to the person holding the camera. At the time the picture was taken people had just started learning Henry's name; nevertheless, he looks very sad.

If you had read *The Birder* in '75, and then flipped to Henry's picture in the back of the book, you would have thought you knew why he looked so sad, but you would have been wrong. Not until *The Girl on the Platform* came out could you have started to understand. The other Henry (James) said that all you needed in order to be a writer was one failed love affair; since you've obviously read those two novels, I'm going to skip the plot summary and tell you what really happened.

* * *

Henry had no intention of turning down that scholarship when he took the bus from New York City to Lancaster at the beginning of the summer of '67. He had just graduated from Columbia University and was only going home for a short visit; two weeks later his girlfriend, Laura, would arrive to meet him so that they could drive across the country and spend the summer together in California. In the fall he was going to begin a two-year fellowship at Pembroke College, Oxford.

Everyone assumed he was going to England to avoid the war. Henry opposed the war, of course; he'd even taken part in a few demonstrations, but it was more as a spectator than anything else. The student leaders were people of a different order—more confident, more stylish, more formed, in every way, than he was. He watched them in awe, and at the same time relished his own independence. Henry's essays explain how, at that age, it seemed crucial to him to avoid becoming one thing or the other. In a way I think he might have been keeping his own ambition a secret, even from himself.

The students he saw ranged across the library steps one afternoon—a small, peaceful demonstration a year and a half before the one that made the front page of the *New York Times*—were perfectly silent. They were holding a long sheet of white butcher paper with tall black letters: U.S. TROOPS OUT OF VIETNAM. There were only fifteen or twenty of them, and Laura was at the very end. She was wearing a green wool coat with a hood, and her hair whipped out to the right of the sign, which snapped and buckled in the strong wind. Her hair and her hood and her skirt unfurled like the drapery on a nineteenth-century bronze; watching from a doorway across the quad, Henry had the feeling that if he took his eyes off her she might complete the transformation, so the next time he'd pass by she'd be fixed there, frozen under a skin of thin green oxide.

It was Laura who suggested that he apply for the Marshall; all of her friends were hurrying to get into graduate school, or join the Peace Corps, or have themselves confirmed homosexual, or insane. Henry presented himself as a candidate for a master's degree in English literature. On the advice of a professor, he said that he wanted to write his thesis on Laurence Sterne's "Sermons of Mr. Yorick." He wrote his essays and forgot about it. When he was accepted that April, Henry panicked. He had tried and failed to finish *Tristram Shandy,* twice. He had never left the country. More significantly, he thought he might be falling in love with Laura.

They talked briefly about her coming to England, but Laura was going to a communal house north of San Francisco, where some of her friends were staying in order to check out the scene. She described it to Henry as a paradise: "They grow their own organic fruit—peaches and figs, I think. And it's warm enough to sleep outside, right next to the Pacific Ocean." Henry didn't have any particular fondness for the Pacific Ocean, but he knew that he wanted to sleep next to Laura, as many nights as possible. In the end they planned that they would drive across the country, and spend a couple of weeks together (with her friends), before he had to leave for Oxford. Henry was at once contemptuous of Laura's friends and intimidated by them; he told himself that their politics were thrown on as casually as their clothing, that they were like a herd of sleek and utterly predictable animals. These observations didn't help when Laura reintroduced him to people who all seemed to come from New York, Boston, or D.C., to have attended the same East Coast preparatory schools, and who could never seem to remember that they'd met him several times before. He couldn't picture himself eating figs with them, organic or otherwise, in a commune overlooking the Pacific Ocean.

The strange thing was that he didn't believe he was going to England either. The only thing he was looking forward to was driving across the country with Laura. He couldn't wait to see the desert. He had the odd but persistent idea that between Lancaster and Berkeley something would happen to show him what he should do.

On the bus that rainy afternoon, Henry read "The Short, Happy Life of Francis Macomber." He noted, near the bottom of page twenty-five, that no real person changes his mind as quickly and completely as Francis Macomber does after hunting the buffalo, and that Hemingway condensed things that way, for effect. He loved the idea that courage was a tangible quality, which could been seen in men as well as other animals; he also loved the idea of gimlets in the dining tent as the sun set over the bush, followed by an early-morning trip in the Jeep with the gun-bearers and the skinner and the porters. He had almost succeeded in forgetting entirely where he was, when he looked up and saw four soldiers, jogging across the slick cement. He continued reading, but he could hear them climbing on board the bus, vivid and loud and wet.

"Henry Marks!"

It was Billy Coleman. He'd gone to school with Billy for twelve years, but the only things he could remember about him were that he'd claimed to have made it with a girl named Helen Snyder in high school (but certainly hadn't) and, much earlier, had peed in someone's black rain boot in the coat closet of the elementary school.

"Coleman."

"You going home too?" Coleman asked, sliding into the seat next to him. Henry could see him taking in the perfectly worn leather shoulder bag (a gift from Laura, bought secondhand in the Village), his jeans and his vest, and his used copy of *The Complete Short Stories*.

"For a couple of weeks," Henry said. "You?"

"We got a ride here, straight from Fort Dix." Coleman glanced across the aisle at his friend, who gave him a disgusted look, as if Coleman might've been slightly more discreet. Not that they could've been coming from anywhere else, with those haircuts.

"We're shipping out in ten days," Coleman said. He watched Henry in an open, almost childish way.

"Soon," Henry managed.

Coleman nodded, encouraged. "We're just going home for a week. Schwartz and them're from Philly. Schwartz knows French and he's going to learn goo—Vietnamese too. He can speak French already—hey, Alan, speak some French."

Alan shook his head, just barely.

"Come on. He's got this amazing memory."

"Baise ta mère."

"Which one is that?"

" 'You look very beautiful tonight,' " Schwartz said. "It's what you'll tell all the girls, next time you're in Paris."

Coleman hesitantly laughed. Turning back to Henry, he said, "You're in college, right?"

"I just finished," Henry said. "I have a scholarship. I'm going to graduate school—in England." The minute he said it he wished he hadn't.

Coleman punched him lightly on the arm. "Hey, man, that's *great*. Congratulations. I should've guessed. You were always smart at school." There wasn't a hint of envy in it. "Schwartz's been to college too. He got out last year, and then he got his number." Coleman lowered his voice. "I'm not going to be sitting in some office, though, you know? You know what I'm doing?"

Henry shook his head.

"Come on, guess?"

"I don't really—"

Coleman grinned. "Forward artillery spotter."

"That's what they told you?"

"I volunteered—it's just you out there, you know? And I'm a kind of solitary guy. Aren't I? Hey, Schwartz, aren't I a kind of solitary guy?"

But Schwartz didn't turn around. He seemed to be memorizing Ephrata, Pennsylvania.

"You remember Susan Tammeny?"

"Uh—no. I don't think so."

"We split up for a while, but now we're back together." Coleman lifted his pelvis off the seat and reached into his back pocket for his wallet. He opened it and flipped expertly to a picture of Susan, under plastic. She was a soft-looking, rounded blond girl, wearing shorts over her checked bathing suit and sticking out her hip in a bashful Marilyn imitation. You couldn't see her eyes under her sunglasses, but you got the sense that she'd put them on only a moment before, for the photo. She didn't look even vaguely familiar.

"Oh, right," said Henry. "How is she?"

"She's great," said Coleman. "I'm gonna see her this week. I'm

going to go home for dinner, and then I'm going to go to Susie's."
He grinned. "I may not go home for dinner anymore, after that."

When Coleman asked, Henry told him about Laura and how they
were planning to drive to California. Coleman wanted to see a
photo; but when Henry said he didn't carry one, Coleman patted his
arm consolingly, as if Henry had said he didn't have a girlfriend
at all.

• • •

You'll recognize that scene from *Private George Johnson,* and the one
after it, in which George decides to enlist. He and Eddie Foster
(Billy Coleman in real life) walk home together from the bus station, since it turns out that their houses are only blocks apart. Foster's mother is waiting at the window; as they approach Foster's
house, she opens the door and cries out, "Eddie!" as if he's already
been in the war. Foster slaps George hard on the arm and says,
"Good luck." He saunters casually across the lawn, kicking a weep-
ing sprinkler (as if reminding himself of a chore), and allows his
mother to embrace him, looking back over his shoulder at George as
if to say, "Women—what can you do?"

George Johnson thinks at that moment: "I have to save him."

Henry's hero pays later for his idealistic moment on the lawn.
(This is the kind of reversal for which Henry is famous). He curses
Foster and his mother again and again, until the name "Foster" becomes slang in George's mind for anything particularly stupid and
pointless. In the thirteen months that George spends in Saigon,
there are many, many Fosters—until one day he opens the *Stars and
Stripes* and Foster's name is on the list. He gets up, walks to the window, and looks out at the street full of bicycles, and women with
baskets of vegetables on their heads, and (the one weird detail that
makes you know it's real) a hand coming out of a room across the
street, so low and narrow he can't believe someone lives there, dangling a red and orange paper snake on a stick.

And he thinks that Foster went to Vietnam for two reasons—vanity and stupidity. And he thinks: "Fuck you, Eddie Foster. *Baise ta mère.*"

• • •

Henry has explained in his letters that his thoughts about Eddie Foster (Billy Coleman) were real, but the moment on the lawn is invented. In real life Henry didn't think about enlisting until very late that first night in Lancaster, after dinner with his parents, his brother, Sam, Sam's wife, Karen, and their two daughters. Everyone was curious about Oxford; his mother wanted to know what kind of food he was going to get there, and whether he would have a hot plate in his room, in case he got hungry between meals.

"I guess the food is pretty awful over there?" Sam speculated.

"Why would it be awful?" his mother asked. They both looked at him eagerly, for information.

Karen, who had gotten up, came back into the kitchen and stood shyly in the doorway with the baby.

"Do they make you wear those robes?" Karen had a napkin over her shoulder to protect her blouse from the baby's spit.

"Not every day," he said.

"I saw a movie," Karen said doubtfully. "I think it was Oxford. In the movie they were wearing them all the time."

"Why would they wear them all the time?" Sam said. "Jesus."

Henry had no idea when you wore your robes, or whether you could have a hot plate; in fact, when he thought about Oxford he got a sick feeling just below his rib cage. He was relieved to leave his family and go up to his old room, with the sloped ceiling and the tan carpeting, the Columbia pennant and the baseball trophies and all his old books, everything from the Hardy Boys to *The Catcher in the Rye.*

He was thinking about Coleman, who might now be fucking Susan Tammeny in a car somewhere, and wondering whether it would be possible to go down the hall and call Laura without waking his parents. Instead he settled himself on the floor with his back against the bed, where he could stretch out his legs, and opened the Hemingway. He'd skipped the preface before; now he read Hemingway's thoughts about experience for the first time:

> *In going where you have to go, and doing what you have to do, and seeing what you have to see, you dull and blunt the instrument you write with. But I would rather have it bent and dull and know I had to put it on the grindstone again and hammer it into shape and put a whetstone to it, and know that I had something to write about, than to have it bright and shining and nothing to say, or smooth and well-oiled in the closet, but unused.*

Henry copied out that passage for me, since it doesn't appear in *Private George Johnson*. He said that those two sentences were the reason he enlisted, and that in the few moments it took him to read them, he changed his mind completely.

* * *

Henry is nervous about *The Last Bastion*—the first book he's written that has absolutely nothing to do with Vietnam—but I don't think he should worry. He's made his reputation writing about Vietnam, but if you look at the last thirty years of his life, they've had much more to do with teenage girls than with the war. At this point I might mention that although there are several very attractive young ladies in his workshops, Henry maintains strict professional boundaries. He's been very frank with me on this point. He thinks that a seventeen-year-old girl who is going to be his friend—or whatever it is we are—should know that he doesn't have relationships with his students, who are a little older than I am, but not much.

The question I have is whether Henry would tell me if he *did* have affairs. And if not, what does he have? He's been so precise about his schedule, accounting for every hour, including the ones just before bed, that I wonder whether he may have left some things out.

If so, I wish he would tell me. Maybe he thinks I have delicate ears. I may be young but I'm not delicate. I like some sports, especially tennis (I play on the junior varsity team at school), and when it's not tennis season I go jogging in the mornings. I am skinny, but flat-chested, and my ankles are too thick. My hair is blond and stops at my chin, and I have very big eyes, which are light blue and require glasses. I once told my mother that I had fish eyes, and she laughed and said I certainly did not, but that's when she started calling me "Miss Fish." She says this is not because my eyes are too big but because I watch people, including her. She says that I am a smart, slippery kind of girl.

I should tell you that I'm not a virgin anymore. This is a pretty recent development, as of last Monday. I had sworn that I wouldn't be by the time I turned seventeen, but I turned seventeen in April and I still was. It wasn't that I didn't have a boyfriend—I did, Curtis Moreno—or that he didn't want to—he did, very much—but I guess I just never imagined it would happen in our apartment (my mom's and mine) in the afternoon with a guy like Curtis. My imagination is one of my big problems, according to my mother. My mother says that if you're always thinking about how things are going to be in your life, you can never be happy. That's what she says, but I know she imagines things too. I can tell by the way she gets dressed up when we go to church on Sundays, in a skirt and a blouse with a pin (a bee, with cubic zirconium eyes) and the way she does her Jane Fonda tape every other morning on our living room carpet, even though she's been doing that tape for at least ten years, and it must be starting to make her crazy, the way Jane comes into the exercise studio and says: "O-*kay,* are we ready to *work?*"

Anyway, that Monday afternoon for no reason I just decided. That's the way I am (like with this letter, which I didn't know I was going to write until I got home from tennis practice today and saw the application from your college on the table). My mother was at work, but she'd left the application where I couldn't miss it. For a while I did think about letting my average slip a little so that she would stop bothering me, but it's hard to do badly once you've gotten used to doing well. I'm not applying to your school, but I don't mind telling you that I have a 3.97 and that everyone says I'm going to be the valedictorian.

Curtis could be the salutatorian if he didn't smoke so much pot. He says school is too easy to bother trying hard, which I think is an excuse he uses to explain to himself why I get better grades than he does. Curtis also plays the guitar and he's cute; he's Italian. He has very nice brown eyes with long eyelashes, and longish hair (just below his ears). He wants to be a musician, and he really admires Neil Young, The Band, Jerry Garcia, and Bob Dylan, a lot, even though that isn't the music people listen to at our school. I don't mind when Curtis comes over after school and plays his guitar, but now that I've heard the songs he writes I think it might be smart for him to choose something as a backup, like optometry. I'm looking for a tactful way to tell him that.

When Curtis got here that Monday, Mrs. Glick was out in the yard, standing with her hands on her hips and looking at the impatiens.

"Hello, Mrs. Glick," I said. My mother says we should try to stay on the bright side of the Glicks, since Mr. Glick is not only our neighbor but our landlord and our mayor.

Mrs. Glick shaded her eyes and squinted up at us. "Oh, hello, Curtis." Then she said to me: "I see it's company day." That's something she says whenever someone comes to our house, so that later she can ask what the person was doing here. In this case, Curtis and I did not enlighten her.

Curtis and I each had a little bit of sherry, which is the only kind of alcohol my mother keeps in the house, from a shot glass with a picture of a pig on it that says I LOVE IOWA. This was at about two-thirty in the afternoon on a Monday, when we would've been in school if it hadn't been Memorial Day. My mother doesn't get Memorial Day off and she usually comes home around six, so Curtis and I had plenty of time. We went into my bedroom and started fooling around, and Curtis let me choose the music, which is *very* rare. I'm not sure how to describe what happened next. In a way it was like being two people: myself (my name is on the envelope, if you're curious) and someone else (for example, Miss Fish) at the same time. One person was feeling very strange, and the other was thinking very hard about what was happening, and those feelings and thoughts were very different.

What Miss Fish thought was: they shouldn't have canceled Health class. The parents who did it said that it was because we live in a conservative community. It's true that you see Amish and Mennonites here, especially at the covered market on Saturdays, but those people mostly teach their kids at home. It's the ones who don't wear any special costume—who drive all the way out to the Calvary Monument Bible Church in Paradise—who got it canceled. My mother doesn't agree with them, but talking about sex brings up all kinds of other things that my mother and I settled a long time ago, and I think she was glad when I told her I'd learned all about it on my own. She said: "Miss Fish, you are one smart cookie."

In Health class I've heard that you saw movies and even put condoms on bananas. The way I learned about sex was by looking up one word after another in the dictionary. It was time-consuming. I started simply, with "sperm," properly "spermatozoon," which led me to "spermatic cord" and "testis." I could pretty much picture those, although the "scrotum" turned out to be much, much uglier than its definition suggested. None of the words that I looked up had a picture, which I thought was weird in an illustrated dictionary that showed you a "scrimshaw: a carved or engraved article, especially of whale ivory, whalebone, walrus tusks or the like, made by whalers as a leisure occupation," not to mention a "testudo." The "vas deferens" was helpful, especially because it led me to the "epididymis: a long, narrow, flattened convoluted body that is part of the spermatic duct system, lying on the lateral edge of the posterior border of the testis." That really tied it all together for me and also, in a way, made me feel tenderly toward the epididymis and almost identify with it—I know that sounds weird, but I was also a long, narrow, flattened, and convoluted body, under Curtis. Maybe if we'd had Health, or if there had been a picture of something besides an "epergne" on that page of the dictionary, I wouldn't have gotten such a strange idea. (You, Sir or Madam, will identify the epergne immediately as "a large table centerpiece consisting of a frame with extended arms or branches supporting holders, as for flowers, fruit, or sweetmeats.")

· · ·

The above is what Miss Fish thought. What I thought was: I am going to cry. Curtis closed his eyes and so I did too, but then I opened them because I couldn't help it. Curtis was making a face I didn't like, and so I looked at the ceiling over his shoulder and I think it might have been the ceiling that made me almost cry. Our ceiling is off-white, very low, and whipped like frosting. It's the same all over the apartment, which my mom wishes were bigger. I wish I didn't know that she wished that, because otherwise I think I'd like our apartment. She complains about the AstroTurf on the steps outside, but every time I see that AstroTurf I think of Fredericka, our gray rabbit, who lived in a hutch that my mother built right outside our front door.

That was on a Saturday morning, when I was about ten. My mother got up early and went downstairs to borrow Mr. Glick's tool belt. While Mr. Glick was helping her adjust it to fit her waist, I heard Mrs. Glick saying:

"It's not that there's no pets in the lease that I mind, but that you have to do this kind of work yourself." Then Mr. Glick offered to build the hutch for us, and Mrs. Glick said: "You!" And then she said to my mother, "It's not enough that he's a good businessman and a good mayor—he has to be a good Samaritan too!"

And my mother said, "But Linda, no one needs to be a good Samaritan. I like having a project."

While I was having sex with Curtis I remembered Fredericka, and that must've been what made my nose tingle on the sides, and all of a sudden Curtis opened his eyes and said: "Are you watching me?" His "male organ of copulation in higher vertebrates" was inside me, but I thought that he hated me. That's when I really thought I would cry, but I just said I wasn't watching him, and he closed his eyes again and finished. I knew Curtis wasn't experienced, but I expected it to take longer than that—from 3:12 to 3:21 on my alarm clock. I just rolled over and pulled my knees up, and I was surprised when Curtis put his arm over me. We lay like that for a couple of minutes, on top of the bedspread, and I was thinking about my breathing, trying to keep it regular and calm.

"Thank you," Curtis said.

I didn't say anything.

"I love you," Curtis said.

"I love Iowa," I said.

Or that's what I thought. I always think of a better thing to say later, which is why I like letters. I would've liked for Curtis to disappear the second we were finished, and then maybe to write him a letter later. At the time, though—last Monday, May 27, Memorial Day—I was so relieved that Curtis didn't hate me that what I said was: "I love you, too."

But now I wish I hadn't been such a coward.

•   •   •

I haven't been in love yet, but you don't have to have been in love to be a good optometrist. Henry, famously, has been in love only once.

He tells his students that, and if they ask more about it he says, "It's in the book." By which he means *The Girl on the Platform.* In that novel, Henry gives up the pseudonym George Johnson and writes about a man called Henry Marks, who meets a girl, leaves her, and then falls in love with her again after it's too late. The girl's name is Laura.

Henry used to write letters to Laura too. He wrote the first one before he even left for Basic and he kept writing, every three or four days, the entire time that he was in Vietnam. He was the one who'd said that he didn't expect her to wait for him, or even to write to him, unless she felt like it. You can imagine what Laura thought of his decision, made just a week before they were supposed to go on their cross-country trip. Henry didn't expect her to understand, and when she asked him calmly to explain his reasons, it annoyed him. He might have preferred it if she'd raged and cried. In the book Laura is silent for six months, as she was in life, before she begins to write.

He was a little surprised that she'd gone to California without him. The commune, called Seagate, was situated a little north of the city in Bolinas, on a hill overlooking the Pacific. It was on four acres, with the aforementioned fruit trees, a vegetable garden, and a cedar sauna. The population was international and included a Bolivian named Andreas who was teaching Laura Spanish, a language she wished she'd studied in school in place of French, because of the indescribable way you felt when you spoke it. She wished she were as good a writer as Henry was (she wrote), so that she would be able to put it into words.

Seagate was not a typical commune, she assured him in the next letter. It wasn't what he thought: there were no drugs, except for grass, and people who were doing other stuff had to do it outside. Everyone had separate bedrooms, even the couples. It also wasn't a typical commune in *that* way; Henry shouldn't worry that she'd changed *that* much. For the most part people who had "paired off" did it outside in the woods, which according to Andreas was also very common on his grandfather's sugar plantation in Bolivia.

People at Seagate who were critical of Andreas because of his grandfather's plantation—worked by Indian peasants who migrated from their villages in the mountains for the growing season—should just realize that things were different in Bolivia and that when it came down to it, America was basically the feudal plantation owner of the entire world. That was Laura's idea, she emphasized, not Andreas's. Andreas had simply told her about the softness of the grass by the river that ran through his grandfather's property, and the smell of sugar in the cooling breeze from the Pilcomayo as you lay on your back at night, admiring the inverted constellations of the rich Bolivian sky.

What was it like in Vietnam?, she just had to ask in another letter, even though she knew that there were a lot of things he couldn't tell her. She hadn't told anyone in the house about him—not because she was ashamed, but maybe because she didn't really understand herself. She knew Henry wasn't out there killing kids and old people, lining them up against their huts and shooting them point-blank, just because they wanted a system of government that the United States of America didn't happen to agree with, but she would like to know what he *was* doing there so that she could explain it to the other people at Seagate, especially Andreas, who was foreign and therefore much more open-minded than some of her new friends.

•　•　•

Of course, everyone who's read *Private George Johnson* knows exactly what Henry was doing—sitting in an office writing statements that were delivered to members of the press at JUSPAO every afternoon. He'd embellished his tour to Laura (he wrote that he couldn't tell her about the interesting part of his job, except that it involved "reconnaissance"). In fact, the only reconnaissance Henry did regularly was with MACV, where he had to go for the special form needed to requisition typewriter ribbons for the ancient machines in his office. In his free hours, he would wander the convoluted streets and markets imagining Laura naked, satisfied and cool in the sweet river breezes of the Bolivian night. He was in Vietnam, with a blunted instrument and no experience of the war beyond the kind of statistics delivered to a brand-new second lieutenant information officer. According to his commanding officer, he was supposed to make these "clear, logical, and goddamn encouraging." It would've been a big job had Henry been forced to tell the truth.

He had imagined that Saigon would be the perfect place to become a writer. For the first few weeks he stayed late at his office, while his colleagues were out at the bars on Tu Do, or went back to the empty BOQ and stood by the window, listening to the street sounds—how were the nighttime sounds different from the daytime ones, and at what hour, exactly, did they change over?—writing and rewriting impressionistic paragraphs that trailed off into nothing. They were only background, and they made no sense without the war Billy Coleman had seen: the firefights and the night patrols and the tunnels. It was like talking about sex before you'd done it; no matter how good a talker you were, anyone with real experience would know in a second that you were full of shit.

After a few weeks the only thing he could bear to write were the letters to Laura. Sometimes he thought it didn't even matter that they were addressed to her—as long as they were addressed to someone, with a salutation and a closing. He tried to vary these: "Yours sincerely," became "Yours despondently," became "Yours malarially" (he exaggerated), became "I am, your devoted," became simply: "I am." In a letter Henry knew where he was going.

One afternoon he crossed a bridge over a fetid canal, ignoring the vendors of pencil-thin black eels and freshwater turtles who falsely grinned at him, gesturing at the swarming buckets, and found himself in a narrow alley of noodle shops open to the street. He was so busy negotiating the bicycle and foot traffic, pretending not to notice the curious stares of the pedestrians around him, that he didn't see the white man in the shop until he was nearly upon him. When Henry nodded, the man turned away. He was sitting on a low, wooden block, with his legs crossed underneath a child-sized table. Henry could see right away that he wasn't American. He didn't know what the man was, especially when he looked up and said something in rapid Vietnamese, which made a beautiful woman in blue pajamas laugh.

Now, when he thinks about it, Henry can hardly believe that he went into the shop and sat down at the next table, just as if he were stopping in at the Linden Diner for a hamburger, and asked for *pho* in his very tentative Vietnamese. The woman disappeared behind a curtain. In a moment an old man came out and stared. Henry tried his French, and the old man retreated as well. The European looked up from his paper, as if he were being interrupted by a particularly irritating child. He repeated Henry's two sentences, in Vietnamese and then in French, correcting his pronunciation.

"Thank you," Henry said.

The man went back to his book. Henry covertly strained to see the cover: it was Turgenev's *First Love.*

Henry felt a kind of irrational excitement. In the last seven months, he'd met only army men, but the person sitting next to him was distinctly unmilitary. He was wearing a white linen shirt, rolled up to the elbows and far from clean, and a pair of leather sandals with heavy gold buckles. He had longish brown hair and a few days of stubble. Henry was trying to determine his age—older than Henry but younger than forty—when the man finished the novella and stood up. He bowed to the waitress, who bowed more deeply in return.

"Excuse me." He had no idea what the right opener would be: *"Vous habitez ici?"*

"You should speak English," the man said. "Or even Vietnamese. Your French pronunciation is outrageous."

"A Parisian woman once told me that I spoke like a Belgian cow." That was true, although she'd been his French teacher.

The man smiled, and Henry pressed his advantage. "I noticed your book. I—"

"You like Turgenev?"

"Especially that one."

"Why?"

Henry thought for a minute. All he could remember about *First Love* were a few unconnected details—a game with a hat, a midnight tryst, a horsewhip—and that while he was reading the story it had seemed profoundly true. "The way he establishes his authority is really modern—with all of them telling their stories about the first time they fell in love."

"And yet only one story is worth telling. The one with fear and humiliation in it, from the beginning."

Henry wasn't sure what to say to that.

"Are you a soldier?"

Henry held out his hand. "Lieutenant Henry Marks."

The man introduced himself as François Metrailler. "You've been up to Danang, then?"

"I've only been here," Henry admitted.

"Good," François said. There was none of the bitterness you got from grunts who'd been up-country, who would smirk at each other and call you "lucky." Henry waited for François to tell him what he was doing in Vietnam, but no information was forthcoming.

"Are you working for—with the Americans here?"

François gave a mock salute. "Who else?"

As casually as he could, Henry asked, "You're in intelligence?"

François laughed. "That's very generous. I was a translator." He pushed his bowl away, and the girl appeared instantly to clear it. "Although my father was SDECE—you know what that is?"

"It's like the CIA."

"Only French," François said. "So you can imagine."

Henry nodded, although he couldn't really.

"Ghosts, as you call them?" François continued.

"No—spooks." He couldn't tell whether his new friend was having him on.

"*Spooks.* That's the right description. My father was there, he was gone—you never knew."

"That must have been hard for you."

"Hard for my mother," François said. "She was from your country. A more precise people, no? Where are you from, exactly?"

Henry lied without thinking. "New York."

"Ah. My mother was from New York. *Une jolie débutante.* She came to Europe for *her* tour, where she had the misfortune to meet my father, in a café. He was a failed poet and a failed painter before he became a remarkably successful spy." François was extracting something from the pouch under his shirt. "I was born in Hanoi. From my mother I have this—" He flashed the familiar passport. "But in exchange, perhaps, no home. It seems I keep coming back here."

The shop was humid with a rich combination of smells—lemongrass, fresh coriander, and mint. Henry had never heard of a life like the one François had just described, but he knew he wanted to hear more. Already he was imagining a child in a white suit, running through rooms of antiques—silk, teak, porcelain—while a gauzily attired society beauty lounged on velvet cushions, reading a novel.

François interrupted this fantasy. "What are you doing in this quarter, if I may ask?"

"Looking for a good *pho.*" Henry's bowl steamed, untouched, in front of him. Pink, lightly cooked shrimp floated in the clear broth, flecked with mint and basil.

François spit in the street. "It's not good here."

"Why do you come, then?"

François nodded at the curtain, as if it were obvious.

The girl had been watching them. When Henry looked up she dropped her eyes to the floor and flushed slightly at each cheekbone. Her mouth was tiny but full, and her eyebrows were thin and peaked, as if they'd been plucked. He could not determine anything about her figure underneath her pajamas; she was barefoot and hid her hands in her sleeves.

He didn't think she looked like a prostitute, but you often couldn't tell. Perhaps François had simply made an arrangement with her. "She's very beautiful."

François seemed to know what Henry was thinking. "I come every day. She serves me; sometimes she laughs. That is it—*c'est assez.*" He nodded to Henry, picked up his book, and said something to the girl. Without waiting for her answer he dropped lightly into the street and made his way through the frenzied foot traffic, stopping once to buy a pack of matches. The people expressed no surprise at the presence of the tall foreigner in the crowd. Henry watched until he disappeared, suppressing an urge to get up and follow him. He realized that he was already composing a letter, and that meeting François was the first thing he could tell Laura with pleasure, in answer to her question, "What are you doing over there?"

*   *   *

Henry's letters arrive in heavy envelopes, addressed in a loopy, almost feminine script. The first one came last September, right after I'd started my junior year. A few weeks after that I received a chapter of *The Last Bastion,* about a teacher at a small college in New England. For a while I thought about showing my mom the letters and chapters, which have been arriving regularly since then, but I decided against it, at least for the time being. I always get home earlier than her on weekdays and on Saturdays I stand by the mailbox waiting for our postman, who is Chinese. My mother doesn't ask me about things that she can see I'd like to keep private, unlike Mrs. Glick, who, when she sees me waiting by the mailbox, will say:

"Expecting something?" Then she stands there frowning, as if she thinks I'm one of the junior high school boys who go around putting stink bombs in with peoples' letters.

"My optometry school acceptances."

"Acceptances," Mrs. Glick says. "Aren't we sure of ourself!"

I ignore her, although to tell you the truth, I'm thinking of waiting until next year before I apply to optometry school. I'd like to use a little bit of my leftover college money to see some of the world— or at least someplace farther away than Philadelphia. I haven't told my mother, or even Curtis, but I've been thinking about California.

Some people have the same names in Henry's letters and in his novels—François Metrailler, for example. Henry's not even sure whether that was a real name, since he's been looking for his friend without success now for thirty-three years, and given Henry's reputation—not to mention the research skills of the department secretary—anyone he doesn't find probably doesn't want to be found. He's told me that after what happened to them in 1969, in Laos, François's unwillingness to be found was "clear and logical, but still goddamn discouraging."

François never had any trouble finding Henry. He would show up at the Continental, or more often in the street, all of a sudden slipping out of a shop, joining him as if they'd been interrupted for a moment instead of a few days or a week. In addition to Turgenev, they discussed Dostoevsky, Henry James, James Joyce, and Virginia Woolf. François learned that this was Henry's first trip outside the continental United States; that he'd thought seriously of becoming a writer, and had imagined that his service in Vietnam might afford him the necessary experiences; that he had a girlfriend who lived on a commune. He told François that before he left America he hadn't known he was in love; that now he knew he was in love; that his girlfriend was considering a trip to Bolivia.

"She's fucking someone else," François said, as if he knew this for a fact. They were at a *bia om* bar, in one of the streets behind the French opera house, watching two young women performing together on one black velvet platform. Their oiled skin, already the color of honey, was bathed in a golden spotlight.

Henry (who explains in his letters that he didn't often go to this kind of place) said nothing, trying to make François feel that he'd stepped over a boundary. The girl closest to Henry was using a donated American coin to demonstrate her control and dexterity to the appreciative audience.

"This place is no good," François said.

"She says she's learning Spanish," Henry ventured.

François made a sound of disgust. "In Vientiane you get the real thing."

Henry looked at him. "Have you been there?"

François watched the dancers, which Henry took as a yes.

"Were you working as a translator?"

"At that time, yes," François said. "But before that I was in the countryside."

"But what were you doing?"

"The only good thing I've ever done." François signaled for the waiter, a boy in white whose part of the action was certainly not limited to serving cocktails. "Yessir," the boy whispered, kneeling too close to them.

"Two White Horse—ice, no soda," François said brusquely. When the boy was gone he turned to Henry. *"J'habitais un village. J'étais en train de construire une école."*

* * *

François's school was in a Hmong village ten miles south of the Plain of Jars. He'd arrived in the country in the winter of '61, as a volunteer with the American IVS. He showed Henry the place on a twenty-year-old French map. He'd lived in the back room of a house owned by an old woman who sat at the window all day, cross-stitching elaborate, jewel-colored patterns into the traditional *pa ndou*. François immersed himself in the language and culture of the village and immediately began planning the school. It was slow going, even with the enormous goodwill of the tribe, because there were almost no young men in the village. They had already been recruited by the famous general, Vang Pao. When François asked what the men were doing, the women pronounced the word in the French way, *"Reconnaissance."*

François and the children harvested bamboo and laid it to dry in the sun. They lashed the structure together with handmade ropes and set about weaving the bamboo walls. When the walls were completed, an old man arrived from another village with a cartful of dry, gray thatch. The thatch was arranged, and the children began sawing the plentiful teak for benches and desks. The project was nearing completion when the North Vietnamese army took over the Plain of Jars, and François was forced to leave. He spent the next two years working at a refugee camp in the mountains southwest of the plain, waiting for a chance to go back to the village. One afternoon in Xieng Khoungville, where he'd gone to buy White Horse whiskey, François met an American officer who invited him for a drink. The officer was impressed to learn that François spoke not only English, French, and Russian but also Hmong and Vietnamese. A month later, a letter arrived by Jeep in the camp, strongly urging François to come to Vientiane and work for the Americans. The letter added that if he wanted to go, permission had already been granted by his bosses at USAID.

"I was under the illusion that you could do more from within the system," François said. "I believed I was making a personal sacrifice."

Almost immediately he had regretted his decision. Vientiane was full of American military personnel, many of whom couldn't find the Plain of Jars—not to mention François's village—on a map. François translated radio reports, and NVA propaganda leaflets. Occasionally he accompanied American politicians on official visits. He waited what he thought was an appropriate amount of time and then reapplied to the USAID office in Vientiane. He knew he'd done excellent work in the village; he thought that his USAID colleagues would agree with him that in Vientiane he was missing his calling. But when he visited the office, his boss told him that the situation around the Plain of Jars was still too risky for François to return to the village. Politely, François told him that he would take that chance. They went back and forth for nearly an hour before the man admitted that, given the sorts of documents François had been handling for the last several months, there was no possibility of returning to a village less than ten miles from the NVA.

"They hadn't even sent another teacher," François said. "They swore they were going to do that, but they never did."

Disgusted, François had returned in '66 to Saigon and resolved to wait. Now, three years later, things looked hopeful for Vang Pao and his forces. François believed that the general was going to retake the plain, and that he would be able to go back to the village that winter. One evening in August, after a rainstorm that had left the streets around the Binh Tay market sparkling and steaming, smelling of crushed vegetables, heat, and fish guts, François asked whether Henry would be interested in coming with him.

Henry knew about the planes that had been taking off from Udorn and Vientiane on strafing runs above an obscure sight in eastern Laos: a plain littered with oversized, ancient stone urns. He'd heard the standard line on Vang Pao, the native general who supposedly had gotten rich on poppy, who supposedly led a guerilla army of teenage headhunting tribals and disposed of his enemies in spiked underground pits. He'd even read the Mission's version of these events to bored reporters at JUSPAO: "At the request of the Royal Laotian Government, the United States is conducting unarmed reconnaissance flights accompanied by armed escorts who have the right to return fire if fired upon." But he'd never thought he would have an opportunity to see the Other War for himself.

He wrote a letter to Laura saying he was thinking of taking a short trip, as soon as his tour was finished, with a friend who was extremely knowledgeable about the region. He said that it was an unusual opportunity. What Henry didn't say, because he almost didn't believe it himself, was that he was feeling a little apprehensive about going home, and particularly about seeing Laura. He'd grown accustomed to the happiness of *waiting* to see her. A letter from her could change an impossible day into a bearable one, illuminate a drunken walk back from the Continental with dazzling visions of their reunion. The desire to postpone that reunion—to savor it a little longer in his imagination—grew stronger as the months went by and his tour crept to a close.

A few weeks after he sent his letter, Henry received a reply. Laura thought Laos was an excellent idea: why not see as many countries as possible, as long as he was sure it would be safe? She was dying to see him, she wrote, but unfortunately she might not be in the country when he got back. She was doing some traveling too, spending the spring semester in Bolivia—presumably to improve her Spanish.

He had a photograph of Laura now—not a very flattering one—in which she was standing on a cliff in front of the Pacific Ocean. It was hastily composed, at a scenic spot on the edge of the highway, and Laura had a blue bandana over her hair and one hand on the bandana to keep it from blowing away. She was wearing a blue blouse he recognized and a patchwork skirt that he did not. Henry looked at it approximately fifteen times a day, although it frightened him. Perhaps it was only the sun in her eyes, but Laura seemed impatient.

She was looking at the photographer (who was the photographer?) as if to ask why he was stopping to take this picture now. She seemed to demand some explanation.

* * *

In September, as François had predicted, the Hmong general retook the Plain of Jars. Three months later the two of them were boarding a twin-engine Beechcraft, operated by an American commercial pilot, to Wattay in Vientiane, where they switched on the tarmac to a Pilatus Porter. There were none of the problems Henry had anticipated. In Saigon, where François paid the pilot with a small airmail envelope of high-quality hash, Henry was introduced as a journalist, and François was his translator. In Vientiane François exchanged another envelope, this time full of American dollars, with a Thai PARU pilot named Pornchai who was doing a routine resupply flight to Xieng Khoungville. They were the only two passengers on the plane; the backseats had been unscrewed and removed to make room for burlap sacks stamped U.S. ARMY. Henry expected the brown sacks to be full of ammunition, or perhaps even cotton, hiding precious gummy balls of black opium; he was surprised to see, through a slight tear in the burlap, a trickle of the stubby Asian rice, scattering, a few grains at a time, as the plane banked and dove in the white, spiderweb clouds.

The city was submerged immediately under a thick jungle cover, with only the temple stupas showing luminous and gold in the black velvet hills. For most of the short flight Henry looked down on the hills and the twisted silver river, and then, just before landing, they left the river and the ground was bleached gray in larger and larger patches.

Sections of hillside had been deforested; huge craters had been ripped out of the flat sections, which appeared now, through the tiny circular windows, like bulldozed and abandoned construction sites.

"Holy mother of God."

Henry panicked. "What?"

François pointed at a rust-colored mountain looming on their right, its western slope hatched with skeletal black trees. "See that? All of that was green."

Henry tried to conceal his relief: no one was shooting at them, and there was nothing wrong with the plane. "How long has it been since you were here?"

"Three years," François said, incredulous. "*Less* than three years."

Henry was about to say something sympathetic when they suddenly dropped and skimmed the tree line; he closed his eyes instead, and concentrated hard on not throwing up. This is what I wanted, he thought, and God is giving it to me: now I'm going to die a thousand miles away from home, in Laos. But that was only a feeling, and it wasn't a surprise when the wheels hit the dirt airstrip and the plane began its long, bouncing taxi. Henry opened his eyes to see François, still staring out the window.

"I knew, but you don't know. Not until you see it."

"I thought we were dead," Henry said simply.

François looked at him with disgust. "*We* are not in any danger."

Because he'd closed his eyes, Henry's first glimpse of the base was from the airstrip. Along its eastern and southern edges were a couple of tented field offices, and behind them the ruins of the town. Henry could just see the standing walls of empty, roofless buildings, the piles of scrap lumber, the shell of an abandoned enemy tank. A local driver was waiting for them on the airstrip, smoking. The only other human being in sight was a Thai officer in fatigues and sunglasses; he didn't signal to them but stood absolutely still just inside one of the tents, observing their progress toward the open Jeep.

"Did you see that big fucking hole in the ground? Northwest?"

Henry shook his head, but François didn't seem to be talking to anyone besides himself.

"I imagined—what did I imagine? I imagined something different."

. . .

An hour outside of Xieng Khoung, the driver stopped suddenly in the road.

"He wants us to get out here," François said. The sun was at its fiercest point above the jeep; to their left a field stretched out peacefully to the next ridge of hills. The driver pointed up ahead, where their road suddenly jogged to the west, making a wiggly brown line across the valley. A tiny black rectangle was traveling along the line in their direction.

"What's that?" Henry asked.

"A truck," François said.

"But whose is it?"

François shrugged.

"Not enemy though?"

At François's suggestion, Henry was carrying a .45 that he'd purchased in a shop in Bangkok, in an alley behind a temple noted for its amulet market. After you bought your weapon, the owner of the shop directed you to the market, where you could pick up a bronze or enamel Buddha to hang around your neck.

Like the amulet against his chest, the gun was a charm. Henry had absolutely no intention of firing it, certainly not at a soldier from the Pathet Lao. (The possibility that there were North Vietnamese troops in the area had been summarily dismissed by François the night before in the capital, where they'd sat in a café drinking "tourist-strength" *lao-lao,* watching the red sun drop between black spikes of palm.)

Now, as the unidentified truck crept like a slow, poisonous insect over the landscape, Henry was less sure. The driver said something to François.

"*Ces sont tes frères,*" said François, who had a habit of shedding whichever nationality became inconvenient. Squinting at the tiny truck, Henry didn't see how the driver could tell it was American. You couldn't hear the engine yet; only birds loud in the field. Wildflowers trembled in the crevices of the rock, which split just ahead of them, forming a dry ravine. The driver indicated the path up the hill through the ravine, with an urgent version of the local gesture: arm outstretched and fingers beckoning, palm down.

"The road's not wide enough for the two of them," François explained. "He doesn't want to have to get off the road."

"But what'll we do?"

"This is another way to the village," François said.

"Do you remember it?"

"I trust him."

The driver waited, one hand vibrating on the gearshift. François handed him two bills and got down.

Henry hesitated with his left hand on the Jeep. "He's coming back for us?"

François barely nodded, turned, and crossed the road to the path. Having run out of questions, Henry reluctantly followed.

• • •

Instead of telling you what happened next, I am including a scene—the climax—of Henry's most famous novel, *The Birder.* Probably it will be familiar to you, but it's important that you remember the details exactly. Henry has cautioned me against learning history from books, but he forgets that books are often the only means available. Once I asked my friend Katie's dad what it was like to be a marine, but Katie's mom told me that the Vietnam War wasn't something for the dinner table. Last year I thought we would finally hear about it in tenth-grade American history, but that unit was right at the end of the year and we didn't get to it.

I don't see why I shouldn't learn about these things from

Henry—or from Henry's books—since he's explained in his essays that the setting, characters, and plot of *The Birder* are nearly identical to those he experienced, in December 1969, in Laos. The following section begins on page two hundred and twelve of the paperback edition (the one with the blue cover and the black silhouette of a boy):

François spots the Hmong boy before George does. The boy is standing in the middle of the path, wearing black farmer's pants and a rifle over his shoulder. His body is the size of a six-year-old's but the shape of someone twice that age, with a flat, hard belly, thin arms and legs, and a large head. In his left hand he holds a rusted circle of wire with two dead birds, speckled black and white, strung upside down by their feet.

François talks to the boy in his language. George listens to the truck coming closer and closer: he can hear its diesel whine. And then the sound stops and he hears only the birds—hiding from the small hunter in the grass. George knows exactly what kinds of munitions might be concealed in the elephant grass along the trail—mortar shells, white phosphorus, the U.S.-made cluster bombs locally known as bombi.

"He wanted to be our guide," François says. "He remembers me."

"You said no?" The boy stands up straight in the long grass, his bare chest thrust out proudly. George smiles at him; he thinks they could use a local guide.

"He doesn't have time," François says sharply. "He says he's been hunting for three hours, and look—that's all he's got."

They hike for an hour under the forked trees, seeing no one else. The fact that he doesn't know whether the truck has passed makes George turn back often, although they can no longer see the road. He becomes aware of some kind of water to his left, and then a pair of water buffalo, watching, submerged in the mud. The path softens, until they come to a grove of undistinguished young trees, their thin trunks growing out of the ground at a diagonal. The pool on their left is nearly still, with a skin of dust on the surface. In the deepest shadows on the opposite bank are three motionless tribeswomen, surrounded by their laundry. Their own skirts are half filled with air, floating on top of the water with the clothes.

François calls out a greeting and they giggle. The whole glade seems to be in motion, as if they are swinging in a hammock: an illusion caused by a soft wind in the trees, the lapping of the water, and the constant sound of insects. As the leaves shift, bright chips of sunlight rearrange themselves on the sandy soil.

A noise right behind George makes him whirl: the snap of leaves, black pajamas, a long, rusted barrel in the grass. He hears the shot; faster than he's ever drawn he draws and shoots and in a second it's over; a softer shape squeaks, collapses in the grass.

His friend is standing next to him unhurt and unarmed. Vaguely, he can hear the women splash and scream. George pulls François roughly off the road, down into the nettles and the perilous grass.

"Others!" he croaks. But François springs across the road. George is dizzy and there are suddenly mosquitoes, an army of them, rising up from the nettles into his sleeves, hair, ears, onto his eyelids and his hands.

"François," he says, "François," but François is standing now like a paper target. He waits for the shot but there is no shot. Only when the women reach them—their arms full of wet cloth, their brown legs wet, and their hair in long wet twists down their backs—does François drop to his knees, then his face, prostrating himself before them, with his hands in prayer against his forehead. A woman cries out, a long, sustained call. The others join it.

From his place in the grass, George watches the odd ritual. He can't see the man—wounded or killed?—in the grass behind François. There are no more shots. Cautiously he runs his hand across the back of his neck and feels the smashed bodies of insects, wipes his own blood on the leg of his pants. François unfolds himself and stands.

"Come out," he says, in French. "You've killed a child."

Henry says that a novel is a letter you write to someone you don't know; or someone you do know who is separated from you for whatever reason. Henry's first book was dedicated to Billy Coleman. He wrote *Private George Johnson* while he was at Oxford and sold it to a small publisher on his return to New York. He'd taken an apartment near his old campus, on 103rd and Amsterdam. He had a second-shift copyediting job at a business magazine; he arrived at the office at three in the afternoon and often didn't leave until one or two in the morning. These hours suited Henry perfectly, leaving his mornings free for *The Birder.*

While Henry's first book had happened painfully, over three years, with many false starts and compromises, *The Birder* seemed to flow from him effortlessly. Early in the mornings he moved from his bed to his desk, as if into another kind of dream. He heard the trucks rumbling downtown and the grates of the bodegas going up; pigeons patrolled his windowsill with their mysterious low cooing, as if to say that there was mystery and meaning underneath the cluttered, everyday world outside. In the middle of the morning he walked to the deli and bought an egg sandwich, which he ate standing up at the counter with the *New York Post.* He was too excited for serious news; he wanted to read about murders; to stand next to the immigrant cabbies; to smell the unfamiliar food and watch the Spanish girls through the window, pushing their babies. He loved the way they dressed up even in the mornings, in tight summer shorts and cheap gold jewelry and platform shoes, and their precisely oiled and braided hair. He loved his neighborhood, where things had all the promise of a story he someday would attempt to write.

You, Sir or Madam, will remember what happened when *The Birder* was published in 1975, because that was the year you hired Henry to teach at your college. The response to the book was terrific. Henry seemed to read on every college campus in America. He read at bookstores and coffeehouses, drawing audiences like a folksinger. His readings inspired discussions and debates; on one occasion the well-known activist and former IVS volunteer Fred

Branfmann showed up to shake Henry's hand. Henry also developed a passionate following of literary young women, many of whom told him his book had made them cry, some of whom cried in his presence, and nearly all of whom seemed to want to help him heal himself.

In his letters to me, Henry admits only that he didn't mind this attention. I want to know more. (What did their hair look like? Their clothes, their breasts? Did they wear slips under their skirts, or were slips already a thing of the past? Where did Henry go with them—and how, exactly, did it happen? Did you do different things in the seventies than we do now?) But Henry's letters skip quickly over these details, to a reading at a coffeehouse in Berkeley, in the spring of '76.

Henry had already begun the section (his own copy fell open to it now) that culminates in the Hmong village when he raised his eyes—the girls thought, "It wasn't his fault! We forgive you! Let *me* forgive you!"—and saw her standing just inside the door. She was wearing a thin white blouse and jeans, and although it was nighttime, she had sunglasses pushed back on her head. She hugged her arms and listened, and Henry read to her. When he finished, she was crying, as were many other people in the audience.

Henry signed twenty or thirty books before she was able to make her way to the front of the room.

"Hi," Laura said.

"Hi." He had imagined something like this, but now that it was happening he felt ashamed of the fantasy. People were watching them.

"I didn't even know you were—"

"Yeah."

"Do you live at that same place?"

"Oh, God no," she said. "I have an apartment in the city. I'm in graduate school now."

"Literature?"

"Art history. I'm writing my dissertation."

"About what?" He was afraid that if he stopped asking questions, she might go away.

"Paul Klee. Are you—"

"Just tonight," Henry said. "Tomorrow I'm going to Los Angeles, but—"

"I could wait."

"It should just be a minute."

"However long," Laura said. "It's fine—I'll just. . . ." She flipped her hand toward the door, accidentally catching a piece of her hair between her fingers. Her hair was very dark brown, almost black, and wavy, against the fashion. It was so soft, he could feel it without even touching it. She was holding his book, which was worn along the spine.

"Could I write something?"

"Yes, please."

But he discovered that he didn't know what he wanted to write. He chose to err on the side of ridiculous understatement:

"I missed you. Love, Henry"

After the reading, they went back to her apartment, which was overheated and filled with healthy green plants. Now that they were alone he could look at her more carefully; her skin was more tanned than he remembered, her lips fuller and a darker color. There was also something sad about her face—he didn't flatter himself that it had anything to do with him—but she had grown up since he'd seen her last; a certain distracted girlishness had been replaced by confidence, or disappointment.

"Lapsang Souchang, or mint?"

"Whatever you want."

Laura smiled. "Let's have mint." She was using actual tea leaves and a strainer. She held the strainer delicately with her right hand and poured with her left; he'd forgotten that she was left-handed.

"This is nice," Henry said. "Really. I can never have plants, because I forget to water them, but they're great. You must water them—do you have a roommate?" That sounded as if he were prying. He was prying.

She shook her head. "I was living with someone, but not anymore."

He thought of the Bolivian.

"Can I ask you something?"

Henry nodded. He felt like he was going to sneeze.

"Is it hard to keep reading that, night after night?"

"It's a little boring."

"But I mean, do you find that you go through the experience again—when you read it?"

Henry couldn't figure out what the right answer was. He was sweating and trying not to sneeze. The sneeze was rolling in anyway, a small nasal thunderstorm. He suppressed it; it tingled electrically. He must not sneeze. He felt that his welcome hung on that fine a thread. She handed him a very hot, handleless ceramic cup. Her brown eyes were fixed on him, waiting for an answer.

Henry sneezed. The tea spilled, staining the fabric of the couch.

"Oh no," Laura said. She sounded genuinely alarmed.

That's it, Henry thought, I've ruined it. "I'm so sorry," he said. She was standing under the light in the kitchenette.

"Come here," she said. "Quick."

"If you have paper towels, or something?"

"Don't be stupid."

It took him a moment to understand that she was worried about his hand. "Run it under the water," she said. "Here."

"Oh, I'm fine," Henry said. "Really."

But then they were standing together in the kitchenette, which was only big enough for one person. His left thigh was against her hip and she was holding his hand under the tap, examining the place where he'd been burnt. She didn't even know what she was doing. His face was extremely close to her hair, which smelled like wood smoke. Had she been lying on the floor in front of a fireplace with someone? With the Bolivian? It seemed likely. Just because she didn't live with him didn't mean anything. It just meant that she was independent—one more good quality. He couldn't stand all of her good qualities.

"My grandmother says you should put butter on it."

"What?"

"Except I don't have any." She smiled at him. "I'm vegan now."

She was vegan. That was a whole world of things—pulses, gluten, kale—that he knew nothing about. Could the Bolivian know about them? Probably he pretended to eat like that with her and then went home to steak fajitas. Probably he had another girlfriend back home—one who cooked for him. If that were the case, Henry personally would kill him. He wondered if there was a subtle way to warn Laura about the perils of her situation.

"Does it hurt?"

"No."

She turned off the tap and released his hand.

"I guess it hurts a little."

"Do you think you need to go to the emergency—"

"No," he said quickly. "I'm fine. Drink your tea—unless—you're probably tired. Are you tired?"

Laura shook her head. Holding his gaze she lifted his hand to her lips, slipped the two injured fingers into her mouth. He was surprised by a small moaning sound, which seemed to have come from him. Her tongue ran around his fingers; she slid them out and blew gently on his finger.

"Does that hurt?"

"No!"

She laughed. "I'm not tired," she said. "But I think we should wait a little."

She wanted to wait. Which meant that there was something they were waiting *for.* He had never been so happy in his life.

"Thank you."

"What for?"

"Just thank you," he said.

The apartment buzzed with its own warm, dim atmosphere. He felt as if everything in it, including the couch and the green carpet and the Japanese teacups, was breathing. A gray cat had wandered out of the bedroom and was twining in and out between their legs.

"This is Petra," Laura said.

Henry knelt down. "Hi, Petra."

"Say hello to Henry," Laura instructed the cat. "He's been away such a long time."

* * *

They probably should have taken things more slowly. But it's like the instructor probably used to tell his students in Health class: in the heat of the moment, you'll forget. Laura picked right up and moved with Henry to New York City. In the apartment on 103rd Street, they began to eat vegan and sleep on the floor. Laura got a job at the information desk of the Metropolitan Museum of Art, where she could be near the Klees. At lunchtime she would take her vegan brown bag out to the steps with the other girls, where they would eat and smoke and make fun of the tourists buying hot dogs and having their photographs taken, with their hair standing up in the wind like little wings.

Laura told the girls at the information desk that her boyfriend was a writer. She told them that she couldn't go home until after six (even though her shift ended at three-thirty) because Henry was working. The girls sympathized and said it was awful, but Laura corrected them: she said that she respected what Henry was trying to do. What Henry was trying to do was to write a book about Laura. It was going to be called *The Girl on the Platform,* and it would tell the story of a soldier who imagines his girl again and again, down to the last detail, as she waits for his train on the platform of the railroad station in their hometown, only to find, when he finally does return home, a Dear John letter waiting for him there. Years later, the soldier meets the girl in a five-and-dime, and is shocked by the difference between what he's been imagining and the woman standing before him. He's been conducting an angry, one-sided argument with a teenager in a checked bathing suit, wearing her hair in bangs, and this is a professional woman in her late twenties, with a husband and a baby. They commence an affair, and eventually she leaves her husband for the soldier. Whether or not their relationship is successful—Henry still didn't know. Henry told Laura that if you knew the end while you were writing, it basically meant that your book was shit.

Laura absorbed that information and tried to stay out of Henry's way. After work she went to the main branch of the New York Public Library, where she took neat but absentminded notes about Paul Klee. She looked up often at the high blue windows of the reading room, where it seemed that Klee's *Angelus Novus* might at any moment appear. She could see him flapping madly against the glass like a new kind of Gabriel, dropping in so suddenly that even he would look surprised.

Of course, eventually, they would have a baby. She could imagine an older version of Henry whose moods would not depend on the number of pages he'd written during the day; who took the baby to the park and recited poetry to it; who wrote his novels perhaps in the summers. Although they hadn't talked about Henry's new teaching job in the fall—not officially—Laura didn't see how they could live apart from each other now.

Henry's good moods were amazing. They would cook together and often take their plates out to the fire escape, leaving a candle burning inside on the sill. After the tempeh or bok choi was finished, they listened to Laura's records or sometimes Henry would read aloud to her. If they had wine, they would drink it, beginning with good intentions and often finishing the whole bottle. Then they would make love for long stretches, with gaps of talking and stroking each other in between. Hungry again afterward, they liked to get up and walk out into the city, still hot at midnight, past the couples sitting on the steps and the radios playing soft merengue and crooners that bled one into the other through the smallest hours, to the all-night deli on Broadway, where, truthfully, they often fell off the vegan wagon—bought black-and-whites or almond lace and a quart of ice-cold milk.

Laura allowed herself to forget the bad days. When Henry was unhappy, he became silent, looked at her like someone on the other side of a one-way mirror, who could see the shape of a person there but not which person it was.

"Are you all right?" she would ask him.

"Yes." (Accusatory, as if the question were not only rude but stupid.)

"It's just you seem—"

"No."

"I'm going to the library." She would stand a little bit behind the typewriter, waiting for some kind of acknowledgment and wondering whether he was playing a game with her, or whether it was possible that he really hadn't heard. As it turned out it was neither; Henry was finishing a thought. The typewriter keys sounded to her like loud, terrible birds. When he finished he would swivel around on the black chair on wheels, fix his flat eyes on the wall behind her (where she'd hung a framed reproduction of the *Angelus Novus*), and say, "See you."

* * *

She came home one afternoon in August with the renewal of the lease on her San Francisco apartment in her purse. It was four-fifteen. He heard her in the hall, dropping her canvas bag, which looked to him like the just-milked udder of a cow. The bag held her lipstick and a few old Kleenex, brochures from the museum, her notebook, pens, Tic Tacs, caps of pens, and, as he discovered once (while doing research for a short story), a raisin. The same raisin was probably still there.

"Hen?"

The day had got started late and was going to be a washout any-way. But the thing he'd discovered was that you had to write through the bad days, purge them out in order to make room for the good ones and the very rare spectacular ones. Now, by stopping him at four-seventeen, she'd put another bad day in front of him tomor-row. It could linger on into the weekend, like humidity. And she was calling him Hen again!

He didn't answer. He would've liked to keep typing, except that he couldn't think of a single thing to put down. He decided it was worth typing nonsense, just to prove to her that he was seri-ous.

"Hen—sorry. I know I'm early, but listen to what happened?"

"Don't call me Hen."

She seemed not to hear him, dropping heavily into the chair and resting her arms, one on top of the other, along its back. Her arms were tanned and three-dimensional. He typed:

Sometimes when she comes in, Henry feels as if he is a dead person, whom she animates by her presence. Or half animates: he is a pale and pathetic inhabitant of Purgatory, visited by a lumbering, live thing. How pink her arms are! They are like blood sausages, resting one on top of the other on the back of her chair.

"What are you working on?"

"Nothing now." But he leaves the paper in.

"Oh, Hen. I am sorry. But listen to what happened on the subway. Because I *wasn't* going to bother you; I *was* going to the library, and then just as I was getting off at Grand Central, there was this horrible screaming.

If she were to appear silently, he imagines that she might see the typewriter keys moving up and down without him, like a player piano. Why are there no player typewriters? Because the act of writing is not dramatic.

"Listen to me for one minute," Laura said. "Everyone thought there was a bomb."

"What was it?"

"Nothing, I guess. I saw the girls who started it—teenagers. Black girls. They were laughing."

Henry wonders what it would be like to fuck a black girl. He never has. Would he live his whole life without knowing what it was like to fuck a black girl?

She grabbed the paper, which must've been what he wanted to happen. Henry watched her with interest; he was still in his dreamy writing state, where he'd determined there should be no rules. She began to smile, and her eyes became round and glassy. She choked on one of his phrases—he wanted to know which one—and then looked up, dangling the paper between her index finger and her thumb.

"It's nothing," he said. "It's free writing—whatever pops into your head."

"I thought it was anger."

"No."

"Well, this is worse."

She was standing above him; it was sexy. He knew that if he was going to manage this fight, and have it end where he wanted it to end, he had to start paying attention, thinking a couple of moves ahead. "I was having a bad day. You were early—it doesn't mean anything."

"It's not what you think," Laura said. "It's not the black girls, which is perfectly normal—kind of banal, actually—or the thing about my arms, which is . . . well, you know what that is."

"I love your arms." He wasn't doing very well.

"It's this supernatural impression you have of yourself." She shook the paper. "Of this. You're not a ghost. You're just a writer."

"I know."

"Do you?"

"I was just having a bad day—I'm sorry."

"Well, I was having a good day," she said. "I was going to tear up my lease renewal."

"And now you're not?"

She crumples into the chair, with her hair sprouting out from the thing she's tied it in, and bends down to unbuckle her shoes. Her feet are dirty from the sidewalk and the subway, where there could've been a bomb. Her feet are very small. "I don't know," she says.

She looks stricken. He hadn't known it was possible to love someone this much and still not know what you wanted from her. He wanted to touch her arm but at the last second refrained. She looked up. "What do you want me to do?"

"I don't know," he said honestly. "I don't want to lose you."

"You might, though." Then she started to cry. "I would have to kiss you so many times—a million times, if we were going to . . ."

They went on like this for several hours, until they were sitting in the real dark. The traffic seemed louder than usual. Neither of them mentioned dinner. His desire had seeped away with the light, but he still wanted to be in bed with her. "Do you want to lie down for a little while?"

She nodded without looking at him and took her hair down. This little vanity, in the midst of their sorrow, touched him. He followed her into the bedroom, noticing the lovely hourglass curve. "You're so beautiful," he said.

She was suddenly in his arms with a tremendous force. "Henry," she whispered into his neck. "Henry, please let me come with you. I don't want to break up. I can't. I don't know what I'd do."

"Shh," he said. "We'll talk about it. Let's talk about it later."

That, he realized, was the last moment he could've changed it. Laura might have realized it too. She fell asleep almost immediately, like a kid trying to shut out some horrific event. He held her and felt her breathing and thought about what he would have to say to her tomorrow, and all the time he was noticing what this felt like, and thinking it was not going to be for nothing.

*   *   *

You, Sir or Madam, will recognize the scene above, give or take a line or two. Henry finished *The Girl on the Platform* in December of that year, working late at night when the longing for Laura was strongest, alone in the house that the college had lent him. He nursed that longing until he could use it like a tool; while he was writing the final paragraphs he began to cry. There were no lights on in his house, and the paragraphs were about the snow that he was watching out the window, and the sounds of appliances in his kitchen, and the absolute impossibility of anyone coming up the walk at this hour with an urgent, human need for him.

He walked out North Pleasant Street, turning right just north of the campus and nearly missing the turnoff to the trail, which was covered with a couple inches of old snow. It was snowing lightly that night, but there was a moon behind the clouds, and enough light to walk by. Henry hadn't worn a jacket, and by the time he got down to the reservoir his fingers were numb. He crossed his arms and stuck his hands in his armpits. For a few minutes after he'd finished a book, when he knew it was good but before anyone else had seen it, he felt no pressure to exist at all; the book existed for him. It was like being invisible in the silent woods, so strange a figure that someone passing on the trail above him would only with great difficulty focus on him and think: That is a man. Instead they would see a shadow or a storm-broken tree and move on. Henry didn't need the flask he'd brought, ice cold through the cotton pocket of his shirt; he didn't need to walk out onto the thin, black ice. He was not intending to kill himself, only to enjoy a complete disregard for his own person. He knew it wouldn't last, but for these few, charmed moments, looking at the frozen reservoir, Henry felt that things had been put in order; nothing could touch him; he was outside of everything, and at peace.

* * *

Laura didn't go back to San Francisco in the fall. She stayed in her parents' brownstone on Seventy-seventh Street, where she eventually became so thin that she needed new clothes, and women in the street directed unfriendly looks at her upper arms. Perhaps because of this rapid decrease in body mass (subclinical anorexia nervosa), Laura did not get her period for two months after Henry left. When it occurred to her that she might be pregnant, she got out of bed and began to eat. She ate a balanced, nonvegan diet that included steak, chicken, legumes, grains in their natural state, and a great deal of fruit. She treated herself to an ice cream sundae. She made an appointment with the doctor.

Three days before her doctor's appointment, Laura developed

cramps in her abdomen and thighs; the day before, a sudden wet-
ness between her legs made her panic that she was miscarrying.
She went into her parents' bathroom, where she was shocked
(because she'd become so used to the idea that she was carrying
Henry's child) to discover that she was simply bleeding in the
most familiar way. Mechanically she retrieved a napkin from a box
beneath her mother's sink; mechanically she took four aspirin and
went to bed.

That scene is not in *The Girl on the Platform.* I include it here, Sir
or Madam, only because of its relationship to my own story. It's true
that no one told me (or Henry) that it happened, and if it were really
important I'm sure Henry would've put it in his novel. Henry
would've done a better job describing the eyelet curtains and pale
green wallpaper of Laura's childhood bedroom and the glass eyes of
her antique dolls, and he would've known the name of the artist
scratched at the bottom of the lithograph hanging just outside her
bathroom door—things I can only guess at. I guess the main difference between girls like Laura and girls like me is that girls like
Laura always seem to get their periods, even when they wish it were
otherwise.

Now that it is three weeks since Memorial Day, I might as well
tell you that my period is late.

. . .

Do you remember Maggie Straub? It's OK, almost no one does. She
was the secretary whom Renée replaced on page four of this letter,
an efficient, soft-spoken woman of lower-middle-class origins and a
great admirer of Henry's, who hoped that her successor wouldn't do
the job quite as well as she had. You won't recognize her in any of
Henry's books. Maggie certainly never expected to get into Henry's
books, or even into his consciousness; their acquaintance began in
the mid-eighties, at the height of Henry's dissatisfaction with his

students. At around this time a famous writer came to speak at your college.

Maggie was watching from the doorway, counting herself lucky to hear the Visiting Scholar, and thinking at the same time that the Hello Dollys she'd made at home on her own time ought to be taken out of the department fridge before the students came pouring into the reception hall in search of the Gallo. When the writer began to speak, Henry, who was standing at the back of the room leaning against a bookshelf—visiting writers always made him a little uneasy—happened to turn his head toward the door, where his eyes accidentally fell on Maggie Straub, a thirty-three-year-old blonde in a cream-colored silk-poly blouse with padded shoulders, and a slim-fitting houndstooth miniskirt. Her hair, newly permed, was slightly unruly in contrast to the correctness of her outfit; she had pinned it back unsuccessfully with two rhinestone barrettes.

At the reception, on his way back for a second Hello Dolly, as his students crowded around the writer, Henry smiled at Maggie, who blushed.

"We used to have these when I was a kid," Henry said charitably.

"They're easy," Maggie told him. "They take a little time in the fridge, though—you have to wait for the layers to set." Feeling she'd gone on about the Hello Dollys, Maggie stopped abruptly. Henry wished she would keep talking. There was something familiar about her voice. Out of the corner of his eye he could see a particularly irritating pair of graduate students approaching the table.

"You made them for this?" he asked Maggie, through a mouthful of Hello Dolly.

"It wasn't any trouble."

"Henry!" The students had found him. "We've been looking for you everywhere. We're trying to settle a dispute about the intentional fallacy."

"I'm sorry," Henry said. "I can't help you. I'm getting a recipe."

"Oh no, Professor Marks—I'll write it down for you. I'll put it in your box."

"I'd rather take it now," Henry said, but the students wouldn't leave them alone.

"Do you think Barthes intends 'The Death of the Author' to apply to critics too? I mean because then it just seems to become an infinite regression."

"No fair using the term 'intends'!"

"If you'll excuse us," Henry said firmly. The students moved off, shooting interested, backward glances. Henry decided to ignore them. "Is it a family recipe?"

Poor Maggie was blushing uncontrollably now. "I don't know," she whispered. "It could be Pennsylvania Dutch?"

"Are you from Pennsylvania?"

"Lancaster—you wouldn't have heard of it."

"LHS, class of sixty-three."

It took Maggie a moment to process this information. (Unlike the town of Lancaster which claims Henry at every opportunity, Henry rarely brings up his origins, and Maggie, who'd left home directly after high school, was not aware of them.) Now her eyes opened wide. "Gosh, really? Me too. I mean, not that class."

"I'm dating myself."

"I was never very good in math."

Henry smiled at the department secretary, wondering why he hadn't noticed her until tonight. He tried a joke: "Not too many people are lucky enough to be from Lancaster."

"I love Lancaster." Maggie paused, and then said something that would make her moan in agony that night while failing to fall asleep: "Sometimes I think it's the last bastion of decency in the mid-Atlantic states."

* * *

Hello Dollys are not Pennsylvania Dutch, but shoofly pie is. The following week Maggie brought a large piece of this molasses-and-crumb delicacy, wrapped in brown paper, which Henry sampled and proclaimed delicious. (When you think about what a departure it was from the lunchtime routine of turkey and Swiss on seven-grain, you begin to understand how Henry was feeling about Maggie Straub. Also, there was the sweet anachronism of brown paper, as opposed to Saran Wrap or tinfoil.) One evening Henry drove his car into the next, much less picturesque town, where Maggie had a rented condominium. She had decided, after much soul-searching, not to cook Pennsylvania Dutch.

After an Italian dinner that might have baffled an Italian but that was, for Henry, a bite-by-bite tour through the sunlit six o'clock dinners of his childhood, they went into the living room, where they drank enough of Maggie's terrible Zinfandel for dancing to seem natural. Even later they moved into the bedroom, where to Henry's surprise and delight, Maggie was matter-of-fact and demanding and vocal, and more open-minded than many (I'm sorry to omit details to which I haven't been privy) of the women Henry had been involved with in the recent past.

Henry hadn't allowed himself to think about what he was doing, beyond the fact that it was easier and more pleasant to be with Maggie than with any other woman he knew. Maggie liked to cook, and take walks. She liked Mahler's Ninth Symphony, or said she did. Familiar with Henry's schedule, she respected it without question and was glad to get calls at obscure times, when Henry was feeling lonely and wanted an interruption. On none of those occasions did she mention Roland Barthes.

Soon, as will happen in college towns, people began to speculate. A relationship with a graduate student would've made a small, mildly scandalous splash, but this was unusual. When the gossip

got back to Henry, it only strengthened his resolve. He liked to surprise people. Also, he genuinely liked Maggie. He couldn't imagine
fighting with her, or feeling beholden to her in any way—which
was strange given the conversation they had on one of those very
early walks, down to the dam (you, Sir or Madam, know the place),
where you can sit on the stone wall and feel the cool air coming off
the rushing water, and occasionally see a turtle slip over the drop-off
and skid like a grenade over the streaming stones.

"I got a note today from Professor Chandler." Maggie was wearing a peach-colored short-sleeved sweater and a white pleated skirt
with a wide belt. She was wearing white ballet flats to match the
belt, a gold bracelet, and above her right breast a gold pin shaped
like a bee, with cubic zirconium eyes. After the walk, they were
planning to have dinner at the Old Mill Café.

"She said that I should remember to collate the syllabuses for the
summer school prospectuses and deliver them to the department by
the end of the week."

"'Syllabi' is more common—although interestingly both are correct."

"Syllabi."

"You can tell Chandler I don't need another 'Aristotle and the
Idea of Beauty' syllabus—I have her last five efforts. If there's anyone less qualified to teach a class on—"

"She said you hadn't gotten it."

"Gotten what?"

"The prospecti."

"Prospectuses. You were right the first time."

Maggie looked at him.

"I'm sorry," he said.

"It's only that you're not paying attention."

"I was distracted by how pretty you look." Henry had been distracted by the idea that Maggie looked like Peach Melba, and then

by wondering whether he actually knew what Peach Melba was. He'd learned his lesson, however, about comparing women to food items, and so said only: "You have extraordinary eyes."

"Did you get it, though?"

"I'm sure I did. I might have lost it. How does Chandler know what I got?"

"She says she asked you."

"I'll tell her I got it."

"No!" Maggie grabbed his arm so forcefully that Henry had to brace himself on the wall. "Don't say anything to her. She's only saying that to get me to talk about you."

"Well, I could talk to her about that," Henry suggested.

Maggie shook her head. "I have to fight my own battles."

But the possibility of reaming out old Chandler, whom he out-ranked despite the difference in their ages, and who, in fact, had no legitimate basis on which to object to his relationship with Maggie, was immensely appealing. He wondered if he might have an opportunity to call her a classist. A classist classicist. He smiled to himself.

"It's not funny," Maggie said. Sitting on the wall, she managed to look both formidable and picturesque. Her ballet flats didn't touch the grass in front of them. The sun was in her perm.

"I'm sorry," Henry said. "Why do you even put up with me?"

It was a rhetorical question, but Maggie didn't take it that way. She shaded her eyes, so all Henry could see of them was shadow.

"Because," she said, "I want to have a baby."

•　•　•

They did not go to dinner at the Old Mill Café. They walked up Market Street, turning left on Center and right on Summer, to his house, where they sat on the same shabby blue velveteen couch that he had bought for his long-ago apartment on 103rd Street while

Henry explained why, under no circumstances, ever, did he want to be a father. He gave her capsule summaries of *Private George Johnson* and *The Birder.*

"I know," Maggie said. "I read them."

"You did? Why didn't you say anything?"

The living room was getting dark; automatically, Maggie got up and turned on the lamps. Before sitting down again she ran her hand over the back of her skirt, so as not to crush her pleats.

"You didn't like them?"

"Oh no," Maggie said. "I did. They were sad, though."

"There's a lot of sadness in the world. I don't want to be responsible for any more of it." Henry delivered these thoughts with quiet force. Truth be told, he'd had occasion to deliver them before.

Maggie nodded. "But how are you responsible?"

Henry looked at her.

"I mean, did those things happen to *you*?"

In the last ten years, Henry had talked a great deal about his experiences in Vietnam, but this was the first time anyone had asked him that question directly. People simply assumed that he was Private George Johnson. He remembered when he'd made the decision to use his own name in *The Girl on the Platform,* and how he'd seen himself moving closer to his own experience, accepting it and atoning for it. And yet sometimes he thought it was a kind of slight to his imagination, that his readers assumed it must've happened just as he wrote it. It touched him that Maggie was ready to believe it was all invention.

"You know what I like about you?"

Maggie shook her head.

"You're smarter than anyone else around here."

"Then why don't you want to have a baby with me?"

"I don't want to get married."

"We wouldn't have to get married."

"Of course we would."

"I've been reading this book—*Looking for Mr. Right*?" She blushed fiercely but continued. "They say women are too focused on getting married."

"Who are 'they'?"

"Some psychiatrists or psychologists or something. They say that as long as you're satisfied with your career, you don't need to wait for Mr. Right."

"I think it's a little more complicated than that."

Maggie nodded. "I'd like it to be yours, though. To have your genes."

"*My* genes." (But Henry was pleased.) "You could do better. Not just in terms of money. You need someone who's going to be a father—who really wants to do that."

"I can do it myself," Maggie said. "I know I can."

"I'm sorry." He watched her play with her bracelet, turning it around and around on her wrist.

"OK," she finally said.

He looked at her closely, but she didn't seem upset. It seemed to be what she'd expected. She yawned fully, stretching her arms above her head. He wondered whether it would be very inappropriate to try to sleep with her tonight.

"Do you want to go home?"

Maggie looked startled. "Do you want me to?"

"No," Henry said. "But I mean—does this change things for you?"

"No."

"You don't think you should be looking for Mr. Right?"

"That's the whole point of the book," Maggie explained. "There is no Mr. Right."

"Right—but there might be someone righter."

"I already *found* Mr. Writer."

Henry found himself smiling for longer than was warranted by this pun.

* * *

My mother collects angels. There are angels all over our apartment, with little sayings on them. BE NOT FORGETFUL TO ENTERTAIN STRANGERS, FOR THEREBY SOME HAVE ENTERTAINED AN-GELS UNAWARES is painted on a china cherub in the kitchen window; and above the washing machine is: WE SHALL FIND PEACE. WE SHALL HEAR THE ANGELS, WE SHALL SEE THE SKY SPARKLING WITH DIAMONDS. (Those are from the Bible and An-ton Chekhov, respectively.) Angels, my mother says, are babies on the other side, waiting to be born. They're waiting for the right woman to come through to us.

This is the way Henry feels about the future. He imagines that the future is there on the other side with the babies. Like the babies, the future is waiting for the right person to come through to us. That's something Henry's noticed about writing novels: even when you make things up, they tend to come true eventually.

You'll remember that in *The Accident* George Johnson's son meets his namesake, François Metrailler, who lives in a small apartment above a parakeet shop. Slowly, in his conversations with François, the son begins to understand the way that a series of accidents (including an antiwar demonstration, a bus ride, an invented enthusiasm for Sterne and a real one for Turgenev) led to the war crimes to which his father, a famous writer, has publicly confessed. Everything about the book happened just as he described it in his letters to me, except, of course, that it was Henry himself who took the trip, and even Henry was not able to find François Metrailler. The final scene of the novel—in which the son wanders through the market, is solicited by a vendor of eels, stares into the bucket and in that moment knows that he is going to write a book to redeem his father, an account that will secure the writer's reputation, both personal and literary—is therefore invented. That account would be difficult to write anyway. If you want to tell the true story of your own life, you have to include not only all the things you have done but all the things you haven't; and from my correspondence with Henry, I've learned that the second category can be much harder to describe than the first.

Henry thinks that people are much more interested in guilt than in redemption—just compare *Paradise Lost* to the one that nobody reads (and I do intend to check those out, almost every time I go to our library). Even though he jokes about it, I can tell that the failure of *The Accident* practically destroyed him. Henry tends to be hard on himself. I've read all of Henry's books, some more than once, and I'm not sure redemption is the problem. I think there might be a simpler reason: something Henry has told me about the way that his most famous book is different from what happened in his life.

You, Sir or Madam, who do not collect angels, who do not remember Maggie Straub (who left your college in 1984, due to an accident), have probably never asked Henry: "Did those things happen to you?" Should you have to ask? Shouldn't it be clear to you from the texts that you've studied so carefully that Henry did meet a man who said his name was François Metrailler, in a noodle shop run by a pretty girl; that they became friends in Saigon; that François took Henry along, not for practical reasons (in fact, having Henry along made things more difficult, bribes higher) but in order to educate him about the war that he'd wanted to use as a whetstone?

And doesn't it make sense that Henry, more nervous than he'd been up to that point and at the same time more determined, went to a notorious market in the Banglamphu section of Bangkok to purchase a gun and an amulet? And, never having fired a gun at anything more sinister than a paper man in black pajamas, doesn't it seem right that Henry was petrified and imagined, all the way up to the Hmong village, that he could hear the little men dropping off the back of their truck and creeping along the side of the trail, invisible in the elephant grass and shifting shadows of the high jungle trees?

The glade *was* brown and gold. The women at the other side of the pool did call out to François, and François answered in their language. The clothes were floating in the water and the women let them drift there because there was nowhere they could go. The trees here weren't so tall but they were closer together; the place was like one of the enchanted spots Henry had found as a child on his grandfather's farm, down by the creek where he planned to hide out if anything ever happened, to defend the farm himself (he carried a big, forked branch because his grandfather wouldn't let him take the gun), crouching for what seemed like hours in the wild raspberry bushes, waiting for the crashing of a buck in the dead oaks. The insects in the glade where the women were washing clothes sounded the same as the ones in Lancaster. Henry's nerves had made him hypersensitive and alert. He touched the gun at his side again and again, so that it was natural for him to draw it at the sound behind him, to spin and aim, for the woman to cry out and for François to yell, "Stop."

And natural for Henry, who'd been such a good student, to hesitate long enough for this voice to tunnel its way into his ear, where a moment later he would slap a mosquito and draw blood. There was no fire. The boy who'd wanted to be their guide stepped out and aimed at Henry with his own muzzle-loader rifle, the kind the pilots brought back as souvenirs, grinning shyly at his own joke. The women laughed, and the moment before this one was erased, as it always is in that part of the world. Only François held what had almost happened in his mind, and the look he gave Henry went straight into the novel that made Henry's fortune and his name.

• • •

I'm not a writer like my father. (I'm not a writer, even though this letter has gone on longer than I expected.) If I were one, though, I would be careful what I wrote to people I don't know very well. Even if you trust the person one hundred percent, you can't control things once you've put them down. I made that mistake myself, recently, when I wrote to Curtis and told him how I'd spent $35.99 for the test and used all three strips, and how all of the strips had said the same thing. And what are we going to do now, because I believe in science, but my mother, whom I love so much—you wouldn't believe how much I love her, like I want to have a parade for her and compose a song about her and then make everyone in our town stand around in the parking lot of the Safeway serenading her when she stops there to pick up our dinner on her way home from work—my mother believes in angels.

If Henry and my mother agree about one thing, it's that they want me to go to a school like yours. Which is the reason I've written you this letter, to explain why that won't be possible. Even if you were to pass this on to him in his office, which I imagine is in the oldest, fanciest building, and he were to read it and suddenly stand up—go to the parking space with his name on it and get out his map and start to drive, drive all day and come eventually to West Lemon Street, when the lights on the Dragon Boat Restaurant are actually fighting with the light in the sky, which is bright pink, as if our town were some kind of Vegas instead of the last bastion of decency in the mid-Atlantic; and park his car around the corner, outside Glick's Drugs, so Mrs. Glick would open the curtains and say: "It's company day," and watch my father's cropped gray head and then his mole, the collar of his white linen shirt and the bronze Buddha against his neck, his trousers and his sneakers that protect him from his shinsplints; and ring the buzzer that Maggie has outfitted with a little china dog's head, and I were to stand up from the table and go to the door, and let him in so that he could see the shape and color of my extraordinary eyes—I'm afraid I wouldn't want to go to your school, no offense. I'm going to be an optometrist.

Maggie will be home soon and I should put on the lights. The kitchen is purple now, the way I like it: the windows are violet, pulsing squares. (Do you like the way I described that? Actually it's an optical illusion. The windows appear to pulse because of the contrast between the dark inside and the light outside; your eye keeps making adjustments because it thinks you're going to choose one or the other. It doesn't have any memory, your eye, so even though it's a very sophisticated organ, it can wear itself out doing that, and it's better to choose either the window or the room.) I should put away these papers too, because if Maggie sees me with the application she's going to think I'm filling it out and get her hopes up. Do you remember that about my mother, the way she could keep her hopes up?

I hear the car door, and even though I don't see it with my eyes, I can see Mrs. Glick checking and saying, without turning, "It's Maggie home from work." I hear my mother on the sidewalk and now at the bottom of the stairs, and I flip on the lights and shove the application in a drawer under the counter with the greeting cards, so my back is turned while the feet are coming up the steps.

If it *had* been you, I could have just handed it to you, and you could have read it right here at the table. That would have been funny, after all of your letters, for you to finally lay eyes on me and then spend your time in Lancaster reading a letter. But it might've been the best way, so I could have a real look at you, without worrying about staring. Everyone looks different in real life than they do in pictures, just the way that they sound different in writing than they do when they talk. People disagree about which one is more honest. Personally, I like having time to figure out what I mean before I say it: that's probably something we have in common.

Maggie says that I get my disillusionment from you, but I don't really believe that you inherit abstract things like that. I think it's my interest in science that allows me to be dispassionate. If you were here, I would want you to be the same way. I would ask you to read this letter with a critical eye and make your red notes in the margins. You wouldn't have to tell me what you thought, unless you felt like it.

Yours very sincerely,
Miss Fish

With very sincere thanks to Emma Freudenberger, Vanessa Reisen, and Benjamin Kunkel for their advice and encouragement; to the MacDowell Colony and Yaddo for their support; and to Bill Buford, Amanda Urban, and Daniel Halpern, for their enormous help.